A QUEST FOR SOLACE

What price success? What is success?
What does it mean to feel at home?

A QUEST FOR SOLACE

What price success? What is success?
What does it mean to feel at home?

SOLA ODEMUYIWA

It shouldn't matter materially whether they like you or not.

CHAPTER ONE

'Professor Sharp to ITU, Professor Sharp to ITU.'

The voice on the Tannoy crackled with foreboding. Os gulped down the mug of black coffee, snatched Comfort, her big black bag, off the floor and raced down the corridor. In ITU, the patient, a Nigerian police officer, lay supine and tilted head down, his blood pressure and oxygen saturations plunging through the sparkling floor.

Ossy, you don't need the IMF to tell you that Mr. Shoot-de-lot-of-dem won't make it back to Lagos alive. Not without a major bailout. Was that why his aide de camp was kneeling outside giving the double stringed rosary such a desperate wank?

'Back in theatre now,' she said. In burst a dozen members of the team and, in a few hectic minutes, amongst the sharp whispers and cursing, the drats and shits and sucking of teeth, the not there – there!, not there's but here's, and hissed rebukes, pointed requests, curt shakes of heads, clashes between elbows and egos, they rushed the patient back to theatre.

Whilst they cranked his chest open again, Os tapped her favourite Beethoven CD into the player, then skipped next door to get scrubbed and gowned. She signalled for a stool to stand on as she waltzed back into the operating room, her gloved size 5 palms clasped in front of her chest as if in prayer. Radio pips for the six o'clock news mingled with the percussive laughter ringing from an adjoining room, syncopating with the portentous thrum of Beethoven's 5th Da Da Da Dah-ing from the stereo. Os glanced down at the dusky heart. Cradled by the man's pair of soot-spangled lungs, it looked like a distended bladder, rather than a muscular pump. *Why hadn't they called Cody Hayes? It's always you, muggins Ossy.* She lifted the heart. *How did the extraordinary Lord Cody miss these fistulas?* She hunkered down, time itself seeming to hover to watch her improvisations, the sutures gliding nimbly through her fingers. Soon she came to the home straight – grafting the proximal ends to the aorta. Like a snooker player clearing the coloured balls, she'd done this hundreds of times. Some, like her friend Drinkstain, claimed that she could do it in her sleep, blindfolded with her back to the patient, or with her teeth – like Hendrix playing guitar at Woodstock. Os, or Professor Konibaje Oritsejolomi Osese Sharp, to give her her full name, didn't believe a word of it. Her stepmother H-Mum had seen to that.

'Ok, let's see if he'll come off bypass,' she said, her usually silky voice a rasp. She replaced the heart with studious care and, in a show of much greater alacrity than the banging in her chest suggested, clicked her fingers for the perfusionist to rewarm the patient. Time to shine – a few more brownie points on the old CV wouldn't do any harm. Os applied the paddles and, on her nod, the nurse pressed the defibrillator button. The heart of the Nigerian police officer squirmed and fell still. Os raised the paddles for inspection and stared at the nurse.

'Madame in the bluecap, please tell me that there was adrenaline in the syringe and not pissing orange juice,' she said.

Ignoring the nurse's daggers, Os gave the patient's heart a quick knead with her left hand. *Genies gimme strength, please wake this lot up. Yes, that one, the wide-bodied one with the long hair. Phew, she's got the message. Yes, you regina blinking brontosaurus. In your own geological time. Please, madam, the syringe. Behind you, hand it over, like, now! No, you don't need that. You'd think she was pulling pints of gulf sea oil.*

'Ah, ventricular fibrillation. Better than nothing,' Os said aloud. Ten times she applied the defibrillator paddles to the heart and ten times the wicked man's defiant heart thumped out a recognisable beat, flicking blood pressure up for a few seconds before wriggling back to a lifeless halt.

'Try again, shall I?' Sweat puddled inside her gloves. *Why couldn't*

Cody clear up his own mess? Typical Cody, nicking loaded overseas patients then doing a runner when things went fucking belly up. He must have thought the Nigerian had an oil well on tap in the Niger Delta. Well, maybe you deserve each other. Lord Cody and Sir Shoot-de-lot, who blows the heads off rough sleepers at the Lekki toll gate. What will the man say when he wakes up, if he wakes up, to find that a woman laid her fingers on him without permission?

'Another shot of adrenaline?' said Os, to nobody in particular. A surgical colleague sidled in, sensed the tension, and his granite face lit up. He folded his arms across his chest and leaned against a worktop, tapping his triceps with his fingers. *Genies wept! Another one from the bush telegraph. Bet he'll run off to plaster my mug in a dunce's cap over Instagram – the blinking blundering woman who can't darn a sock without tearing it apart.*

For want of anything better to do, Os turned the heart one way then the other, giving it the odd squeeze whilst she pummelled her mind for inspiration. As she straightened up to ease the ache in her back, someone squeaked. Os's hungry eyes shot to the screen and the heart in her palm set off at a canter for thirty-one suspenseful seconds, before settling into a slow and effective beat. 'Blood gases are not bad, not bad at all. My infusion must have done the trick,' said the intensivist on duty, a middle-aged white man with brilliant brown teeth.

Just as Os slid her palm out from under the thumping heart, in walked a stooped sandy-haired man.

'Great work. Cody's patient, was he? Thanks to you…'

'Ian, I can't thank me enough either,' Os said, bowing her head and slipping off her gloves. When she hopped off the stool, she barely came up to her boss's shoulder. Whilst he waited, Os scribbled her signature on a prescription then dictated a quick summary of the intraoperative findings.

'You were right about Cody,' Ian said as they made their way back down the sloping corridor. On Os's quiet say-so, Ian Kennedy - the Geordie giant of Cardiac Surgery - had taken Cody, kicking and emailing, off the prestigious rota for complex cardiac surgery. 'But going back to our discussion the other day, I'm hanging up the old gloves. Not quite made up my mind whether to go before or after the Olympics this summer. Timing, as they say, is everything.'

Sparklers went off in Os's head. Pinch me Genies, was this it? Little Ossy, from New Cross to the prestigious Head of Amalgamated Department of Surgery at the South London University Trust. Behind Ian's oceanic desk? Between the hard wood arms of his chair. Her back rubbing that button-tufted red leather? Rolling her fingers on the antique brass nail-head trim whilst she held court? Insane, as the kids would say. H-Mum would claim credit for the decades she spent praying for Os to reach this promised seat at the top, where she'd find plenty of room to be at home. Ian said she'd walk it, on paper. And so did everyone else. That was all very well but, unless you are a printer cartridge, when your name is Osese, life is not played on paper. H-Mum said it was more like trying to drop your tears through the eye of a needle.

'Timing is nothing without the right notes in place,' she said, apropos nothing in particular. 'You'll be missed,' she added, blushing, hoping she sounded as if she meant it, which she did. There couldn't be that many surgeons whose boss had found them a second husband. But just before she gathered her wits to ask him for a reference, Ian set off to answer a call, his mobile phone pressed against his thick sandy beard. Os ducked through the door of the female changing room to peel off her sweaty togs. Ten minutes later, she was dictating her surgical notes in the consultants' common room when Cody Hayes appeared in the doorway. Carrying a bulging briefcase containing papers from his role as Medical Director, he was wearing a trademark brilliant white shirt open at the neck and rolled up to the elbows. At six foot five he was a foot taller than Os, with a thick neck that reminded her of a viaduct.

'Quite extraordinary. Ian's becoming a bleeding liability. I heard you had to take his guy back in,' he said. 'And he has the nerve to jerk me around.' He leaned forward and added, growling, 'Mark my words, you'll be next if you're not careful. *Genies wept, this was the sort of guy who walks backwards in the snow to marvel at his beautiful footsteps. He's got a nerve. Can't even bring himself to say thanks. They probably didn't call him back to theatre because they knew he'd buggered off and would only send a trainee to clear up after him.*

'How do you know he hasn't jerked me around already?' she said.

'I've got my beady blue eyes on him, that's why. Can't have the same thing that did for me happening to you, can we?' he said. He dropped his bejewelled drawl to a complicit whisper. 'You *are* going to apply when he eventually packs it in? We'd love your input drafting a job description…'

Os hesitated. *If it sounds too good to be true, there's probably something in it for someone; but not for you.* 'I'm probably undecided,' she said, knowing full well that she would apply and that John, he indoors, would almost certainly not like it.

CHAPTER TWO

Meanwhile, the deadly coronavirus made landfall. When the first of Her Majesty's loyal subjects died, cabinet ministers said not to worry, they had underlying conditions, bad luck and all that. But the wards soon overflowed with ordinary everyday people: parents, grandparents, sons and daughters, brothers, sisters, computer programmers and project managers, engineers and accountants, quizzers, teachers and carers, soaked in sweat, air gasping through what little lung it found in their chests, patients too weak to make a thumbprint in runny yolk if you paid them. Os howled at her car radio. *Really? Gimme strength. We should all huddle together under your stiff upper canopy of guff. Death from this Covid thing must be a blinking lifestyle choice, then. Like installing underfloor heating in Equatorial Guinea, or plastering the office with anaglypta, or - the sort of thing David would do - jumping into an empty swimming pool to teach his itchy head a lesson.*

The three bedroom flat where she lived belonged to John's much wealthier elder brother, Gary. Its L-shaped reception room, part living room, part diner and kitchen, overlooked an eight-lane section of the A3 and was stacked deep and ceiling high with boxes of books which John insisted it would be philistine to leave behind. As she entered the room, a knot in her chest pulled tight because David's photo lay face down on the window ledge. Os barged through a tiny gap between the maroon sofas to clasp the photo to her chest for a moment before she stood it back up on its fin. A brooding wariness lurked in the then-5-year-old David's eyes. She slapped down a stinging memory and turned away. Beside a crossword puzzle on the wooden dining table sat Os's mail, sorted by John into personal and professional. Os wished he wouldn't keep doing that. John had marked the letter of invitation from the Women's Medical Federation with a big red cross. Lazy identity mongers he called them. Why hyphenate humans? Colour, ancestry, race, ethnicity were all made up. When it comes down to it, we are simply like trees raised in different forests, under differing prevailing winds. When he saved the little boy from thugs outside the school gates, did he care what skin the boy was wearing? Does algebra or quantum physics or relativity give a toss about inclusivity and diversity? Does a molecule on your brake pad ask if you're Osese or Monica before it applies itself to the spinning disc? Does a bra ask what colour breast to support, or does it express its doubts by letting you down? Then he'd throw his head back and his jaws would convulse in a belly laugh.

Years earlier, when they first met at a soiree put on by her boss, Os (broke and broken, single-mothered by Lamide, career shattered by Cody) believed that you were either black, BEM, black ethnic minority, or white, WEM, white ethnic majority, with nothing in between. Yes, she agreed that it was ridiculously absurd to lump Jew and Indian and Arab and Armenian together, but this rough and ready reaction, a counterbalance to the overwhelming culture, got her through each day. In spite of her initial impressions - she thought John somewhat pompous and dry - she agreed to go out with him because she didn't want to think that she did not go out with him because he was white. Did he make her laugh? She cannot remember. But he did intrigue her. For one, there seemed to be nothing he didn't know or hadn't thought about. They began to date and, in those intense, tactile, tactical early manoeuvres common to all relationships, she kept her views to herself. Why spoil it when the man seems to want to test the air before he breathes it in. And this was crucial; David took to him. One night, as they waited for a taxi after seeing Madame Butterfly, John locked Os with his passionate olive-green eyes and said that he loved her and *he* (unlike Lamide) would never let her down. As they got out of the taxi, he said he knew how David felt because he had sailed in a similar boat himself. And still was, sort of. His mother, Matilda, could be so cruel, with her ego-stripping put-downs, that he'd come to the conclusion she wished she hadn't had him.

That reference to a mother who was there, but could not care, did it for Os. She fell in love. Beguiled by his air of injured innocence, enthralled by his eclectic tastes and effortless social graces - and because he made her feel special and David feel safe - she discarded her angry Made in New Cross absolutist black and white view of the world and replaced it with John's simple "people are people." She didn't mind or notice then that John was less curious about her than she was about him.

On the tailwinds of the Great Recession, came the hostile ambience of Teresa May, and Os found that tucking yourself away with your olive-eyed Adonis and two kids in a Surrey mansion surrounded by laurel and leylandii – where the closest thing to knife crime was a blunt pair of secateurs – would not shield her from resurgent Enoch Powellism. At first, Os put her rising blood pressure down to a West African predisposition, not the hostile environment. *You are working too hard woman.* But a tiny voice in the back of her mind kept intruding. *Use your high-browed loaf, Ossy. It is because you don't quite fit in, not like John, but, never mind, your kids will be when they grow up.* Or so she fervently hoped. Yet she noted that, for all the talk about taking back sovereignty, not a tiny thread of reassurance for the common health or wealth of the ones called ethnic, or BEM, came from the mouth of any of the leading lights of the Brexit bunch. Quite the contrary. After Jo Cox was murdered, for the first time in her life, when Os went out - for the same reason, she told herself, that Thatcher took her handbag to Bruges and countries mushroomed nuclear weapons - she carried a surgical scalpel inside Comfort, her black bag, only to give it up weeks later for fear of stabbing someone by accident; a hobo waving a mouldy loaf of bread at her, or a hysterical young man fleeing the police.

She peered over the balcony. Two ambulances screamed down the A3 leaving, in their wake, the simmering pre-apocalyptic serenity of lockdown in bright sunshine, achingly tantalising thanks to Covid restrictions. A couple of neighbours on the rationed daily walk exchanged greetings from across the slip road, one pair eyeing an approaching jogger with trepidation, as if this could be the one to pump them full of Covid.

Os swayed furtively to Beethoven's violin concerto playing on the kitchen radio, the rails hot under her hands. Back in the day, she could dance to the sound of a dentist's drill but John disapproved: it was not becoming of her as an academic. She was wearing a pink blouse because John didn't like her in dark tops. Her stomach burned at the thought of what she'd shrugged off to suit his ways. Yet, after what happened with Lamide, was it not natural to yield a bit of yourself? She refastened her watch. Quarter to eight. Another ambulance banshee wailed up the A3. Then another. Os hoped the occupants had *only* a broken bone or two. A passing car tooted, rainbow flags fluttering out of its back window. She waved back, turned, to see David in the balcony door and wearing the shirt she bought him, showing the white Peter Norman, against the silhouettes of Tommie Smith and John Carlos giving the famous salute at the 1968 Olympics. Her head spun when her eyes met his.

'Hi, Mum,' he said. His skin had a starry blackness and he emitted a rich sleepy drawl, like his dad's. Easy on the ears of the girls.

'Hey, my blabby dabidoo! What are you going to bang for The Clap?' she said, to a pleasurable ache welling up in her chest.

'Urgh, Mum, do you kinda want to rephrase?' He crept up closer. 'Told him yet?' he asked, making her feel like a head girl caught smoking in the office of the head teacher.

'Let's clap for workers first,' she said. 'Might cheer John up... He's not happy, shipment of school equipment from China's gone AWOL... He blames Somali pirates...'

David seemed about to speak but held his tongue and smiled. Os was going to ask David if he wanted a drink when his sister, the lissom Louise, cantered up, headphones twittering round her neck, hair in neat cornrows. 'They haven't gone and started without me?'

'Your hair's neat. I thought the salons were closed?' said Os.

'I invented this, like a machine. Set the program you want, put it on your head and it's done in fifty minutes. It's called David,' she said, olive eyes sparkling at her brother.

David tutted and his face creased into a bashful frown. No big deal. He learned how to braid from Grannie H-Mum over WhatsApp. Her real name was Ifeolepoju, meaning 'you can't have too much love', but they called her H-Mum behind her back because she added h to words, like houtside, hequation, HeNHS, rephublican. A retired schoolteacher, in her 70s, H-Mum loved nothing more than weaving Louise's hair into intricate geometric designs whilst she told stories about Lagos, *Eko ile*, the sleepless city of vaunting daydreams, where she grew up. She was going to return to Lagos as soon as Os "settled down."

'Ready, Mum?' David said. He tapped a hip hop riff on the balcony. 'Great to see the happy faces,' he said, bopping his head at the groups standing ready to clap or drum on anything for two minutes.

'Has she told dad?' said Louise.

'Keep up the revision, dear, just in case, you never know with…' said Os in response to her son's puff of cheeks at the kitchen radio. The government seemed about to announce another U-turn on A-levels.

'Mr. Winkelman and Ofqual are bound to cut us less slack,' said David, because his school did not have a great tradition for sending students to medical school. Years earlier, Mr. Winkelman had placed David in a lower attaining set and wasn't too pleased when Os and John got the school to reverse the decision. Some of the girls at Louise's school had butlers but John insisted on a state school for David because the private sector would give the boys airs. Os was desperate for David to get the grades to ease her guilt for his bad start to life, for one. In her dark days as a cardiology reg, when Cody was on her case and Lamide flaky (an understatement), a son who could write his name let alone go to uni seemed as likely as a camel winning the figure skating gold medal at the Sahara Olympics. But her boy knuckled down and, with John's support, here was David on the threshold of medical school. Smashing, as Ian Kennedy would say. In her quiet moments alone in her cab, the exciting thought of a Dr. David Bamisetiti maybe even working in the same theatre made Os screech out loud.

'I think lockdown, like, sucks,' said Louise, frustrated because she couldn't see her new friend Kelvin. Or was it Calvin? *Please, Genies, let them only brush backhands!* Yet at that age only the threat of nuclear fallout would stop Os's ardent pursuit of the Brockley footballer. Hypocrisy and parenthood go together, like eyes and tears.

'I won't lie, my little pretty, the reason you can't get on with life as usual is because other lives depend on it.'

'That's blackmail,' said Louise, thumping the balcony rail.

Os shrugged. 'It's life. You don't clean your teeth, they fall out. You don't work, you don't eat. And so on…'

'If you are old or not well, you are not part of the economy,' said David, moments before John sauntered into the living room, the previous day's crossword puzzle in his hand.

'Ah, you're just in time,' Os said, hoping that he hadn't heard what David said.

John waved his newspaper at the line of neighbours waiting to cheer outside. 'Virtue signalling churned up by the media to assuage the guilt of the shirking from home. What are we clapping for exactly? For the clapped-out cathedrals or the sanctimonious busy bodies?'

'For the dead porters and bus drivers and nurses,' Os said. John stopped dead, narrowing his eyes and grinding his jaw. He looked like Michelle Obama when Barack took that selfie with the Norwegian woman at Mandela's funeral. *Bloody smashing, Ossy. What is the fucking matter with you, snapping in front of the kids?* She didn't see the harm in remembering fallen colleagues but could do without the billionaire-owned media's wishy-washy, pat-on-the-shoulder, military metaphors in lieu of a proper salary. NHS workers were not soldiers on a Pathe newsreel, but terrified ordinary people trying not to catch a chill from their flapping empty pockets. Down on the ground almost directly below Os, a boy aged about seven, wearing a replica Spurs t-shirt, ogled Os's red cab.

'Poor thing, that's child abuse, Mum. Shouldn't let anyone follow a football team until they can – '

'Vote?' said Os. She rubbed a sore spot on her left elbow.

'The NHS martyr thing's been overdone,' said John, waving his newspaper at the flatscreen TV on the wall. 'And the language they use. The insinuating imprecision, execrable hysterical reporting and syntax. What do they mean by "disproportionately affecting some more?"'

Os sighed. *Love you, John, but you don't half talk as if the world sailed on your farts.* Lately, since their simmering divergence during the referendum campaign, Os had begun to tilt back towards her old worldview that people were human in different ways and they didn't need the likes of John sticking a label of uniformity on all of them.

But before she could reply, David clapped his hands and mimed a sash in the air. 'Mum's epitaph.' He stamped his feet as if tapdancing. 'She was only pretending. And she was good at it, or she wouldn't be lying here,' he added. 'Don't look at me like that, Louise. He agreed with John that it *was*, kinda, massively irresponsible to bang on about poor people getting Covid because that only made the clamour to re-open the country from some on the Right all the louder. Had Louise read about the yellow fever epidemic in Philadelphia?

'You got me there,' said Louise, an admittance of ignorance that seemed to stick in her craw. They loved catching each other out.

David rolled his gleaming eyes at the ceiling and said, 'They put the black nurses on the frontline in Philadelphia because they were supposed to have what was called natural immunity. I know what you are going to say: they were lucky to have jobs,' he added. 'I can just hear the loud chants from white people, going: "What do we want? What the blacks have! When do we want it? Now!"' He broke into song, clapping his hands in time.

'Keep it down,' said Os. Her stomach writhed in acrid juices, yet she agreed with David. Any baby genie in a bottle could tell you that all that dying from Covid stuff was for mugs trapped in high rise multigenerational households, strapped for cash and vitamin D without an orangery or two and acres to laze on. She raised her hand as if to speak but gratefully gave way to Louise.

Louise waved her headphones in the air. 'Hey, hang on, David, are some, like, people more susceptible or more exposed? Exceptions to the rule may, like, hold the key? Genes, that sort of thing, I read about genotypes from neanderthals…' she said.

Os sighed, stroked her girl's free hand. 'Don't you think you should consider reading Medicine? You can still be a game show host,' said Os, scared to think of her daughter in the public eye in an era of vicious social media and culture wars.

'It's electronic pixels not scalpels for me, leave the medical healing to David,' said Louise, then turned to Os to mime a question: had she told dad about the job?

Os coughed and gave her chest several ostentatious thumps. 'Kettle?' she said, turning to John who tutted and said he would do it himself. As he slapped the tap on, in the sharp shadows cast by sunlight he looked so much darker than Louise that in the old days he might have had trouble getting into apartheid South Africa, or, nowadays Poland or Hungary, and a few other countries which wanted another go at a version of what Os called Fundamentalist Whiteanity – an intoxicating and galvanising amalgam of Christianity, economic myth making and white supremacy. Paradoxically to some, but patently logical in Os's view, this religion now welcomed and promoted black recruits. Was imitation not the best form of flattery?

Steaming mug of strong tea in his hand, John hung back, as if he didn't want anyone to see him in Gary's flat. A honk went up from a saxophone on the ground floor and the clapping for carers and key workers started, the echoey cacophony rising to a poignant fraternal crescendo of beating drums, plastic toys, bovine femurs on carcasses at the butchers down the road and, from Louise and David, a saucepan pummelled with wooden spoons. When the din faded, Os stepped back out of the sun to flick through the menu of a takeaway restaurant and plan a strategy. Would it be better to butter him up by letting him order up his favourite dish, a curry, then find a suitable opening to tell him that she was going to apply? Or should she just wing it and see how the evening unfolded? What would H-Mum do?

'If he doesn't have exams, I don't want David spending summer playing games of chance on his laptop,' said John. He snapped a broadsheet open and put on his impression of Churchillian gravitas, grunts, puffs and all. 'The likes of Fairybet247 seek teenage boys and girls in the pubs and bedrooms and empty their pockets. Which brings their families closer.' He signalled his imminent punchline by turning to David. 'Because the house gets smaller, that's why,' he said. David had lost money gambling on the internet.

David's face wilted like a plastic bag in a furnace. Os bristled and cocked her head at John. Genies wept, it was John's blinking idea to have the house done up and she was the one bloody paying for it in more ways than money could buy. Before she could speak, David sighed and speared Os with a sideways glance, dropped the wooden spoon, and sloped off to his bedroom. Louise bustled after him, headphones swinging from her neck. Os leaned back over the balcony, biting her lips, upbraiding herself, churning inside like a faulty washing machine. After three minutes of searing silence, she crept to the bedroom.

***

David was sitting on his bed under the giant posters of Kobe Bryant and Tupac, leafing through a chemistry notebook. His eyelashes were shiny and wet.

'Go away.' He rubbed the shoulder he had banged against the wall in his hop away from Os. Louise was sitting a foot away from him on the stool David used as a makeshift desk. She gave Os a silent dressing down and slinked from the room. Os lowered herself onto David's bed, inching her hand towards his. Although he did not repel her, he refused to look her in the eye. 'You know what John is like, wants everything just so. He got you the exemption, didn't he? And the extra tuition for the GCSEs. And -'

'Did he have to have the house done up during my A-level year? There's not enough room for my sneakers to do a three-point turn. Boxes everywhere. Trying to make it sound as if it's my fault and -'

'John wasn't to know lockdown was coming.'

'Nor did his government. Now we know why. Maybe H-Mum was right. It's just like Nigeria...'

H-Mum claimed to find so many similarities between Nigeria and its birthmother, Britain. She had a point. In Nigeria, General Gowon, held *his* lavish state nuptials during the catastrophic Biafran war and was sorry that Umuahia fell a few days later as it had been intended as a wedding present. In Britain, Johnson returned from Mustique to dance in the Chinese New Year then retreated to his grace and favour country pile with his pregnant fiancée. Days after the Cheltenham Festival, on Monday March 23rd, after much umming and ahhing and sloganising – Get It Done, Kill the Virus, Control the Virus, Wash Your Hands - the same Boris Johnson put on a sad Humpty Dumpty face, combed through 'the science', ruffled his hair into the scruffy pineapple look and appeared on TV. He gave the impression that his decision to impose lockdown rules was the result of a long and agonising deliberation between warring libertarian instincts: but these same instincts folded like a recliner chair during the assault by his friends in the press on the independence of the Bench. Brace yourselves, he had said, I'm not Latin coating it, you are going to lose loved ones.

'Particularly if they are old and poor,' David had commented, tongue in cheek, to H-Mum, who told him to wash his mouth out. In her support for Boris, H-Mum vied with Nadine Dorries for the top one or two spots.

David snapped a thread on his jeans. 'You always take John's side. H-Mum was kinda spot on about that too.' He sighed and looked up at the ceiling. A shouting match erupted from the floor or two above.

'H-Mum should keep her bloody prejudices to herself,' said Os, stung by the sudden memory of a story Louise had told her. One day Louise's sleeve was about to drop onto a side plate at dinner. John had rolled it up so nicely for her and said it wouldn't do to have a dirty shirt at a job interview or at school. The next week, they were doing their homework before tea and David had smudged ink on his page. When David had asked John what he thought he should do - tear the page out and start again or carry on down the page? - John had said to ask the teacher. 'Like he didn't want to, like, engage?' Louise said. She had put her arm round David to ask if she could help but he just smiled and shook his head, his eyes like dusty masking tape, dull and rough and sad.

Os shuddered at the memory of her cowardly slapping-down of Louise's story at the time, insisting that the girl was mistaken. She could still see the colour bleaching from her daughter's face.

'We are *family*, a team,' Os said, words greeted by her son's half smile. 'You two mean the world to me, you know that,' she added. But, asked David, if everything was so cool and tickety boo why hadn't she told John about the job?

Touché. Os squinted against a flash of sunlight reflected off the windows of a passing bus. Before she could reply, John and Louise called Dinner. David grabbed Os's wrist. 'Promise you'll tell him.' He fixed his big compelling eyes on hers.

'Ah, look.' She pointed at the satchel in the corner. 'Louise and I got them from the loft when we were looking for H-Mum's stuff. Remember the stories I used to make up?' She fetched the bag and sat down again, hugging it to the throb in her chest. Poignant memories were segueing into pining for as happy an ending for her boy, her girl, for them all, as those in her home-spun stories about Genie Thunder and Lightning and chickens with flapping teeth instead of feathers to gnash foxes with until there was not a shred of vulpine fur left for forensics.

'I just haven't found the right mood, his and mine,' she said, pausing for a moment to put on a happy face before she sailed into the kitchen to proclaim, 'Smells hot, as in peppery hot. John Sharp's democratic curry, all parts of the mouth get an equal chance of burning to death.' She was hoping to get a laugh from Louise at least. It was just after nine o'clock, the stacked boxes of John's precious books, the TV screen, and the sofas, were all tinged orange by the setting sun.

'Your first fulsome compliment to me in a week and it's backhanded,' John said.

'It's the only type of compliment she, like, know's? said Louise. Os started back. As she heaped her fork with mushy peas, David mimed at her again. When was she going to tell him? *Genies wept, David! Would he just give it a rest!*

At the table, Louise sat to Os's right, combining her desultory prodding at her carefully assembled plate of fish and chips with wounded glances at Os. A phone, concealed somewhere on Louise's body, let out the occasional chime which set Os on edge. At the head of the table, with his back to the main door, John hogged the cruet in defiance of Os's advice to cut down on salt. David wafted at the fly on the table but missed. Louise smiled and said they had too many eyes to be caught by a mere two-eyed human schoolboy. Talking of eyes, she'd found Mum's receipt for the dashcam lying around.

'Does it work?' said David. Mum owed him because he'd paid for the repairs with his credit card.

'What's wrong with Dad?' asked Louise, because John bleated, dropped the bottle of brown vinegar, spilling some, and scampered to the toilet.

David cleared his throat and put on the squeaky voice of his biology teacher. 'Some of us endure briefer intervals to urgent micturitions.' He laughed at himself for not quite pulling off the impression. 'Louise, it's on the list of things we males don't look forward to,' he said, making the "we males" rhyme with the word "female" in a friendly dig at what he considered his sister's constant moaning about her hormones. Then his brows knitted again. He leaned across the table and growled at Os. 'When are you going to tell him…'

'Tell me what?' John said as he sat back down and frowned at the empty spot where he had left the salt cellar – which Os had put away.

'Er, we saw our neighbour, the upstairs one…he had a black eye,' said Louise. 'Must have walked into one of those lamp posts you don't like here in slumburbia…' John coined the term slumburbia for the endless rows of boxy houses, nestling hideous clusters of satellite dishes amongst which he was trapped by Covid restrictions.

David grinned. 'I bet his black eye is one that now sees the world differently.'

John emitted a grunt and his knife tore through the plaice and made a squeaky sound on the plate. They fell into a silence cold enough to make their freezer shiver. Os was aiming for a phatic comment about the kitchen cabinets when, 'This is really warped,' Louise said. 'Shall I or will you?' she said across the table, to her brother.

'To what are we referring?' said John.

'It's Ian. I was saying that I love him to bits, but I wish he hadn't asked me to give some Yank students a lift the other day,' she said, squirming under David's disapproving glare.

'Jesus, Ossy, I wasn't born yesterday, you know.' said John. 'That was nothing to do with the Yanks.'

David nodded I-told-you-so at his mum.

Heat rushed to Os's face. 'I'm going to apply,' she said.

John rocked his chair back on two legs so far that Os's hand shot out. The chair crashed back square on all four legs.

'Knew it. You promised. No more clambering up the snake rope or whatever you call it...' John's voice rose to a petulant whine. He puffed his vinous cheeks, his olive-green eyes freckled with rust, aflame. She was always going to, wasn't she? He conceded he had his moments too, but this was a stretch too far. Where were her priorities? Her son was gambling for Chrissake. Her daughter was under the cosh of the impressions her peers had of her and what did her mum go and do? Chuck responsibilities to the wind in pursuit of yet another moving mirage. Did Os for one minute think that his repeated overslaugh at school had nothing to do with his unstinting discharge of strenuous double domestic commitments? Now David was off to university was she going to abandon a teenage daughter for him to look after on his own?

Os wagged her hand at him but could not speak for the rock in her throat. Genies wept, and she was supposed to be the highly strung one, the one with a wafer-thin skin, as Cody once said at work.

'That's not fair on Mum,' said Louise. John harrumphed at Louise. Maybe his mum was right about Os all along.

Matilda's objections gave Os all the more reason to apply. 'We know where Matilda stands, where does her boy?' said Os, placing the stress on boy.

John jabbed his fork down. 'After all we've been through.' He filled his glass, sipped, grimaced because he'd poured himself vinegar not wine. He'd read Os's unintelligible psychobabbling CV. Enhancing organisational connectivity, translational integrity, sustained psycho-creative meritocratic networks. That was not the Os he always knew and she knew it herself. Os should look herself in the mirror and tell him he was wrong.

Os seethed. *Didn't he get it?* Maybe for others the prestige and the out-of-joint nose of *their* rivals was good enough but she needed this job as much as a newborn needed the first breath. The oven bleeped. As she leaned over to take the dishes out, she squinted over her shoulder. *Genies wept, just look at his face, it is as if I've killed someone. It's called going up in the world.* She bet Brody or Martin or Philip didn't get the third degree when they applied for jobs they were not qualified for. She served David and Louise large chunks of apple pie with cream. As Os poured him custard, John tapped the table with his pencil and said, 'Ok, take for example Louise's prescriptions? Who, sort of, picked them up? Moi…always….'

'What prescriptions?' said David, about to bite into a slice of apple pie.

Louise chuckled. 'To stop me laying eggs.'

'Free range or battery?' said David in a faux headmasterly tone.

'Hybrid,' said Louise. 'Dad was…'

'As I was trying to say before the anatomical digressions. Can we hear your mum's response to…'

'It's because she is a woman, isn't it?' said David, looking John straight in the eye.

'Absolutely, categorically not the case,' said John. He raised his eyes to the heavens. 'You can't breathe nowadays for people banging on about their right to be represented, as if we're choosing colours of paint from a catalogue. A bit of Africa, Arab and Muslim with holy splashes of Roman Catholicism, and a smattering of north of Watford gap talent? That way no one will feel left out…'

'You mean like poor Real Madrid?' said Louise, winking at David.

'But their jersey's spotless white,' said David.

'What's this got to do with the rising price of shrinking loo roll, darling?' said Os, scratching her elbow. She feared for her boy. Too full-on for his own good: but then she was no different at his age, wearing her heart on her sleeve and taking on the role of the defender of the weak like a rite of passage. How similar they were too in the exceptions they took. Once, he'd marched his team off the pitch during a home school match because he thought the officials, who came from his school, favoured his team.

But John Sharp could be quite the Ayatollah too. If the kids and Os talked about hip hop or afrobeats, or about their coiled or frizzy curls, or whether they should take vitamin D supplements in winter, he sulked and wanted to change the topic to "more mainstream." When Louise wanted to put the instrumental section of the 4th movement of Beethoven's choral symphony to the words of H-Mum's African hymn, John, the phlegmatic good listener - good listener only to himself, according to David - put his foot down, almost literally on the score, his big chin a-quiver. No, no, no, this was Western canon, not for appropriation. Louise's choice of Winifred Atwell for a musical project? His foot went down again. Genies wept, Dad, give a girl a break. Winifred Atwell was the first and only female instrumentalist, BEM or WEM, to have a number one UK hit. Yet she wasn't mainstream enough for dad? Louise went ahead with her project anyway.

'If Mum's the real deal, why shouldn't she apply?' David made a blubbery noise with his lips, then fell silent. Os, got up, fixed him in her glare, leaning across as if to see if he wanted more cream.

'But... with respect,' David said, smiling right through Os. He wasn't sure he was going to buy John's line about blind Sharp merit, 'remember when they wanted a new head for the Commonwealth for when the Queen was kinda not here anymore?' David said he screamed at the TV. He was, like, begging, on his knees, to the Africans to get off theirs. Then he got it. Big shout out to the Africans. Stupid him. How did he not see that the Africans were waiting for Buckingham Palace to blink and play their trump race card first. He rolled his big dark eyes at

Os. 'Remember, Mum? That was peak…'

'Not really,' said Os, wringing her toes. 'Yes, you do, Mum. Palace said the post is not hereditary but could it be Charles? And I'm like dhu, I don't get that. If it is not hereditary why does it have to be Charles?' He turned to John whose chin was the colour of an aubergine. 'So it *was* about representation, we owned you once and it's in our blood.' David winked at his sister across the table.

'But,' said Louise, turning to Os. 'Maybe it wasn't about that. She was doing what any mum would do. Backing her son.'

Os blushed. She stole a glance at John, whose knuckles trembled round his fork. His eyelids began to twitch. A bad sign. Louise must have sensed the tension too. 'After all the Charlie Parker dedication Mum put in, why didn't they just let her get on with it?' she said. 'To get it out of her system? If Mum didn't get the job, she'd at least tried. Or she'll, like, regret it forever.'

'Bird would have been a hundred this year,' said David.

'Yeah but I bet you didn't know he practised 15 hours a day for years. And the guy who composed The Entertainers, Scott Joplin, was, er, African American? Did you know that?' she said, to get one over her brother.

'Names are complicated, especially in America,' said Os.

'Complicated name, complicated identity, uncomplicated poverty… was that why they drank so much?' said David.

'They drank because they were inadequates. Given the right treatment, things would have been different for them and they might have been more productive.' John sat straight up as if to compensate for the wheedling notes in his voice. Os knew that he envied David's deep voice.

'You both make valid points,' said Os as she rose with a stack of dirty dishes.

David ignored her blinks and the brief rattle of her head. He tapped the table with each point he made. 'First, "Bird" and friends didn't get the right treatment, then they drank because they didn't get the right treatment, then they kinda didn't get the right treatment because they drank. This is what happens when the system forces you to give up what you are if you want to do something you are good at. And that is exactly what is happening to Mum.' David sucked his teeth, shook his head and flicked an orange from the fruit bowl.

Os gulped. Her boy, bless him, had hit the nail right on its head. Culture was the template on which history repeats. We've always done it this way. They didn't put in an application. We did it on precedent. Which is why she so much yearned for the top job where, as Dad promised, she'd find the room to be at home, to rise above the stink of this toxic culture around her and drag the kids up with her.

Os placed the dirty dishes on the worktop and turned to find three pairs of eyes trained on her. In David's great round orbits nested defiance. John, arms on his chest, navy blue shirt buttoned to the neck, looked like an arrogant judge sizing up the accused and Louise, kneading her lips between her teeth, seemed about to burst either into tears or song. Os feigned a cough. *Genies help, where did her boy get this gift for causing silent wars? From his dad?* Her tongue felt like a sandbag, and she wagged it in her head to see if it worked, drew breath, and in a tone which she hoped John would approve of, spoke to her son as if she did not understand what he was getting at. Wasn't he lucky, darling, to have a roof over his head and ready meals and warm beds and the privilege to let off more global warming gases in 10 minutes than all the kids his age in Lagos could in ten years. Ask H-Mum.

Not until she'd flung the words from her lips and seen David's big wet eyes did she realise, as she shrunk into her blouse and heat zigzagged over her face, that she'd let herself and her son down.

David's scalp glistened with sweat. Sinews sprouted on his neck as his voice rumbled round the cramped room. Did he not get enough of this *be thankful for what you've got, David, you can still stand and talk* outside on the streets even as he walked in the shadow of the statues of those who didn't consider him a man? Why couldn't he say what he thinks in his home?

'Yeah? And since they were kinda making international comparisons, like, ever heard the courts tell the KKK in Virginia to go back where they came from - England, Scotland, Ireland, Germany, Sweden, Holland - if they didn't want one man one vote or blacks to vote at all or to buy a house next door? No, they bought angry people rope to hang the mud people with.' He rolled his big eyes. 'Then they bought film and the cameras to take pictures of their mates gloating under my rotting body as it swings high under a poplar tree.' He ran a finger across his throat as he spoke, and as his voice rose, Os shrivelled all the more in the rays of hurt from his eyes. He said he'd had it up to his fingertips too, with people looking at him as if he was the compilation box set with the song you really wanted missing. He closed his eyes for a moment. 'You cough too loud and there was a risk of someone reporting you to the MET for parking your airpipe illegally.' He sucked his teeth and scraped his chair back along the wooden floor, juggling the orange. Os saw Louise's sour expression and stared at her sweltering feet instead.

Os's phone rang. 'But I'm not on call tonight,' Os said, even as she wondered whether she was not better off at work. John rolled his eyes. 'There goes your mum again, the world is her patient and it shall not want,' he said, but Os ignored him and rushed to the bedroom for a fresh outfit because she didn't have a clean one in the cab. If she could help it, no matter what the time of the night, she never went to the hospital in casual track bottoms lest she be mistaken, as she once was, for a cat burglar.

'Forgot to tell you, the accountant's been trying to get in touch,' said John, as Os raced to the door. 'Says it's not urgent.'

'Then why tell me now?' said Os.

CHAPTER THREE

Thankful that nobody died during the night shift and that, after leaving the headlights on overnight, the car started first time, Os stopped on her way home for groceries. The queue, of about a dozen sundry shoppers, most wearing masks, standing apart at the social distance of at least two metres, was eerily quiet. The empty bench slanting its ghostly shadow across a bare patch on the lawn in early sunlight looked like a dial to Os's daily yearnings. How she ached for freedom from the lockdown restrictions so that they could get back to their own house. Please, Genies, give us peace, let David get his grades and make Louise change her mind and do Medicine too. If only John would lighten up and cut everyone a bit more slack, she'd buy him that super sit-on red lawnmower he set his mind on.

Back in the flat, surrounded again by brown boxes, she peeled the scarf off her sticky scalp and raised the packs of toilet paper as if in triumph, rehearsing the self-deprecatory huffs and shrugs and humblebrags to the felicitous hugs she expected from her sleepy brood. Ah, my pets, queueing at the supermarket since daybreak is nothing as long as your stomach has stuff to drool over. Sorry I had to dash off again, but duty called, a tricuspid valve disintegrating from Staphylococcus Aureus: the worst. The patient, a drug user, was only twenty, with lungs packed with pus. Os fished out the packet of raisins she'd bought for John's "dominics." Os called rock buns "dominics" because she shortened rock buns to RB, as you do, and when she found the letters matched the consonants in Raab the name of the foreign secretary, it was an easy step to amuse herself by naming rock buns after the curiously fascinating Minister of State, who called his compatriots 'The worst idlers in the world.'

She fetched her other peace offerings off the floor – James Baldwin's Collected Essays and a new pair of football boots for David she meant to give him at Christmas. For Louise, an internet radio so she could listen to a wider choice of Jazz music. John would just have to wait for his big present.

After the tiff, John had lapsed into what Os called his DUP mode – no to everything almost before he heard what was on offer. A war movie? Glass of wine? A takeaway? A walk round the block? Praise for shielding the little boy from feral bullies and for saving Marne High, his school, a fortune by doing DIY was met by curt rejection. She could have told him that he smelled and looked like a cross between Adonis and Achilles, and was as wise as Darwin, Einstein and Solomon and his Protestant hero Martin Luther, and it wouldn't have changed a nano-part of his sulk. To John, David had been radicalised by his dad and would take Louise down with him because she clung to every preposterous pronouncement that came leaping out of her brother's mouth. And Os couldn't see it, because she was blinded by guilt and by this misplaced notion that she had to keep climbing a greasy pole. Then, instead of listening to what Os had to say in defence, he'd turn to the bedroom wall and bury his nose in Evelyn Waugh.

Genies wept, who was it who said, 'Emotions are there for a reason; but there are reasons for emotions?' In 70, 80 years did the Queen never get up anybody's nose? She bet nobody lost their temper with the Queen. For a reason. Power, or lack of. The same thing happened at work. Porters didn't as a rule lose their rag with managers. These florid sulks were not spontaneous but to wrongfoot her. She was reminded of a story she told the kids when they were little. It was about a woman who so desperately wanted to be an actress. She was so happy when they offered a walk-on part; but it was as a doormat. When her kids tried to lift her off the floor, stuck in her ways, she tripped them up and broke their necks.

'Genies, gimme shelter, no,' she rasped to herself, horrified at the thought of emulating the tragic protagonist of her fairy story. She needed a reboot with John - a day out, dinner for two, anything. Wincing to a cramp in her belly, she sat at the table behind a vase of wilting chrysanthemums. Genies gimme strength, not enough room in here for your reflection in a mirror. An ambulance screamed past. Then it went quiet, apart from the echoey drip from the kitchen tap into a plastic bowl. The early knockings of a growling match in the flat above stirred an elusive itch in Os's chest, like an imminent sneeze deep inside. Os crept down the gloomy corridor. She cocked an ear against David's bedroom door. Nothing. The unease in her chest spread to her navel. She gave the cheap wooden door a tentative prod, waited a second, grunted a guarded warning - with teenage boys you never know - then barged harder. Wedging the door open with her foot she swung right shoulder first through the gap.

She gasped. What in the name of the Horn of Africa? No, no, no. Her eyes pinged from their sockets.

Ripped window blinds dangled off the pelmet. The trashy white wardrobe John hated straddled the mattress on the floor. Os staggered against the wall, her knees knocking as if in need of mutual support. She tapped her glasses back up her nose even as she darted her terrified eyes around the room. Thank the Genies, no bloodstains. Tearing her eyes from the scene she shouted over her shoulder. 'Louise, Louise.' Outside, a door clicked open. Os squeezed back out and stumbled into the arms of the sobbing Louise.

'Where is your brother, where is he?' said Os, shaking Louise by the wrist. 'Two of them, one man and one woman,' said Louise. 'They handcuffed David, just like on TV.' She had told them her mum was a surgeon and would be back soon, but they weren't listening. Louise shivered and leaned her head against the wall. 'All David needed was the loo, Mum… the stupid loo.'

'Where was your dad?' said Os, to the chaotic chuntering in her head. From the flat above came insistent taps on the ceiling. Louise slid down the wall and crumpled to the floor at Os's feet.

Just then the door of the main bedroom at the end of the corridor brushed open. Out crept John crumpled grey shirt open buttoned up to the neck. 'I needed the bathroom. It sort of got out of hand.' He dipped his jaw at the toilet door and shook his head. 'He was online again, didn't take kindly to me poking my nose in. You know what he can be like,' he said, referring to how David went uber dramatic over a missing delivery from Amazon.

Louise howled at her dad. 'You didn't have to sneak into his room. David was only making a mug of tea?' She raised a cupped palm to her cheek 'And he wasn't gambling, he wasn't.'

After his friend's granddad got shipped off and died destitute in Jamaica, David had misheard Os's telephone conversation and thought H-Mum was on the Home Office radar too for deportation. He had tried to raise the money for H-Mum's legal fees online and fell into the trap of a betting company. Lost a couple of hundred before Os put a stop to it.

'Dad needed the loo again. He said David was taking too long.' Louise said she had heard banging on the door. She was afraid to come out. Then, before she knew it, the police arrived. Tears fanned round the mauve edges of her nose. She jabbed a finger up at her dad. 'We don't kick off when *you* take ages.'

Os lifted Louise back on to her feet whilst John, one hand in a pocket and muttering to himself, brushed past into the living room. *Genies wept, what was he thinking? What had he been reading in his broadsheet paper? He worked with teenage boys for fuck's sake. If he was caught short, why couldn't he piss in a plastic cup? Then we'd all have had a good laugh about it. End of.*

'This is why they won't promote you to head of school, you are too up yourself at times, John,' she said, a dig guaranteed to rile him. Louise had dropped to the floor again, her chest convulsing with sobs. Os dragged her up and, as she dropped her into a dining chair, the floor trembled. Was it a passing lorry? No, it was her legs again, vibrating. If only she'd followed Drinkstain's advice and come straight home or not been so prissy about flashing her NHS badge to jump the queue, or hadn't stopped to talk to that patient, or put her foot down when

John asked for the new swimming pool, or told her mum that she didn't want to be born, or wanted to be born but with a different set of genes under a lucky star, none of this would have happened. Knowing the MET they'd have her boy banged to rights for threatening behaviour and resisting arrest, for foul abusive language and disturbing the peace and for breaking any number of laws randomly cut and pasted into incontrovertible "facts" to make it easy for the hard-pressed impartial judiciary to sum up in time for lunch.

'If anything happens to him...,' Os said as a huge chunk of what she felt for John splashed, hissing, steaming to its death in a spot vaguely between her breastbone and stomach. 'Don't cry darling, you'll make yourself ill,' she said, placing a soft hand on Louise's shoulder.

John tapped a box with his fingers. 'What did you blinking expect me to do? Fight them off? Pat David on the back for not crushing my cranium? A warning was all I, sort of, thought was required from them. We'll just have to leave it to their professional -'

'They took him to boost their figures?' screamed Os. She grabbed her key fob, phone, and Comfort, and dashed to her cab.

***

An hour later and twenty frantic minutes after a wrong turn at Raynes Park junction and another on the South Circular, Os arrived at Stockwell with her head in a hot vice. Tapping her blue-rimmed glasses into place, the midday sunshine stinging the back of her neck as she raced past the mosaic erected in memory of the young Brazilian electrician shot dead by police in 2007. She hopped up the stairs to the police station gripped by fear, Genies Thunder and Lightning, was that not on the friendly Cressida Dick's beat too she thought as she bustled to the counter.

'Excuse me, good afternoon, sorry to disturb, my name is Sharp. I'm looking for my son, David Bamisetiti. He had a barney at home, handbags if you ask me but that's lockdown for you,' she said and, thrumming within, tacked a careful smile to her lips.

'Are you a material witness to the events mentioned?' said the white officer and, without looking up from behind the glass screen, tore a wad of paper in half and chucked them under the counter. Os's spine snapped taut and her smile slipped. Genies wept, was that even a fucking material question? But armed with less leverage than a priest caught pants down in a brothel, Os slowed her breaths down, called on her New Cross days and spoke like a geezer counting out loose change to a foreigner, 'My mistake. I didn't explain myself. I'm his mum. My son is the one called David. Kids are not just to carry for nine months but forever, eh? I'm, like, getting home after my night shift, could do without the aggro... and so could you...by the looks of it,' she said, pointing at the masses of paperwork on the desk.

The officer looked up, but her grey eyes sank back. Os wondered whether to beg or weep or let her sawn-off feelings rip, but her phone's muffled Beethoven 5th ringtone got there first. She snatched the phone out of her black leather bag, Comfort.

It was Lamide, her ex. 'Well done oh, you and your Oyinbo husband. Satisfied now? David told me everything. Where were you? Working?' What was she good at except cultivating bad luck, eh? For all her book learning was she any better than the ignorant village people who left their children in the bush for tigers to eat? 'Figure it out,' he said. Anybody with native cunning can convince a politically correct committee to give her a job on trial but did Os really think, if David had had a choice on the day he was born, he would have picked a selfish woman like Os for a mother?

Os shivered at the thought that David considered her a shitty mother. Her eyes pricked and she cringed at the swell of envy, because David had called Lamide first. 'Take your cheap points down the hole you crept out of.'

'What kind of woman abandons her kids to make no point at all? You think-'

'For fuck's sake, grow up.' Os gestured an apology to the duty officer and made room for two hefty policemen hurling a handcuffed black young man with an afro to the desk. 'Where is my boy?' she said, barking at her phone and wafting away an acrid aroma of nicotine and lager from a pair of young women who marched into the station swearing like sacked backbenchers.

'If it wasn't that domestic polecat who called them, who did? Abraham Lincoln? Freddie Mercury?' Did Os think that if the roles were reversed and he was the black stepfather of a white boy he'd last one minute with the police? Before he as much as opened his mouth they'd have him in handcuffs, fleeced for guns and cocaine, and they'd ransack the house for anything that they later relied on to fit him up at the station. He made a guttural sound. 'Should never have let my boy live under the same roof as that polar bear...'

'You are not fit to suck his snot,' she said, but Lamide chuckled and said she could protest all she wanted but she knew she didn't believe what she said about John either.

Os shuddered, closed the call and shuffled past a new arrival, a round-shouldered black boy in handcuffs, to reach the counter again. The officer wrinkled her pert nose and spoke to a point above and behind Os's head. Due to Covid personnel changes and shortages, they'd put David in what they called temporary holding, in a facility which was a cross between a prison and a youth offenders' centre.

At that news, a leonine padding began inside Os's chest. She stuffed the scribbled note from the officer into her trusty Comfort, and stumbled out onto the deserted street, to mind whipping images of crazed young men in dark cells, of drug abuse, of knuckle dusters hewn from mattress springs, buggery and fights over anything from the look on your face to your place in a queue you didn't know existed.

***

It was past six o'clock the same day and Os had just found that she had had the missing packet of pasta in her left hand all along and was about to return her divided attention to the cooker when the Beethoven ringtone drummed from her phone. It was David.

'I'm fine Mum, got a room on my own for the moment. They let me make this call but on borrowed time,' he said as Louise walked into the dining room dabbing her bloodshot eyes with her fists. 'Lucky to get this place they say, not far from Luton I think, exactly where not sure.'

Lucky? Os imagined bread wrapped in green cling film and genetically modified algae but pure white underneath. Parts of the boiled potatoes would look sky blue. She heard David say he had a bed and a kinda stool or chair. No biro, no pencil. Too dangerous. No jacuzzi yet either, disappointing considering what John thought of these places.

'What was that crunchy noise?' Os said. 'There it is again.' She clasped Louise's hand.

'Cockroach, Mum. It must have missed its train and was rushing home after work but crashed into my heel. I won't tell when they come to assess me tomorrow or they'll mark me down as violent. Black on black cockroach violence.' Os braced herself against the urge to scream at him for taking the mickey. He said they asked if he smoked. Ganja they called it. He told them he didn't drink anything much stronger than black coffee. They asked about his real dad. 'I said he was working in the States as a surgeon but is back home now. What sort of surgeon? Tree, bin, laundry, traffic they asked. 'No, urology, I said and told them it was about bladders and passing wee. Ironic, that's John's problem, isn't it? Prostate? Two of the busies, one had a nose with a left hook on it like Bad Babo's in the story you used to tell us. You should see the face of the senior officer. Big pale watery blue eyes. Your mum's old man, bet he's white isn't he? Nature, innit? Genes is stronger than water, I tell you that or Lassie's my father, she said. I said I didn't do anything wrong but she drew a string in the air. That's how long they might keep me until… Said Pritti Patel the Home Secretary would have her guts for garters if I escaped. She said I should learn to control my natural aggression.' David blew a loud raspberry. 'It's like they feel sorry for John. When I'm the one sitting…'

The phone went dead. Os shook and waved it in the air then slammed it to ear. 'Are you there? Reception or…' she said, stammering in wild incoherence for a minute until she heard his voice again. He said Os needed to be registered as his official visitor then he had to be booked to see this psychologist they chose especially for cases like his. Os's tongue rasped against the roof of her mouth. 'They are not letting you out yet?' she said, beset by the dreadful thought that they'd made up their minds that her boy was mentally ill, which is one way of making you ill; locking you up for any inventive misdemeanour that fits the bill. The more you protest, the madder they say you are until you don't know *who* you are any more. Which is not that different from what happens outside too. What next for her boy? Electric shocks, mind-altering, mind-numbing drugs and preloved straitjackets? She rolled a shoulder to ease the growing ache in the back of her neck. 'I'll put my name down. When can we visit?'

'We? What do you mean *we?*' said David.

The line cut out, for good this time. Os swallowed the steely cold in her throat then half turned to Louise. 'He'll be out soon, says not to diss his rugby shirts… shsh Louise,' said Os. 'Don't cry.' The last as much to herself as to Louise. 'If H-Mum or Jaundiced Matilda ask, say he's in quarantine with a friend.' Os sucked her tongue. 'You think up a better story, then, and I'll ditch this one,' she said, snapping in response to the shadows of doubt on the girl's reddening face.

John had crept up behind them. 'If there is anything I can do,' he said, scratching the back of his head. Os turned round. *Genies gimme strength, my delicate hubby sounds as if it is my boy's first day at a new school.* Picking her way round a riot of angrier retorts, Os fell silent, then gasped to a stabbing question. *What if she could never forgive John for this? Genies wept, this could be the beginning of something terrifying between them, yes?*

'You go listen to your Mahler or have a sip of concentrated sulfuric acid because, honestly, that is how I feel right now,' she said. *And if he as much as breathed a word of advice about how he thought she should feel, she'd wedge that priceless roll of toilet paper she had queued round the block for down his gilded throat.* John leaned back against the wall. Head bowed, he picked at his fingernails, emitting the odd whimper. 'But why didn't you stop them?' said Os. He'd done it before.

Shortly after the move into the six-bedroomed house in Sure Lanes, rural Surrey, a neighbour reported seeing a muscular young black man lurking in the woods. David was only twelve at the time – prompting Scotland Yard to dispatch an immaculate division of high-powered cars, motorbikes and a brand-new helicopter. When Dr. John Sharp PhD opened the door, the uniformed intruders, blasted by his englobed vowels, apologised, turned their day glo coats inside out, reversed their shiny chequered 5 series BMWs and sped off to file a spotless report since copied for syntax, prolixity, and vacuousness by peers around the world. Except for the Nigerians who had a unit called SARS which didn't need to make excuses for repeatedly gunning down innocent compatriots. John could repel a battalion or division, whatever you called that lot, yet sat on his high horse and let them take her son away. For what? Weeing priority.

'Go, just go… I can't honestly take any more of you right now,' she said and punched him away. John mumbled to himself and, as he turned for the bathroom, the sun caught the silvery hairs on the back of his neck and a judder went through Os because she had to agree with Lamide: her husband *did* look like a predatory polar bear.

CHAPTER FOUR

A flawless sea blue sky, caressed by golden sunshine, the wild chorus of birds chirpy cheeping added bounce to Os's mindsteps. A great day beckoned.

'Remember, no tantrums,' John had said earlier when, in her excitement, Os thrust her foot down the wrong hole of her trousers and fell over, crack of skull against the wall prevented by a stack of John's books. By this time tomorrow David would have had three moans at Louise for wrecking his replica rugby shirt and drafted a list of grievances about the detention centre to send to his MP. That's my boy. And if H-Mum was impressed by the verisimilitude in his manuscript he could say he'd spent a night in a youth detention centre as part of a school project.

A bug-eyed white woman with straggly brown hair scowled Os to one of six tables behind screens in a stuffy waiting room, its walls plastered with government posters urging the rest of us to Save the NHS, Control the Virus, Stay at Home. Os smiled to herself. Government by slogan. She made up a few: Cut Tax Cuts, Up Tax Cuts, Down Tax Cuts, Don't Shoot Us, Let Me Breathe, Cash For Masks, No Masks For Plebeians. That was a good one, No Masks For Plebeians directed by the seesaw brothers, Johnson and Sunak. When one goes up the other goes down. Os suppressed a guilty giggle and put a deadpan expression back in place. Genies wept, she was so close, this was no time to jinx David's release with premature jollity. She crimped her mask over her nose to stop her glasses misting up. A couple of truly white white women sat at a table ten feet away exchanging curt whispers.

Good luck, people, whatever yours has done. Mine is coming home. A massive result.

Shortly, two silver doors parted and out shuffled David, shaved head lumpy and scabbed. Trembling, Os leapt out of her chair to hug him, sensed that it was not the done thing with teenagers and, to a pebbly rattling within her, dropped back down into the chair. David looked round, winced like an old man as he lowered himself into the wooden chair on his side of the screen. A bead of pus peeped from the inch-long cut above his left ear. Dull eyes looked out of his bony face. Os smelled iodine and vinegary sweat. Did they shave her boy's hair with a broken bottle and douse him in diesel aftershave? Her hands shot out to hug him, bumped against the glass. Blushing, she bunched her fingers and dropped them on to Comfort.

'Hey Mum, what's up?' said David. He flinched and his head jerked his eyes round the room and Os swung round to follow David's snagged gaze. It was Lamide. A coiled string snapped inside her.

'Ah, ah, why do you make your pancake face as if I be taxman?' said Lamide, in a mock Lagos accent. On a day like this did she expect him to sit at home? Was David not his son? Hand in pocket, he yanked on the leg of his brown trousers. 'We should be over there in that building. I hope they have air conditioning, this English summer heat kinda gets me down,' he said, in a faint transatlantic drawl, patting his thick hair, flecked grey at the temples. With Os grinding her teeth in tow, Lamide marched them all across the gravelled courtyard to a redbrick building.

Dr. Ella Gauge, senior clinical psychologist met them in an airy office. Slim and thirty something, dreadlocked, she was a fist taller than Os, with kind dark brown eyes the same colour as her skin. Despite herself, Os found the way the psychologist swept her fringe back with a toss of the head somewhat endearing, but this didn't stop her feeling, in her baggy grey trousers, a right frump.

'My job is neither to paper over faults nor to join them up but use them as an effective roadmap. You see…' said the psychologist, in an accent betraying stints as a postgraduate student on the European mainland, if Os wasn't deceived.

Lamide cleared his throat. 'After this catastrophe, why should my son share a roof with them for one more second?'

Os vibrated her head at Dr. Gauge then she leaned across the back of David's chair and shot Lamide a glare. 'I came to take advice, not fling it,' she said, winding her tongue back in with Herculean difficulty. *What windy nonsense the man talks: after years AWOL, he's now the big daddy is he? But say that and he had a ready retort – if she was so perfect why did her son end up in this shithole?*

'Understandable, these physiological and psychological reactions, but don't be too hard on yourselves,' said Dr. Gauge.

Genies above, where do they learn this patronising stuff? In the womb? Os wobbled her English breakfast face into place – toasted lips spread over grilled teeth with salty eyes frying behind. 'It's lockdown,' she said, and shrugged, hoping she sounded wise and inscrutable.

'Mum, I wasn't gambling that morning…'

'I know, darling,' said Os, gripped once more by the urge to leap over the barrier and give him a bearhug.

Dr. Gauge beamed. 'Such social awareness. David, you should both be very proud.' She rubbed a DVD with a squirt of strong-smelling sanitizer and passed it over the tinted screen. 'John, is it? Your husband? Give him this. You'll find a section on unconscious bias. It applies to all of us but those in positions of authority. Naturally, their actions have as a consequence, more…if you see…impact?'

Os turned the DVD in her hand. *Jeerie me Genies, another free pass for practising facultative racists.* Forgive them for they did not know what they were doing even when they were told what they were doing and anyway thin-skinned bolshie Che Guevara Os, as Drinkstain called her, what is your gripe? What happened happened a long time ago. Three months. That is at least ninety whole days. How can you judge them by present standards for actions they took in good faith, in the honest belief in their God-given superiority? Yes, they enucleated both your eyes but have they not promised to give you one of them back when they've finished with it? And keep the other for record purposes? Or in case you lose it or they need it for identification because they lost your dental records? But what do you need dental records for when we've kicked your teeth in or shot you dead? We can tell it is you from the healing fractures on the back of your skull. Ossy, my dear, ok, you don't half exaggerate. Slowing her breathing down, Os blessed the DVD with a polite nod and passed it to Lamide who implied by the disgusted wrinkle of lips and nose that the video couldn't possibly apply to anyone but Os's domestic polar bear.

Dr. Gauge tutted and cleared her throat, her smile barely ruffling her smooth cheeks. She was sorry to have to hold them up but David needed a final sign off. 'Ah, here she is.' David half rose from his chair to greet a buxom white woman.

'I'm Iolanthe,' said the new arrival, bumping elbows with Lamide, then turning her close-set pale blue eyes on Os. 'And you must be the professor,' she said and, with a self-regarding puff of the cheeks, sat a social distance away from the desk to the right of Dr. Gauge. In one of those clashes of personal chemistry that turn sparks into conflagrations, Os took an instant dislike, such as her hero Ludwig would take against critics and some noblemen.

'David Bamisettiti. Beautiful name. Philology, linguistics, etymology are so very fascinating, really...' Iolanthe shook her head and closed her eyes. 'Don't tell me what it means...something about future, opportunity? Clearing the way?' She closed her eyes tight, shook her head. 'No, it's gone. Memory like a sieve...really...' From her brown briefcase she dragged a thick folder.

Os started to speak but, 'Mum,' said David, in a higher pitched drawl.

'Thank you, David, interruptions retard us,' said Iolanthe without looking up. 'Need to ensure that we get to the deep roots of the issues involved. Then we can have a meaningful conversation, really...'

Os shifted her weight, dying to flood Iolanthe's ear with boiling expletives. What is deep about locking up teenagers all day? A white boy hung himself a few rooms away from David. Whites were more likely than black boys to take their lives in custody. Disproportionately. That word again. Was it a freak statistic? Or would some of them still be alive if their mothers fed them more mackerel and cockle, omega 3 fatty acids according to the research published by the Oxford group but ignored by Her Majesty's governments? Does anyone give a toss apart from those who lost their sons? Os gripped her bag and made to rise from the chair. 'We've already had a most detailed consultation with Dr. Gauge. It is getting late and we have a long trip…'

'By the way, the trains are kinda so, so,' Lamide said, rolling his wrist. Could he cadge a lift back to London?

'With pleasure,' said Os, after a deliberately long hesitation. A barbed knot formed in her throat.

'Thank you both. If I may add, parental attitude impacts my final assessment,' said Iolanthe, underscoring her unimpeachable authority with a drop in timbre. 'Were the required checks not to occur, who do you think will bear ultimate responsibility? Really?' She tapped her shiny forehead. 'Moi.'

'A word please, Iolanthe,' said Dr. Gauge, her face as dark as the dead of night. For a moment Os held her breath. Five dizzying seconds passed then Dr. Gauge tapped the table. 'I mean now, Iolanthe,' she said.

Iolanthe shrugged and rolled her eyes at Lamide. 'Very well, but I'm afraid in the circumstances your son is not yet free to go,' she said, pointing eyes down her nose at Os.

Lamide's clenched fists shot to his head. 'Shit,' he said. Words ran unopposed from Os's highly sprung throat.

'My son is now a flaming threat to the solar system?' she said, then managing after a struggle to wrestle herself silent and drop her trembling hands onto her lap. She sneaked a glance at David and the slight pursing of his lips, shake of his bowed head. Os could not have felt any worse if she'd been caught on camera stuffing plastic bags down the gills of an endangered Halibut.

***

Os thought some trainees were so up themselves they found it hard to tear their eyes away from their reflections. Jezz was not one of them.

Which is why, despite a head fuzzy with fatigue, Os hung around to help because the knock-on effect of Covid on the emergency cardiac surgical rotas had dropped one Mr. Stevens into the unexpecting fingers of the four-month pregnant registrar.

Os waved her hand and placed it lightly on Jezz's wrist inside the patient's chest. 'That won't work, Jezz,' she said, whispering in the robotic voice she learned from playing computer games with the then six-year-old Louise. The bright lights made her wince to a wave of migraine. Foo Fighters growled from the radio. Foo Fighters? Muddy gravel music as far as she was concerned. Was it any wonder Jezz found herself in a tangle between a graft, a valve, and a literally bleeding heart? Jezz, who was beginning to show, leant one way to have her damp forehead dabbed by a nurse, then towards Os with a plaintive tilt of the head, blue eyes flickering with worry, between the double masked jaws and the pink theatre hood wedged tightly over her bunched hair. 'Difficult case,' she said and began to step aside.

Genies wept, don't let her get away with that, you're her consultant not an avatar. 'Patient, not case,' said Os, nudging Jezz back into position. 'Is this not the twin brother of the guy with aortic disease?'

Jezz nodded. She thought he would share exactly the same anatomy as his brother. 'But he's nothing like…'

'That will teach you, even twins are different. Write that down somewhere, you can quote me and I'm not expecting royalties.' Os signalled to the nurse to stop the din on the stereo. 'That's better,' she said to the sound of tinkling instruments in a silver tray. Handing a pack of fresh dry swabs to Jezz she leaned across to flick at a pale ridge on the front of the patient's heart and heard a crunchy sound. 'Calcium, it gets everywhere except my peri-menopausal bones,' said Os.

'Really?' gasped Jezz under her breath. 'You think he's got constriction as well as…?'

'I *know* he's got pericardial disease. And he's got only one life, unless you tell me he is a rechargeable battery, so let's get this show back on the road.' Os fixed her loupe in place, had the height of the stool adjusted so that she could see over Jezz's shoulder without straining her back. 'First do no harm, close that hole,' said Os, pointing at a tiny rent in a chest wall vein. She grabbed a retractor, acknowledging the nurse with a nod and a wink.

For the next three and a half hours, Os teetered on that crucial and at times nebulous line between training a junior colleague and protecting the patient. She resisted the great urge to save time and take over the operation, dabbing bleeders, discreetly suggesting the right way in or the choice of instrument, whispering or grunting encouragement and gentle admonishments whilst Jezz chipped and peeled the thickened restricting crust of scarred membrane off the heart. 'Great, couldn't have done better and I mean it,' said Os at the end, close to half past one in the morning. 'All for free at the point of use. That is what I call civilized.'

'Wish our pay was civilized…the cost of childcare,' said Jezz, patting her pregnant belly.

Os rolled her eyes. 'Genies wept, nobody but nobody can possibly pay us for what we do. Write that down too. Doctors can only be *repaid* by government on behalf of a -'

'Grateful nation?' said Jezz. 'Anyway thanks for tonight, we are really grateful,' said Jezz, tapping her belly and slapping her bloodied gloves into the proffered bin. 'Fancy a quick cuppa?' she said, her voice muffled by the double masks on her face.

Os shook her head. 'You should be as proud of yourself as I am proud of you, but don't not do it again.'

Jezz blinked and started back. 'What have I not done? Did I take too long?' Her glasses steamed up above her mask.

Os chuckled. 'Only pulling your leg. But you did me two favours tonight. Got me out of the midnight Covid shift.' She scanned the white theatre ceiling. 'This is probably one of the safest parts of the hospital. Clean air, one patient at a time and enough space to joust with barge poles. And we have the odd mask to spare…' As if on cue, a nurse wearing a high visor arrived with a fresh mask for Os. 'How old did you say his mother was again?' said Os to Jezz.

'Geraldine Stevens? Incredible. One hundred and four.'

'Then we better hurry off to tell her what a fantastic job you've done for this son too, before she catches Covid,' said Os. 'And ask her for tips about how to look after them,' she added, pointing to Jezz's bump. 'Don't look at me like that. Geraldine may be a hundred odd but she was like you once: fecund.'

'No… no way…that is uncanny, how did you know that I was having twins?' said Jezz, her eyes glistening like mother of pearl.

'Learned it during a teenage trip to Lagos. It's the curve of your spine,' said Os as she replaced her mask.

Jezz tapped her belly. 'Oops, darling, Professor nearly got your mummy going there. But what was the other favour?'

'You reminded me how it feels to operate without Ludwig. Don't do that to me ever again. Foo Fighters…Genies gimme strength…'

Two days later, Os was in her office redrafting a shirty e-mail to Cody about the inadequate supply of protective equipment when her phone rang for the third time in five minutes.

'Professor? Sharp?' The shrill urgency in the voice quivered one tibia against the other. There'd been an accident.

'What happened? Is he ok?' she heard her semi-detached self ask whilst her stomach tossed about like a bag under the arm of a fleeing shoplifter. *Genies wept, Ossy, wake up. Would Dr. Gauge ring or sound as if she had a rocking chair stuck in her throat if David simply tripped over a cockroach? Was accident a euphemism for a slash and burn of abdominal contents, fencing with toothbrushes, packs of feral young men pulping your skull contents?*

'David is in good hands. But no visitors on account of the Covid situation.' Dr. Gauge gave Os the phone number of the hospital switchboard. *Genies wept, good hands? Hope not in the hands of a mum like me, the cardiac surgeon who let her son slip through her oily hands.* Sweat bombarded her face. She dropped her head into her tingling hands, her knocking knees seemingly swapping places. When she shoved a fist into Comfort for a paper hanky, she dry retched and felt wetness in her underpants – legacy of the birthday of nine-pound three baby Louise. With a desperate Kegel squeeze, she sat up, packed her bag, closed her laptop, packed it up and hopped to the car. When she got home – she did not know how – John was at the dining table cursing a ragged crossword, his silver hair bronzed in the sun's goodbye glow. Os tore her headscarf and flopped against the worktop.

'It's David, in hospital,' she said, her knees beginning to melt again. John folded the crossword puzzle and rose to take Os in his arms.

'I wish you'd let me come with you, might have sort of resisted confrontation with this Iolanthe person…'

Os kicked one shoe off and said, as she aimed the other shoe at him, that she was in no mood for his fucking forensic hindsight. She could also have done without the carping Lamide in the cab on the way back from the detention centre. But she knew nobody wished any of this to happen, not Lamide, not John, except the men who ruptured David's spleen. What could her son have done to get up their sensitive probosces? Told them not to talk rot, looked at them in a wrong way? But did they need an excuse when some may have been programmed to violence from birth, from conception. What is it about the men in her family that attracted such aggro?

She popped a saucepan on to the stove and turned round to find Louise standing in the doorway to the bedroom corridor, wearing one of David's baggy black t-shirts. When Os told her about David, in halting euphemisms, Louise flung her headphones to the floor. 'Mum, you stood right there, and said he'd be ok. Nearly there, getting there, not quite there, couldn't quite manage it, except when it comes to your precious job. Urgh!' She went quiet and board stiff, as if in a clonic seizure, then hurled her fiery green glare across the table at John. 'Proud of yourself now?' she said.

Os turned away to peep into the simmering pot. Was it pasta or was it rice? 'Louise, we've got to stick together. Now more than ever. John?' she said, but John didn't reply. 'I honestly, don't know why I bother,' said Os. Her involuntary prod burst the bag and spewed rice grains into the boiling water. She felt a light tap on her neck. It was Louise, tears and mascara turning her face into a barcode.

'Sorry Mum, didn't mean it...'

Os reached up to wipe her daughter's tears. 'I know,' she said, although the girl had a point. If only she'd been there for the boy none of this would have happened. Her phone rang. It was Dr. Gauge. Os slammed the phone to ear. The psychologist sounded more relaxed than she did the last time they spoke. David was stable after the splenectomy but the centre would immediately – as soon as Covid permitted – carry out a full investigation into what went wrong. 'Lessons must be learned. Thoughts are with you...'

'Lessons to be learned and forgotten,' said Os. *Jeerie me, must think I'm a piece of spray-painted cheese. They'll say in their windy nonsense inquiry that her boy was carrying a suicide bomb in his belly when it went off behind his spleen where he'd tucked it, the other boys rushed to help and deserved the Victoria Cross but were too modest to have their names in the papers.*

'He'll be ok, won't he?' said Louise, a wish more than a question. She searched Os's face for a reaction. 'Oh I forgot, H-Mum called, said she wanted to come see us...like, face to face?' said Louise, fiddling with her headphones. At the mention of H-Mum's name, John, who was at the dining table, looked up, silently flicking blame at Os over the broadsheet, and ordering her to sort it out. Os had told H-Mum that David was in quarantine with friends and wouldn't be released until they all tested negative, but every lie has a sell by date and this version was no longer fit for consumption. If H-Mum smelled *wuru wuru*, as she inevitably would, not John, not Os, not Covid, not the MET would stop her trundling up the A3 in her Classic Citroen DS.

CHAPTER FIVE

H-Mum lived off New Cross Road not far from where, in that momentous year 1981, spontaneous combustion, or a rogue cigarette, or a tactical nuclear weapon, or Sango the Yoruba god of thunder and lightning, or the eponymous and omnipotent Unknown Soldier blamed by Nigerian juntas for any number of atrocities, anyone, anything, but racist arsonists, could have killed the 13 young black children attending a house party. That was the year of "13 dead nothing said", referring to the discombobulating silence from Thatcher and Queenie. And the year Fleet Street journalists mocked and chanted monkey noises at Os and the thousands marching in protest at the inadequate and insensitive official response to the disaster.

That was the year of Botham's Ashes, the year of the Brixton riots, the Toxteth riots, the year Os grew up and flushed away the remains of the naive Sunday School impressions that below a certain nadir of regard for black peoples as fellow human beings, white people will not sink. The year her impression that Blacks and Whites could possibly be worshipping the same God died. The year her faith in any God fatally shattered when, after a week of intense exhortations, Fred, the dishy boy in the year above her who drove a metallic red Capri, went off with Becky, the she-devil blessed with melon breasts; a disaster. The windows of H-Mum's first-floor flat glittered in ferocious sunshine, her block on the shoulder of a gentle rise a brisk five minutes' walk from the High Street. As Os swung the heavy door into the lobby, a citrus aroma wafted from the fading carpet. Averting her eyes from the fateful spot on the skirting board where her dad once banged his head, Os hopped up the stairs to the fusty living room, its avocado green wallpaper tinged orange by the afternoon sunlight streaming through the blinds.

On the bulky TV in the far corner reclined a photograph of a young H-Mum with Kola, he in a double-breasted light grey suit, smile burnished by hopes soon to be gobbled up by fate. Next to it stood one of Os and Lamide in happier times, and another of David, aged six, with Louise. When Os asked why H-Mum did not keep a photo of John, 'It's my house I put up who I want to' was the snapped reply. Os peeled back the blinds and sat on the firm leather sofa feet away from the lacquered upright piano under a stack of mildewed musical scores, the bane of her teenage years. On the side table and against the wall rested H-Mum's precious collection of highlife albums from 1950s and 1960s Lagos. H-Mum insisted that she would return to Lagos as soon as Os "settled down" – a nebulous term which Os took to mean promotion. But Os sensed that H-Mum wanted her to get back with Lamide. Os would rather have a drumstick drilled through her windpipe. A vague aroma of liquid shoe leather evoked memories of an overbearing, often clangorous, past. Os often heard people say they didn't want some grave childhood incident to define them. With respect to you survivors, she'd whisper to the TV or radio, shaking her head or wagging a finger, I think you will find on closer reflection that you are palpably mistaken. You will find that you cannot escape, because how you see it, through what you remember or refuse to forget about it, through what you know, or will never know or cannot recall, it is in there, part of you and will change your journey and make you a new and different you. All you can say is that you do not want what you can recall of the past to drop you too far behind or beneath the rest of those who should be your peers. Which is why, if like a villain in a movie, H-Mum's carriage clock rocked back on one edge and poured a bourbon and said, 'Been expecting you, Ossy,' and began to tick back to the messy start of her life, she'd drop to her knees and beg it not to. Or ask it to take someone else on a trip to tragic memory lane.

From snatches of conversation with H-Mum and her own timorous research, Os learned that her birth mother, Semijeje, grew up in a comfortable family in Lagos. Kola was going to England to study medicine whilst H-Mum, Poju, lived in downtown Mushin on the mainland where she worked as a part-time bargirl. Kola's parents preferred posh Semijeje to H-Mum as a match for their brilliant boy. When Kola left, followed shortly after by Semijeje, heartbroken H-Mum learned to play the keyboards for a Lagos jazz band to raise the money to study in England. Meanwhile, in cold and grey London, Semijeje cracked up, cowering in her room and pining for home. Having a child didn't help. Baby Osese seemed to mock and see through her mother and wind her around her perfect little fingers. To Semijeje this was no swaddled bundle of joy, but a VIP whose idea of constructive feedback consisted of sneers, grunts and power wails. Semijeje's sleepless head turned into a bog she tried to escape by wandering the streets. Meanwhile, at home in her cot, her six-month-old baby stared at the photo of Aretha Franklin in a red dress on the album cover on the mantelpiece.

One weekend Kola came home from medical school to find his precious baby daughter alone, starving, shivering, apathetic, and covered in filth. Devastated, he took time off from his studies, couldn't keep up, failed his exams and dropped out of medical school. He found a job in the maintenance department of a bus company.

Os was three when she found her birth mother, Semijeje, dead in bed. Dad saw the pills and suicide note when he got back from his night shift. Soon after the funeral, H-Mum seemed to come out of nowhere to make up a trio again. Then, on a drizzly Remembrance Day, Os's tenth birthday, Simply Blue and his gang murdered her dad.

That would have been that: orphaned Os packed off for a long pit stop in the care system for unsafe release years later, in adverse conditions and in the distant and treacherous wake of more fortunate peers. But H-Mum did not want dear Kola's daughter as the subject of some TV documentary about black girls or a sham public inquiry long after the bastard abusers, the pervert perps, were cadaveric with age, or dead; nor want to risk Os as a stepdaughter to some *yeye* man who failed to come up to standard.

Armed with her own experience of growing up in a strict household in Lagos, when Os went wrong, well-timed slaps from H-Mum reinforced vital tenets: a child is an experiment you can only run once; it's a jungle out there; practice makes lucky; it's a piano not a typewriter; scales should sing not make me itch; disagree first then check; make your mark but don't expect the glow to last; count your words before you speak; never look the police in the eye; only thing you open to the world is your bowel; never tell those who made or make you sick how you feel; *enia l'aso enia*, meaning friends and family are your protective equipment; and, in what Os came to call the 3Hs, to be happy or at least successful as a human being is to be at home in your head, your home and houtside. You, this girl, *omo yi*, she was not breaking her back cleaning Mr. Aggett's pharmacy or the stripper club for Os to mess up her life. Did Os want a kid at fourteen, two at fifteen then twins at sixteen? Did her late dad not say that there was room at the top if she worked hard? His last few words before he went out in that Union Jack and Nigerian green and white shirt? But God works in mysterious ways and one day Os would thank her hin Jesus's mighty name. Then, if H-Mum felt she'd gone too far with the whip, she'd croak an apology in English and Yoruba, make Os an omelette or pancake and say that in Lagos if you scold a child with the right arm it is with the other you comfort it: provided, of course, the child learns the lesson.

Os checked her phone. Phew, no news from David's hospital. That was something. As she peeled a paperback from a bookcase to read she heard the urgent clatter of a key in the front lock. The door rumbled open and a living room blind flapped to a sucking in of warm breeze. Os closed the windows, blew a speck off her baggy yellow t-shirt, inspected her trousers for creases, glanced in the mirror and slammed her mask on even as her armpits began to itch. They often did in H-Mum's presence.

H-Mum was wearing a navy blue blouse and jacket with button down Union Jack lapels in defiance of the thugs who murdered Kola for wearing the same colours. She kissed the silver crucifix dangling round her neck, to give thanks for arriving home safely. With a dismissive wave at Os's mask, she said, 'I declare you in my bubble, no need for that,' revealing the wide gap between her front teeth: in Lagos, a sign of good luck. A head taller than Os, with batwing ears, a tiny scar from a nick in the left nostril that flared when she got angry, courtesy of a nightclub knife fight when she was in her teens, H-Mum's dark brown face glowed from her walk. Rimless round spectacles shielded eyes which, when turned full on, made Os's blood jag around as if seeking to escape the frightened surges of adrenaline. Semi-retired, Poju, short for Ifeolepoju – meaning 'you can't have too much love' - wore her greying cornrows in four parallel curves. She ran online remedial maths classes for children sent to the referral units, a facility the system once used to exclude black children, many of whom were the children of the Windrush generation.

They knocked forearms and, in almost the same movement, H-Mum skipped across the room for a long look through the window as if to take in the mathematical beauty of the world from the tranquillity and safety of her God-given home in England, detached at last from Brussels. Brussels down, Brussels drowns, London's waves you au revoir, she sang on that Friday morning in June. H-Mum stewed the whole of mainland Europe in the same pot. She voted Leave to keep out those backward people in the east who booed black football players. Keep your primitive chants. When you civilise we will let you henter our Hengland.

'Sit down, Ossy. How is everything going?' she said, giving Os a close once over. She didn't wait for an answer. 'Take off your spectacles and let me see your eyes,' she said, reaching forward but Os took the glasses off herself. 'Look at your eyes. Dry. You are like a toothpick on hunger strike. Should we eat? Omelette? Pancake? Fried rice? Akara? Moinmoin? Eba? I have it all.' She swished out to change into a grey gown and, in a nod to social distancing, sat across the coffee table from Os, with a glass of water, her back to the ancient TV set.

'Can't stay long, came to say we are going to be busy. The council is talking of local restrictions,' said Os, weaving in a little inaccuracy and adding that she'd read that a middle-aged man like John might be more vulnerable to Covid so the fewer contacts the better, unless H-Mum wanted to kill him with Covid. H-Mum pointedly ignored the quip by speaking sotto voce to a hairpin she picked off the floor. Os waited for the itching in her armpit to recede then asked if H-Mum could wait a couple of weeks before she paid a visit. 'Really sorry, honestly.'

H-Mum contemplated Os for what seemed like a decade. 'Hunh, I can read you like that big neon sign at Piccadilly. Is he giving you trouble?' Did John send her? Didn't he want her there? Were they having problems? Was it not her husband's idea to spend all that money on the house? Why was it taking so long when as far as she knew builders were allowed to work during lockdown? H-Mum leaned against the arm of the sofa, her Lagos lilt loaded with wistful notes. 'You see, Osese, this is why I cannot go back to Lagos. Not until you are settled. In Jesus's mighty name.' She bowed her head further and mumbled in Yoruba.

'Always you bring it back to John,' Os said. She slung Comfort over her shoulder and eyed the doorway as if to leave.

H-Mum stepped across and took Os by the hand. 'Osese, *omo mi*, please.' Ah, ah, she'd reached the point in life when there are more hours in the night than there are years left for her. Why waste time on trading petty quarrels? 'Is it not because I care about hall of you that I ask? Not for hany hother reason,' said H-Mum. All she wanted in Jesus's mighty name was to spend more time with Os and the children. Once David goes to university, who knows when she'd see him? 'Wait,' said H-Mum. She skipped to the kitchen and soon returned with two steaming mugs of peppermint tea and a packet of oatmeal biscuits. 'What was I saying? Oh yes, what about your promotion?' Was Covid delaying matters? Covid gets the blame for everything. If you are pregnant they blame Covid. Your car won't start, it's Covid.

'Guess who walked into my clinic last week?' said Os. The job was the last thing she wanted to talk about but she'd heard rumours that Cody Hayes was on the warpath because she'd raised several complaints about the inadequate provision of protective equipment.

'Your clinic? Why not ask the man who does not want us in his house, the house you bought and he is enjoying more than your children?' Os did not rise to the bait. H-Mum went on. 'Ok, let me think. Was it Nelson Mandela?' she said, biting into a biscuit.

'Mason Boardman. Simply Blue.'

H-Mum's started back so hard her glasses fell off her nose. 'What? Him? Where?' she said, tapping the spectacles back into place.

Born of a Nigerian father and New Cross white mother, brought up - seized, rather – with expectations mangled - and managed, rather - by his maternal grandmother, Mason Boardman worked as a gofer in a betting shop, then folded into the gang of his maternal cousin who, emboldened by the hostile environment created by Enochisms, goaded him to race-bait BEMs, especially the recent arrivals with broad African accents.

On Osese's tenth birthday, Armistice Day, when her dad, clad in a shirt made of the Union Jack and the Nigerian green and white, walked past, Simply Blue led the chase after him. Osese heard the door crash open and her dad's loud screams and the sound of his head hitting the skirting board flooded her little body with terror. She bounded down the stairs, half dressed, one shoe on, the other shoe nowhere, to find dad lying pale and sweaty with the books he bought for her birthday slipping from his carrier bag.

Osese cried out, 'Dad,' and pressed the shirt down on the blood spurting from his neck. The cloth squelched and bubbled with blood.

'My little treasure in this world, don't let them get away with it,' he said in a tired whisper. He yawned again. 'Remember…room at the… top,' he said, his bloodless eyes opening, rolling to the ceiling as if to make a point. 'It's cold in here,' he said and yawned. He yawned again.

Osese shook him, begging him to stay awake because she thought she heard the siren of an approaching ambulance. But Simply Blue and his gang blocked the road with burning garbage and the ambulance didn't arrive until it was too late.

'Didn't your busman know it is a provocative action to wear our shirt like that on Remembrance Day?' said the police officer. Subtext: England was theirs, how dare you ask why they owe you a kicking? Neighbours dragged the cursing and screaming H-Mum away from the police station. The investigation into the murder came to nothing. Insufficient evidence. For months after, Simply Blue's gang taunted H-Mum in the street. And, although her granddad Ososanya fought in WWII, Os never again celebrated her birthday during the week of Remembrance Day, moving it around, or skipping it altogether, depending on how she felt.

'Awamaridi, God moves in mysterious ways,' said H-Mum slowly shaking her head.

'Moves in mysterious ways His wonders to perform?' When the man they called Simply Blue – his swearing and bad manners turned the air blue – strode into her consulting room expecting to see Ian, Os recognised him at once. How could she forget the scar across his broken nose and his despicable manners, the lascivious stares at women? Yet, she tried to put the familiar flash of contempt in his eyes when he saw her down to her paranoia, or, as John repeatedly said, her heightened self-consciousness. Others jokingly attributed this instant recognition of subliminal facial expressions to an atavistic reactivation, amongst black people in the diaspora, of a highly conserved evolutionary protective set of genes, or to a meme crucial to social and economic survival in difficult environments.

That morning, as Os fidgeted in her chair, her smile forced into place, the man added to her irritation by insisting that he didn't need a mask and, when he eventually agreed to wear one, shoved it onto his chin and shouted over the top of it. In flashy trainers, his wicked eyes behind thick-rimmed lenses, he sat well back and spread as wide as he could, like Putin did with Hilary Clinton and Angela Merkel. 'Not being funny, miss, can't be too careful, but how many of this bypass lark have you done?' Then he wisecracked about having a fag with his pint as soon as Os sorted him out, that's assuming she was really the boss person and not a stand in, it being the NHS and everyone knew it was for the knacker's yard, unless they give it to Amazon. Os had long forgiven him. Was he not as much a product of the system as any racist killer cop? But she could not wait to kick the door shut after the disgusting man.

'It is my job to treat him,' said Os, anticipating H-Mum's misgivings.

'Jesus forgive me, but what that man did to Kola was, I don't want to call it devil's work because even the devil is not that wicked. But God brought him to your clinic for a reason…*awamaridi*.' She emptied the crumbs from her saucer into her palm.

'Where was awamaridi when he killed my dad?' said Os, instantly regretting the retort because she wanted to make a quick exit before H-Mum tied her in knots over David.

H-Mum clapped her hands and looked to the sky for forgiveness. When Os got home safely in Jesus's mighty name, she should tell Louise and David and John that she was going to have a PCR and lateral flow test and if the result is good come to see them next week.

Os leapt to her feet. Drawing herself up to her full height of 5 ft 4 she said, 'Mummy, ah, I told you they are studying. No Zoom no Teams. No Skype. Nothing.' She backed away to the door.

H-Mum raised her spectacles to the light but did not speak.

'See you soon,' said Os.

CHAPTER SIX

The past does not have to dismount for the present to weigh in.

When Os heard that David had caught Covid she nearly ran a red light by mistake. For one day, he was "stable", as they call it, holding his own. Then he collapsed into multi-organ failure. The works: liver, kidney and of course the athletic elastic lungs that drove his beautiful preacher's voice and prowess on the sports field did not escape the virus.

From the local hospital they rushed him to Northampton. No ITU beds. Then York, where the last bed had just gone. Coventry had no nurses. Nottingham had one bed because, thank the stars, someone had just died. Os couldn't visit because of the Covid restrictions. She kept in touch by calling one of the rushed-off-their-feet nurses, usually Kathryn or Marianne. When she saw her son in ITU lying unconscious with his eyes taped she shook like a pneumatic drill. Then they turned her baby's body prone, face down and all she saw to distinguish him was a curlicue of a scar in a crease of his neck. Tubes everywhere. A black shiny tube down his throat for echocardiograms, tubes in his neck and in his nose for drug delivery and monitoring, and a thin transparent tube in his bladder to receive what little brown urine his kidneys produced. Two larger tubes poked from each side of his chest. Grey monitors hovered from the ceiling. Green wriggly ECG complexes raced across their screens like goblins off to no good. At times they rose and concertinaed or broadened into bizarre shapes or a chaotic cadence, dreaded harbingers of doom, thankfully for the powerless Os not for long because her heart galloped almost as fast as David's, close to the point of blacking out herself, during these storms.

The team talked of dialysis and plasma exchange. H-Mum and her friends started special prayers – life is too thick for reason halone to see through it, said H-Mum. Hope was all Os had, hope and faith in the skill of the doctors and nurses, hope that the play of luck, a chance remark or observation, something they read in a journal or heard the other day or that morning, and his genes would help calm the angry red cells, white cells and starry platelets, ristocetin, arachidonic acid and the fulminant cytokines. *Please, Genies, Providence, forces yet unrecognised, please lead his antibodies out of autoimmune overreactions, rouse him from dependence on ventilation and shield him from more complications. Please Genies let him be, let him live.* She would never again hide her love for him; never again let him feel misunderstood, not by this loving but prodigal mother.

Os sent him a recording of her telling him how much she loved him and a playlist of his favourites: Tupac, Little Simz, Stormzy and Davido and Burna Boy songs. John could wear his sceptical headmaster face if he wanted, but could music not reset myriad cellular rhythms, reach deep structures and limbic systems to revive her son in ways doctors didn't yet understand? During her calls to the ward, John would often hover in the doorway looking rueful and blameworthy, scratching his collar bone with a pencil, or twirling the pencil in his hand, or nursing a mug of tea.

Once, Os beckoned him over to sit next to her, but he had to ruin the moment by hinting that the doctors didn't quite know what they were doing and that he'd read about Ivermectin and Chloroquine. At that, the little patience she had left for him – it fit into half an amoeba with space to spare – collapsed, and she did not try to save it. She told him to shut up and moved into David's room. 'For your safety,' she told John, when he asked why.

A few days later, she thought he looked suicidal and, as she couldn't bear a repeat of what happened to her birth mum, she moved back in with him and once tried to help him with his essay on the GINI coefficient during the first Elizabethan era. Were those the halcyon days, without the wasteful welfare system, that hedge funders such as

Gary wanted to take us back to? John asked. Os couldn't give a toss if Gary and his ilk turned the whole country into a pleasure yacht.

On a damp and drippy evening, David's fourteenth day in hospital, Os was on her laptop in the living room, mind drifting from its futile grasp on the latest confusing hospital directive on PPE to fantasising on how she would inflict subtle delicious vengeance on Simply Blue compatible with the Hippocratic Oath. The awful man was on her list for a triple bypass the next morning. To have to save the life of the man who killed her dad, whilst her son, the victim of similar violence, fought for his life, felt like a gargantuan kick in the teeth. Would it not be fair to mitigate the affront, to suspend pure ethics for a few minutes and have some fun by sneaking up to Simply Blue when he was at his most vulnerable, shivering and half naked in a freezing anteroom, to tell him who she was? Or, as he regained fuzzy consciousness, and didn't know where he was, tell him he'd died and you were the ghost of his New Cross victim? And watch him squirm. She closed the PDF on Trust PPE policy and was about to switch off her laptop when Louise shuffled in without headphones, her face lined like a badly mown lawn.

'Can't seem to find David,' she said and scratched her hair, which looked like a wrecked bird's nest.

Os's back bones quaked. Sweat pumped to her face. She tottered to her feet. What did Louise mean by "can't find him"? *Genies wept, these kids and their Tik Tok stuff. Or probably had her head in the clouds with Kevin or was it Calvin?* Os disconnected her phone from the charger in the kitchen bay and switched it on. Louise hovered, hyperventilating warm air over Os's ear. The ward appeared on the screen. In bed 6, under the dark grey monitor, lay not David but a pale white man with a large tattoo of a naked black woman on his arm.

No. Please, No.

Misty waves shimmered in her eyes. One sign, one sight was all she yearned for. A single tinkle or snore from him or a jingle from his bedside kit; a twitch of his toe or the back of the elbow was not too much to ask. Ah, Os turned to Louise and said perhaps they moved him to another ward, or took him for a scan, or to a step-down room because he was doing well enough. They forgot to call them. They are so busy. Been there myself. You are not thinking of relatives, just the patient in front of you and the patient to come. Louise pointed at the phone. That's the same picture she got too, she said in a tremulous voice. Should they not call the ward? Os snapped at her, huffed an apology, and said of course, but what did Louise think she was trying to do all along? She dialled the hospital switchboard. The man on the other end sounded too breathless for words. Genies gimme strength, only gone and called a blinking jogger. She cut him off and tried again. By this time, her heart had gone berserk. A robotic voice warned that some calls may be recorded for training purposes. Fluttering inside like warring hummingbirds, Os couldn't give a rat's ass what they recorded. If they didn't show her her boy, her heart was going to jump out to look for him itself.

As she swapped the phone from one sweaty palm to the other, on pinged the clear voice of Kathryn, the friendly ITU nurse Os so often spoke to close to the end of the shift. On the hiss of *s* of Kathryn's sorry, Os squeaked and, in that bang, a dark weighty aching searching void hollowed her out.

CHAPTER SEVEN

'Please don't go,' said Louise, sobbing and hanging on to Os's nightie with both hands.

'Be back as soon as…I've got to go, darling,' said Os.

She wished she didn't have to. Had last night truly happened? Was Kathryn mistaken? But why would Louise cry all night? Os teased her nightie from Louise's desperate grip. She sloped up the dark corridor, her head like a brick. David's empty room looked ordinary and tidy, the same as it had the day before and the day before. The walls remained pale, trainers paired, the calendar open, textbooks shelved under his makeshift desk on which sat a few lists. A black biro sat on the stool. Wardrobe doors were closed. In the bathroom she stared into space for five minutes. Her electric toothbrush didn't foam. It took her five minutes to see that she had spread foundation on it instead of toothpaste. She skipped toast and tossed a few grains of coffee down her dry throat. Eating seemed banal. So was adjusting her seat belt and starting the engine, as was turning the steering wheel to avoid a pothole. Or applying the brakes to stop at a pedestrian crossing for a man, who looked the worse for wear, to stagger to his waiting car. Lucky him. He was having a normal day perhaps. Hers was anything but.

She stalled the car at a set of temporary traffic lights. Then she took the wrong left turn off Burmeste Road. For a moment she forgot that she had to pull a ring up on the gearstick to engage reverse. Back shuddered the car into a green wheelie bin. She bit her lip, took a few deep breaths and swung the car round. Lost, she trundled down a tree-lined avenue, turned left, and followed a shrieking ambulance around the one-way system. Please, please, make it be, let it be the right way.

The receptionist cast a worried glance at the theatre clock. Os rolled a Don't Ask look with her eyes. Twelve minutes late. Was that all? Hugging Comfort she pressed open the pale blue door to the ante-room. It was as empty as she felt inside. Her fingers closed round the compact disc. A period instrument performance of Beethoven's 5th. Something familiar, unchanging. It would do to frame the time. She fumbled it into the player. Teeth gritted, with Comfort held to her chest, like a shield, she ducked through a back door into the female changing room.

She crept in to the theatre. The patient was hidden under green drapes. A man in a pointy blue hood leant over her patient. Yet, it was not Ian. Her heart clenched. Blonde Barrie, the bearded Nigerian perfusionist, made a muted gesture and she tore her heavy eyes from the look of concern on his face. The man in the pointy hood turned round. It was Cody Hayes. Os's nerves screeched as if steam cleaned. What in the name of the Horn of Africa? Cody waited for Os to get within whispering range, bowed, and mumbled, 'In the circumstances, really sorry, least I could do…wasn't expecting you…in, but, well…'

Os groaned to herself. 'I see,' she said, her voice roughened by a suppressed sob in the changing room. She battled the powerful temptation to let the tears explode from their bulging sacs. *What did Cody want? How did he know?* She had to do this operation. If not, her head would surely explode. No way was she standing around whilst Cody faffed about. This was her patient, her day in theatre, not his. Narrowly missing an instrument trolley, she staggered to the taps to get scrubbed, counting to a hundred to stop her rushing this important ablution.

'Hang on to this, will you, whilst I have another look round. Nasty three vessel disease, extraordinary,' said Cody, dropping the forceps into the waiting palm of the sleek scrub nurse. 'Could someone do something about the overhead light if it's not too much trouble? This loupe's a right dog. What's this we've got here?' he said, edging Os out of the way once again. Os counted to ten.

'Honestly, I'm touched, but really, honestly I'm fine.' She pointed at the clock on the wall. 'If you stay you'll have to do the student appraisals too,' said Os. Cody saw appraisals as a perverse imposition on his limited time. He tore off his size 8 gloves, whispered condolences again and stalked from the room before Os could ask for a proper handover.

Breathing a little easier, Os dragged up a stool to stand on for a clear view of how far Cody had gone. The patient's heart looked larger than it did on the echocardiogram, but finer details escaped her grasp. She ground her teeth and whispered an exhortation. *Come on, you can do this.* The soaring portentous, fate-defining, fate-defying strings of Beethoven's 5th symphony brought her terrifyingly close to tears. Please. No. She sucked in a breath and counted to ten. Out went her palm to a pear-shaped scrub nurse. In her hand landed the perfectly weighted scalpel which Os had helped design. Os caressed the vein graft for texture, an instinctive habit. She got to work. There was nothing preternaturally metaphysical or automatic about her fingertips today. This was a grind. A battle against the hollow ache dissecting her from within whilst she worked, willing, sweating, slipping, clamping, stumbling, suturing her way up a steep relearning curve. Yet she still completed the operation in a credible ten minutes before the end of the 39-minute symphony. Taking each breath as it came, watching every step she took, tinted glasses pushed well back on her nose, nodding or shaking her head to greetings, avoiding eye contact in an affectation of deep contemplation, she found a quiet spot behind the old three-wheeled old trolley to write up her surgical notes.

When she returned to the operating room, there was no patient. Aargh. Her neck snapped back so hard it gave her headache. Barrie grimaced an apology and turned off Sean Paul on the radio. 'Been in there since before I went for my break. Maybe they can't find the locum because of Covid?' he said, pointing with his mop at the blue double doors to the anaesthetic room. Os peeped through the crack in the door. Firecrackers went off in her head. *Genies no, this cannot be true too.* There were two Mr. Boardmans on the list. The dark eyes of a quivering brown-skinned Simply Blue made four with hers. Yet he was meant to be first on the list. She didn't need a genie to tell her that, if he was here, she must have operated on the wrong patient - the white Mr. Boardman. Cody, or someone, must have swapped the list. The throbbing in her eyes signalled blood pressure going "through the sphyg". She slowed her breaths down and spun away from the deepening frown of concern on Blonde Barrie's dark brown forehead. *Ossy, you know what you have to do. Take the white Boardman back to check you've got it right.* They can whisper behind their hands and tell everyone you've lost it: but as H-Mum says *nothing spoil,* the patient is still breathing is he not? As Os was about to summon help to get the white Mr. Boardman back in to theatre, the siren went off and a curt message on the Tannoy summoning Professor Sharp to the ITU confirmed her fears. She raced to ITU, her heart flapping like a flag in a storm. In ITU she found her first patient, the white Mr. Boardman with his face a deadly shade of pale. He looked as if he did not have long before he joined the ranks of his other departed Spurs supporting mates.

Os wished she could be anything else: a particle, a dust mote, a comma, a bug, or the star of one of those terrible nightmares you wake up from smiling with relief when your partner jabs you out of it with a poke in the ribs. She heard herself bark the orders to get this Mr. Boardman back in. 'Now, as in this very second,' she snapped.

She rushed off to splash cold water over her head and don a fresh pink surgical hood, counting to fifty as slowly as she could whilst she rescrubbed. She stepped back under the bright theatre lights and the curious eyes of her team, except those of the anaesthetist, who sat at the head of the table tutting, twiddling knobs, and wobbling his long head. He couldn't have looked less supportive if they paid him. When Os saw Mr. Boardman's pale and still heart and felt its lumpy base, her strenuously composed self-possession almost collapsed. 'Angio? Show me the angio,' she said, to check her work against the results of the preoperative diagnostic angiogram. But the anaesthetist tapped the head of the cradle.

'Lactate's not great. Bleeding anywhere?'

Os fumed. Did he think she was some wet-behind-the-ear first-year rookie with a big green P on their FRCS certificate? Ever seen her patient bleed before? But standing as she was, in a fashion, in the midst of a conflagration armed only with a leaking spittoon, she lifted Mr. Boardman's flaccid heart in her trembling palms, taking care not to twist the grafts off. 'No leaks, didn't think so,' she said, out of the corner of her mouth, then, when the angiogram appeared on the screen, she spotted to a thud in the back of her head that she'd put two grafts on the wrong segments of a branch of the left anterior descending artery. How? She'd never done that before as far as she could recall. But this was not enough to explain the man's catastrophic collapse. 'I'll revise these branches, take down the y graft,' she said, trying to sound calm, whilst she tore through her rapidly emptying mind for explanations. Had the cranky old bypass circuit let air bubbles in? Fat embolus? Reactivated Tuberculosis? Reperfusion injury? She got back to work, checking again for signs of fresh damage to the heart muscle, then, reeling, held her breath and squeezed her hands together whilst she waited to see if Mr. Boardman's heart would come off bypass. If he didn't, what the hell next? On a better day, yes, she'd find a way, but today was about reflexive cussed determination even as hope threatened to shrink and disappear down a lubricated hole. Then through the ether appeared a thick rubber digit; the thumbs up from Blonde Barrie caught the incredulous corner of her eye. The patient had come off bypass as easy as blood flows from a ram at Ramadam. *Don't ask, just go whilst you are ahead.* Lightheaded, Os scurried out of the room, reaching a dark and quiet corner seconds before the tears exploded from her eyes.

CHAPTER EIGHT

Os was in a dark and dank basement in the Midlands somewhere but couldn't tell you exactly where. Had to be done. She gave the chipped double door a timid single knock and stepped back, suppressing a retch, squeezing her eyes closed, swaying as she swallowed the bitter saliva of nausea. She'd been sick twice that morning in the car. Her eyes rested around a lunate crack at the foot of the grey wall. It looked the same as everything else: the oaks and beech trees in the fields, the hydrangeas in the front gardens, the sports cars roaring past on the highway. All draped in the same monotone. Until a cold squall brushed the left side of her chest, Os didn't know that Comfort had fallen off her shoulder. She let the bag rest there beside her foot on the floor, like a loyal pet, and was summoning the will to knock on the door again when a white woman, aged about thirty and wearing an ankle-length plastic apron over boots - Naomi, according to her NHS badge - tapped her on the shoulder. In almost the same movement, Naomi bumped an elbow into Os's by way of Covid greeting and swiped them both into the mortuary with a blue card.

Shivering in the cold room, Os tucked her cardigan in closer at the waist. Naomi swaggered over to a bank of cubicles, the source of the acrid aroma in the room. She rumbled a long metal trolley into view. From the first glimpse of the toe with the brown label hanging off it, Os knew it was David. She froze, beset by a scene you don't, you won't, you can't, dress rehearse; a scene you bat out of mind when you hear of it or read about it. That is, if you don't skip the scene, because the contemplation of it is suffocating, and you cannot take more than a few seconds of it before you withdraw. That is, if you have a choice.

She didn't.

This was no dream or mistake. This was happening and it was her boy's body under the bedewed sheet, a sliver of the large eyes his dad gave him peeping between swollen eyelids, upper lip peeled away from his perfect teeth as if in mordant pity at the frenetic attempts to save his life. Os only realised that Naomi had been talking to her when she heard a sharp stress on a Midland syllable.

The long-limbed lament of the empty ache within her shrieked anew. Yet she could hear herself speak.

'Yes, it's him.'

Her head seemed to swing back and forth on a thickening neck. Naomi retreated. Os stroked the barely visible scar David got on his left shin when he fell off his teacher's pushbike. She dug her elbows into her chest to stop the tears. Why did she not fucking apologise for tearing a strip off the boy when she learned that he took the bike to fill a prescription for his diabetic friend, Clarence, before the chemist closed? Was it to crave John's approval? Or to reassure dubious neighbours that she had the potential terrorist under control? Or was it to vent her fear that he could have fallen into the fitting cuffs of a capricious cop? Or out of cussed frustration with something else he'd done? Answering back, perhaps, as was his wont? She cupped David's doughy cold right hand in hers. She'd do anything to hear that sardonic baritone once more, live. Her tear dropped on to the back of David's hand. She wiped it at once as if it were desecrating or corrosive or a blight.

Naomi loped up, waited, then took Os by the elbow and guided her away from David's body. Leaving Os standing beside an empty desk, Naomi strode back to the trolley and, with jarring professional deftness, rumbled it one-handed back into its cubicle. The main door to the mortuary purred closed behind Os.

Was that it?

It seemed odd that the world did not stop. Strange that she had no special escorts or dispatch riders or constables to guide her to the hospital exit. Was it not odd that she didn't get a medal or commendation for being the bravest mother of the day. Surely, grief must be written all over her face and in her gait because her legs didn't quite go the way the eyes saw it and her arm swung into the wall of the corridors she hugged for safety.

Somehow, she found herself back under the bright lights of the hospital foyer with most of the shops, flower sellers, cobblers and grocers, closed for lockdown. The revolving doors granted her the first concession to her existence since she left Naomi's presence, by pausing when she got too close. Back in the car, she was looking for the car keys she dropped on the floor when the Beethoven ringtone intruded. It was John.

'You turned it off, didn't you? Then why are you calling me here?' she barked down the phone. She couldn't give a monkeys whether he said she left the iron on the laptop or the laptop on the iron. She lifted Comfort off the floor of the car and placed it on her lap and stared.

***

For the funeral H-Mum had demanded a conventional church service but Os threw a spectacular tantrum worthy of John. No, double underlined upper case *no*, she did not want a blinking service, she screamed at H-Mum. David was her son and she was going to have what she wanted, thank you very much.

Lockdown rules prevailed: H-Mum, Louise, and Os sat socially distanced in the front seat at the Crematorium, Lamide sat a row behind. His eyes like cobwebbed catacombs in a face like crumpled underpants. Os had called him once, not knowing why. They swapped mumbles for a few minutes until she broke down.

John remained in the flat with his mother, Jaundiced Matilda. H-Mum didn't want him at the service. Os didn't either, but a stubborn core of residual loyalty stopped her admitting her declining feelings for John to H-Mum who would only make the situation, not worse, that was not possible, but unmanageable.

Her armpits throbbed in time with each hammer blow of a

heartbeat. Her eyes drifted to the huge photo of a smiling David in rugby colours mounted on his raffia coffin. The hammer blows got heavier. Haloed lights flashed before her eyes. The photo was a concession to his classmates because she hadn't wanted a physical reminder of her loss unless she was in control. Which was why she'd stopped listening to the radio. Once, the three-note motif in the first movement of the Moonlight Sonata took her by surprise. *Oh Da-vid, Oh Da-vid, Oh Da-vid* it sang to her. She pulled off the road sobbing and didn't know she was holding up one of those long lockdown queues for McDonalds you could see from outer space until a waitress tapped on the car window.

Twice, in her distraction, instead of turning off the A3 at Tolworth for the flat, she found herself on Sure Lanes as in the old days, only realising her mistake and that David didn't live there anymore, yards from the house. She made a frantic U- turn before the workmen spotted her cab from the top of the scaffolding and asked their latest cash cow for more dosh.

To be so densely packed with pain yet functioning as a bodily unit, a social entity - sleeping, eating, itching, once or twice smiling, making room for oncoming prams, returning the friendly nods of the creepy fishmonger - she didn't know was possible.

Sometimes, on a long solitary walk in the woods, she'd find herself calling out David's name. She tormented herself with the sad image of young David, after a caustic put-down by John, arms round little scuffed knees, head bowed, weeping silently for his mummy to come home. Or recalled carrying newborn David home, 7 pounds and 8 ounces, his eyes closed between a dark malar flush of downy hair. Or she'd sing the silly song, "apple and cinnamon, eh," as she'd sung it, weaning David onto solids. And on another occasion, she'd remember the radiant pride in his eyes when he saw her going wild with joy on the touchline after he scored his first goal at Barden Park, his spindly right leg almost apologetically giving his toes the permission to prod the ball home. Or how he fondly berated her for missing his spectacular winning volley for the school team because, distracted by the worrying fate of a surgical patient, she had had the camera lens cap on. Or she'd find herself telling someone of her terror when she rushed to pick up the fourteen-year-old after news of a brawl in the centre of Kingston. Or she'd wallow in the image of cute David, aged three, plate perched on his knee, eating his lunch with a plastic fork without spilling a bean. Or a picture would come to mind of him aged five, reciting a poem at school, hands behind his back the way H-Mum taught him. Or of her, Os, combing his hair after his marathon charity cardiac massage to raise money for a defibrillator to place in the town centre. She recalled, to ripples of stomach cramps, the don't-worry-Mum text message he sent her after she had a bad day in theatre and a smile cruised to her face as she drove past the club for his cadets' group or the shop where they both invented the fantasy queue game during lockdown. At the end of the game, usually decided by Os when she was ready to go home, the one who had the greater number of followers in their queue that day won.

Sometimes she stopped in front of a tree as if to find a spot on its trunk against which to dash her brain out and leave her unbearable pain for dead. But there was no escape. It was her life sentence. Nothing, not drink, not drugs, would take it away. And though she was just about hanging on herself by a gossamer thread, she had a duty to set an example of fortitude to Louise.

How H-Mum could say this was all part of a grand plan and that the great designer wouldn't give you a burden you couldn't bear she couldn't say. Gimme shelter, the same designer of the twisty double helix we lug around at great cost? Who instead of shouting 'Fire Fire, Mutation Mutation', and correcting your spelling or his dictation with special powers before you are born, leaves you with motor neurone disease, with Huntingdon's, leads a newborn with one heart chamber instead of four into a warzone and, to rub it in, with back to front plumbing. Or packs your spleen with sticky sickle red cells or air sacs with goo and cancers too many to mention. And gives you a consuming love for your son from the moment you clasp eyes on him, then snatches him away? Or inflicts, on a whole generation of millions, a strong man who knows it all and kills all those who he thinks should know better and those who do. Yet still they come, the likes of H-Mum, singing "Haven't got any truths left today, darling, but here is another God-fearing homily baked for you to eat up and share with your friends, especially those in the poor world."

'Go away, go and bow down for what you want, if you want, but leave me out of it,' she said when H-Mum claimed with absolute certainty that it was grief talking. They fell out, but Louise found a way to pull them together again.

'Mum, we each have our ways of coping with this planet. Whatever floats your mind out of this hell works for me,' said Louise. Os saw the rationale for the consoling religious notion that we will all meet again in some hereafter, but it wasn't for her.

At times David appeared in her tortured dreams as a disembodied voice to tell her that he was still alive, that he staged all this to shake her up and warn her not to repeat the same mistakes with his sister. He'd be back soon to start his medical studies at Cambridge. But she would wake up to her agonising, hollowing out emptiness and weep because it was nothing but a cruel dream.

Yet, the dream came true in parts. Despite his anxieties and the ministerial U-turns, David got in. Early one calm September morning Os drove to her old college, Jesus, to tell the admissions officer that David wouldn't be coming. Why she had to go all the way there to say so she couldn't say. Perhaps it was to imagine him there or for someone to ask about her son and give her an excuse to regale them with stories of his great feats and wisdom, how she used to call him the Perineal Chancellor of the Exchequer because he said, when it comes down to it, freedom is the choice to do what you wanted with your orifices, in private. But the thin man with the thin tie in a thin office at first didn't believe that Os was who she said she was. Then, when she produced a utility bill to confirm her address, said in a catarrhal voice he was sorry to hear about David but was there anything else he could do for her? Brochure? Any other sons? Sorry, daughters? *Genies wept, he could try growing a better deskside manner.* Twice on the slog back to her car she stopped beside an immaculate pitch where a few boys played football or a semblance of cricket, sorrow punching her rib cage because her boy wouldn't be playing football or rugby or arguing his case at the Union here. She'd never see him grow into a much better version of herself, which wouldn't have taken much doing for someone like David.

A tap on the shoulder from the headmaster reeled her back out to the hall. Was Os expecting anyone else? 'Four of us, no…nobody else,' she said, looking over her shoulder at Lamide as if for confirmation. Lamide, in a dark suit and blue t-shirt, looked dazed. The Head of School, Peter Drinkwater, appeared on a screen to give a speech. David Bamisetiti, DB, was nicknamed Aston Martin because he shared the same initials as an iconic model of the marquee. Aston Martin loved fairness, symmetry, and balance which is why he walked round the school clockwise one day, the other way the next. Aston Martin loved siding with the underdog, then changing sides when the underdog got too big for boots. David would have made a fantastic doctor, a cardiac psychiatrist if such an animal existed because he liked to know what made people tick so he could wind them up the right way. David was the best smelling and elusive teenage ball handling centre the rugby world had ever seen, bamboozling opponents with the perfume he borrowed from his mother's dressing table and the potpourri stuffed under his shirt. Surely the other side didn't know which scent to track. A grunt escaped from Os. H-Mum tugged on the golden crucifix hanging round her neck.

Louise went next. She dragged herself past her brother's photo and onto the podium. She said she had lost her best mate, her armour, brakes, engine, and catapult all in one. She said she was bombed out, nothing worked inside, she was just a shell, no light, no heating, nothing inside. Then her face crumpled under an avalanche of tears. She tumbled into H-Mum's arms. H-Mum, warned by Os - on pain of kneecapping - not to go off message, read Psalm 23 and told the story of how David tried to raise money for her because he thought she was going to be deported. She described his marathon cardiac massage on a mannequin to buy a defibrillator for the shopping centre. For a week after that marathon he could not raise his arms above his head.

Then the headmaster's discrete gestures fetched Os to the podium to read the words she'd forced herself to scribble down that morning. David was her beacon and like her PPE and she didn't know it, he showed her fault lines but she looked the other way. When her boy was alive, he was always out there somewhere, but reachable, whatever you wanted to say or do – telling him that you loved him, or that you got it and had been there yourself as a teenager – could always wait. And now he'd gone he was always with her: an unbearable ghostly eviscerating mist she walked through when she got out of bed in the morning and that embraced her last thing at night. A weighty aura of him that went everywhere with her, sat next to her in the loo. 'Sorry, David, for not…,' she said and was going to say more but the text on the page grew fat and furry and she lost her place. 'Thank you all for your support,' she said, perspiring with the effort to contain herself as the hollow ache inside her ballooned.

She heard little of what the headmaster said. After, from recessed speakers, welled her choice, the section of the 3rd movement of Beethoven's Choral Symphony, from glorious fanfare with full orchestra to the elegiac waltz-like finale she thought matched her son's breezy vulnerability. The raffia coffin shrank from view behind the fitful closure of the maroon blinds. Her boy, her little treasure in the world, was gone.

*****

'That was beautifully done by Louise,' said Matilda, her back to the outside window, long legs draped by a bottle green skirt, silver earrings in the form of cricket bats swinging in synchrony as she turned her head to Os and then to H-Mum.

The living room smelled of John's fresh baked dominics, sickly sweet and warm. Os sat at the dining table, alone, her chin wrapped in her palms. She'd lost a pound in a few days and her palms seemed to ride further up her thinned face. What did she have to do for some peace round here? Call the fire brigade? She needed H-Mum and Matilda's brand of moral support, their grinding mutual forbearance, like an intravenous infusion of raw sewage. *Genies wept, was Jaundiced Matilda not going to stop yapping until someone wrung her neck?*

'Poju, you must be proud of her,' said Matilda. John handed his mother a glass of sherry and, whilst he heaved a hamper to Matilda's side of the coffee table, Os scribbled a reminder on a post-it note to write to thank Mr. Perriman, an old patient of hers, for sending the selection of biscuits, cheeses and wine. H-Mum emitted a short sharp sound. She didn't need Matilda's sort of pride. A ray of sunshine picked out David's photo on the sideboard. He was wearing his sixth form blazer that day, the knot in his striped tie perfect because Os helped put it on that morning. First day of term. If only Death had sent her a final warning to change her ways. Maybe that was the secret: live your life as if Death sent you a last warning. But would we listen? The human default programme is denial. It won't happen to you. But it had. It had. Os glanced left towards Louise's bedroom. When she last checked minutes earlier, the girl still lay with head buried under the pillows, headphones nowhere near.

Matilda implied with a wink and a cock of the head that, since Os was closest to the kitchen, she should put the kettle on. Os clamped her lips to stop a come-and-make-it-yourself retort and dragged herself up. The kettle spat and sizzled.

'Needs filling,' said John from the sofa beside his mum, but Os trickled in just enough tap water to make one cup. H-Mum downed the rest of the sherry, and dragged her long torso off the sofa, dangling her car keys.

Os perked up but, '*Awamaridi, odun a jina si ara won,*' said H-Mum, in a sad low voice. For the benefit of the mother and son on the sofa who'd exchanged looks, she repeated what she said louder and added, 'That means: dreadful or bad years like this will be few and far between.' She smoothed her black skirt and sat down again, the clatter of her car keys back onto the coffee table setting off a similar unpleasant percussion inside Os. A cutting silence followed and the room glowed coppery gold in the late afternoon light. An ambulance screamed down the motorway.

H-Mum kissed her crucifix and pursued the vehicle with her prayers. 'What those people are doing to Osese at the hospital is not good, oh. Is it next week? They cannot postpone?' said H-Mum.

John shook his head. 'You know Cody. He is doing his Moby Dick impression in pursuit of the cetacean again.'

'What is the concern of Harold Melvin and the Blue Whale in this matter?' said H-Mum.

'Herman Melville actually,' said John, right from the top of the scale of pomposity.

H-Mum sighed. She was only testing but as usual John did not disappoint. Of course, she knew her Melville from her Melvin's but, because the cost of their education could feed a village for a year and they could speak a little Latin, some people think they are the first to ever open a book she said, grumbling as she swivelled to make the point to Os. Hanyway, what was the clever man doing to help his wife's situation at work? She heard that Cody and the CEO were going to cause trouble because she wrote emails about the lack of PPE? Can this be true? In this same England? Does that mean Os will not get a promotion? If they were in Lagos, and it was John having trouble with some local, *omo onile*, she and Os would be the first to the door of the permanent secretary or commissioner, hanyone who could help. H-Mum raised her voice in the Lagos demotic. 'No, but instead of helping their wife, dem siddon for one place, looking for grammar to correct.' She puffed her cheeks at the ceiling.

Cody's behaviour troubled Os. She couldn't explain why he came to help her in theatre the morning after David died. Was it a simple act of camaraderie? Why did he swap the list? Was the white Mr. Boardman going to be more straightforward? Or was it because Simply Blue lost his nerve and needed more time? Or was it a trap? Or, as she recognised herself, was that her grief-fuelled panoramic paranoia intruding? Os tried to warn John with a subtle shake of the head.

'It is probably not as bad as it sounds,' she said, to give John time to think up something equally harmless to say in reply to H-Mum's caustic aside.

But John fished at a bar of chocolate in the hamper and said, 'This is not Lagos. Things are done very differently here.'

'Nigeria, is it?' said Matilda, nodding. 'I hear they are fantastically corrupt,' she said, quoting David Cameron, Greensill's friend, and sounding considerably more up herself than her son was.

'Yehpah.' H-Mum's eyes bulged as if punched from behind. May David forgive her but she couldn't sit here as hif her tongue had turned to wood. She waved her hand at the A3 in the general direction of Whitehall, pointed at her temple, and ignored Os's desperate eye signals. Gripping John in a fiery gaze she said, 'Of course you don't have corruption,' she said. When they *dashed* the probation service to their friends and it failed, it was her pension that bailed them out. When they gave their friends the railway and it failed and the clever man said pay me or I will block the line with my coaches, maybe he didn't say it like that but that is what he meant, it was her pension that again clattered to the rescue. When the banks seized up, it was her savings that suffered. When they shrink margarine inside the container until it looks like a used bar of soap and the toilet paper is overdosed on slimming pills but they say no inflation. When they gave a contract to a ferry company that did not have a single boat, and the contract to supply masks to the friends of the ruling party, her party, she agrees, money that bought masks that you would be mad to put on your face. And those who got the contract are laughing at us from the mansions they bought with her pension money, yet doctors and nurses are dying and we are clapping and they want to crucify her daughter, her daughter who lost her son, and it is not corruption. When Cameron was texting Sunak it is not corruption, it is, what is the word again? Cronyism. Because they both have money. What they call rigging in Lagos, you call elevation, to the House of Lords. Same thing, different packaging. 'It is on a cronatic scale, not corruption scale. Don't tell me what is not because I don't want my mouth to dance today, of all days...'

Matilda recrossed her long legs and fiddled with her earrings. 'I'm sure John didn't mean offence, *I* certainly didn't...' Her voice tailed off, then seemed to be caught up in a wave of bonus material from the back of her brain. 'Shame, because you, Poju, and John have a lot more in common than you think.' She leaned forward, glass in hand, a mischievous glow on the fringes of her green eyes. 'Take the referendum. Same side as Poju, weren't you, John?' She leaned back with a satisfied beam in her eyes. 'Though if you ask me, we in the EU spent years doing exactly what Putin wanted, arguing the toss over who was going to bat at number five or number six, throwing our pads and jockstraps out of the pavilion whilst he's doping his fast bowlers to the eyeballs with Ivanova supplements and Vladimir whatnements and got his heavy rollers on the pitch at Crimea, knocking over the little sides first whilst we're rolling around drunk on piped oil and gas. Now he's got us exactly where he wants us, split up, cobbling bats out of glued up wood shavings...'

'Mum's got a fantastically rewilded imagination,' said John, his chin turning the white colour of the chocolate bar melting in his palm.

'Coffee anyone?' Os said, her navel riding up.

'Upset you, darling? You were sitting in my kitchen drinking my best brew in your Saracens mug,' said Matilda, pointing at her cup of coffee. 'You said you shouldn't have made the silly pact with Ossy in the first place, dammit, without doubt were your very words. John was so keen that he asked if could use my address for the postal ballot. Said he had a word with Jenny at work. You know, Jenny, Ossy, don't you?' said Matilda.

Jenny was an ex of John's who thought she knew everything about Africa because she'd been on one Safari. Os started forward. How could he? She tried to catch John's eye but at that moment Louise crept into the living room, her dark orange shirt lined by tears.

'Did we wake you darling?' said Os, offering her arms up for a hug. Louise leaned against her.

'Mum, can you get my prescription? Two days till I run out. Progestin whatever...'

Os blushed under three contemptuous stares. H-Mum swung out of the chair, grabbed her bag, then on the way out sent John the dirtiest look in Christendom since the Spanish Inquisition. 'No wonder.' She swung her bowed head away from him.

Matilda waved at the bright sunshine outside. 'Poju wait, it's not six yet, they need us,' she said, but John hustled both women through the door. Louise rolled her eyes and made a shove off gesture at the departing pair then backed away to her bedroom. Os stood before the dishwasher with a plate and a knife in hand not sure what she was doing. A saucer rolled off the work surface and crashed to the floor between her feet. She cursed the piercing pain of a shard in her left ankle. John leapt to her side.

'You sit, I'll clear up,' he said.

'Leave me be,' she said, ripping her arm away. 'Honestly, I wish you'd slept with her and got it over with. It didn't mean anything, she made me do it, I was sad, I was mad, it was my mum's ego stripping me to the bones that made me seek validation or revalidation, my wife doesn't understand, my wife is sad, you've got thousands to choose from, but going behind my back to vote because Jenny said so... you've given that some thought.' She fended him off again, reproaching herself for her childish truculence, for exhibiting the insecurity - perhaps to Louise's hearing and disadvantage, poor thing - she decried in other black women. Yet after David's death, even as she cringed in self-repugnance at the thought, she'd often asked herself if she fell for John because his whiter shade of skin held the promise of an easier life for them all, including David. Or was it because she was in love with his love for her? Love is blind, they say, but is it unguided?

'What's their problem?' said John, tiptoeing over broken crockery to answer the door.

'Where are you off...'

A pair of uniformed white police officers, one man, one woman, stood outside the door. When he saw John, the male officer shuffled back a foot. Os swore and her heart reared up and neighed. Could these be the same two officers who arrested her boy?

'We heard of a disturbance at this location,' said the thickset male officer as he flipped a notebook open. His female colleague craned her neck for a better view of the room. John dragged Os back to a dining chair and gestured over his shoulder.

'Ah, only a misapprehension between kneecap and dishwasher… sort of not been a good day.' John straightened his collar and pulled himself up straight. 'Funeral,' he said.

'Very well, if that be the case Mr…erh…'

'Sharp, Doctor Sharp, actually, for my sins,' said John, peering into a crate of his books.

'I'll leave you to it then, doc. Any problems give us a bell.' Notebook returned to pocket. 'Good day madam, sorry for your loss,' said the male police officer and his colleague nodded her cocked head at Os and looked disappointed not to make an arrest. Perhaps they paid them bonuses per arrested head or head arrested. Modern day bounty hunters. That would explain a lot.

'I don't get it. How did they know to come? Are we bugged?' said Os, looking round the room. Huge tears weighed her eyes down.

Meanwhile John had pressed the door closed. He waited for the officers' footsteps to fade out of earshot, then crouched under the table to reach a broken saucer. 'Where on earth are you going?' he said, jerking his head up.

Os pointed at the ceiling. 'To have a word.'

CHAPTER NINE

Os's neighbours in the flat above looked genuinely shocked to hear that David died. After that they toned down their noisy rows and went out of their way to ask if Os needed any help. At work, though, apart from Blonde Barrie who sent her an English translation of a Yoruba dirge, most of the rest of the department avoided Os. On her approach they dived down the nearest alleyway or struck up a loud and improbable conversation with anyone nearby. Os got it. They didn't mean to be cruel, just didn't know what to say to her. But she'd overheard whispers of disdain and pity for her as the mother of a stabbed drug dealer. That stung more than a jackhammer drilling the solar plexus. If she ever caught the rat who started the rumour she'd rip the shitty mouth from its neckrest.

A week after the funeral and a number of uncomfortable encounters with Cody and Georgina over Os's complaints about PPE, they called her in to treat a moribund black boy with a carving knife in his heart. Futile said the gasman. Os's hands leapt to her ears. *Futile? As in let him die? He's the same age as David, for fuck's sake. Not that it should matter. What to tell his mum? Sorry, we let him go because it was too hard, cost too much?*

'Futile? Futile, futile,' she muttered as she charged off to get scrubbed. But after four hours of surgical toil death won 1-0, and it wasn't as close as the scoreline suggests; the operation was like trying to knit a jumper out of black pudding with a garden fork.

Afterwards, drenched and drained, Os tore her gloves off and slung them into the bin, wishing she'd been able to give Dorcas what she wished for herself – her son back. She punched her palm. What words to dangle for choice before his grieving mum? That H-Mum insists to this day that God does not give you a burden you cannot bear? Really? Your thoughts are with her? Bullshit. That you've been there too, yes, but it's not about you dammit, and what consolation is that to anyone. How do you keep these endangered boys safe, especially through their teenage years? Cuff them sedated to their beds? Homeschool them 24/7 until they are grey?

Os sat with Dorcas wringing her hands in hers. She tried not to cry for David, but one choking hiccup and a poignant football story about Mason ripped the tears down her face with such force that the grieving mother sought to console the surgeon. Os felt a fraud sitting there, ostensibly keeping the distraught Dorcas company, when she was in truth seeking to ease her own anguish by mingling it with that of another similarly bereaved woman. Mason's elder sister arrived at 6 a.m. with her hair all over the place. When Dorcas, through puffed-up lips shone by tears, told her daughter how kind this top lady surgeon had been to spend so much time with her, Os's face twitched from guilt. She waited five minutes, angry with herself for being angry with Dorcas for making her feel the fraud. Her fist clenching around Comfort, she muttered something about it being the least she could do, it was her calling as a public servant, then sloped off to her car as the first rays of dawn settled over South London University Hospital.

As she drove home, Os had never found the hospital buildings more depressing. The main block, ten storeys of flaky once ivory, now greying paint, overhanging gutters and narrow windows evoked the cannons and arrow slits of West African slave forts. To the south of the 15-acre site festered an arc of dense terraced housing, cracked pavements, boarded up fast food eateries, a dozen ferociously competitive and profitable betting agents to facilitate responsible gambling. Three massage parlours, two nail clinics, no green spaces, and that was it. All woven through with contraflow systems you needed a four figure IQ to navigate. Which was the point, thought Os, to keep the salt of the earth trapped here.

Meanwhile, word of the imminent retirement of the Geordie giant of Cardiac Surgery had set off the predictably ugly jostle to succeed him. Battle lines were recast, burnished, feuds disinterred between ancient hospitals: between South London and North; between London surgeons and the rest; Scot- versus English-trained; Scottish versus English born; State versus privately educated; British versus foreigners, old versus recent former foreigners; men versus women. Os versus everyone.

After another barbed exchange with Cody and Georgina over the provision of PPE, Os went to see her friend Dr. Bade Ragoye. She wanted his advice about the job because she didn't know what to do. It was close to the end of an overnight shift and he was catching his breath in front of the blue doors of the IOU overflow unit after attending a cardiac arrest when she found him. His face wore the sheen of success because the patient had done well. Ten years older than Os, one of hundreds mislaid by Nigeria in the diaspora, he'd crisscrossed Great Britain in pursuit of training posts, picking cherries in Sussex farms for a pittance at one point, reapplying to extend his visa, until, in the interval between Amber Rudd taking the rap for Teresa's hostile environment policy and the shoving of steel capped knees under the Home Office desk by Pritti Patel, a British passport landed in his hands. He'd escaped Nigeria by a fraction of a heartbeat from those who wanted him dead because he doubted the veracity of a post-mortem report. The powers that be wanted him to ignore the bullets in the fatty apron of a heavyweight politician's ample abdomen. Yet, like many Nigerians in the diaspora, he loved strong leadership and was a "proper" Thatcherite. He considered racism something esoteric, like existentialism, dreamt up by overpaid and over here Caribbean intellectuals. Bade rarely took anything the wrong way, even when the warning not to take what was coming the wrong way meant he should walk away. Os called him Dr. Inkstain, shortened to Drinkstain, because, scrub as they might, Georgina and her team of panjandrums couldn't get rid of him. He had retired in his own time. But when Matron Monty called him to help during the pandemic, he tucked his slippers away and returned to work; only to catch Covid. Drinkstain spent ten days fighting for his life. The Trust docked his pay that month because he didn't put in a full shift. Os didn't tell him, but she thought he'd been windrushed. To be windrushed didn't mean racing to the toilet with flatulent diarrhoea but being asked to do a job others don't want in return for a good kicking in the teeth before your forcible removal or incarceration.

Drinkstain grabbed Os and gave her a long warm hug in his stout arms. '*Pele*,' he said once again, a Yoruba word expressing various forms of fellow feeling and for which there is no English equivalent. He smelled of the freshly laundered hospital togs he was wearing and faintly of sandalwood aftershave and lime air freshener. Drinkstain was only a few inches taller than Os with a round face and a moderate beer belly, in Lagos a sign of good living.

'Why are you putting poison in your lungs?' she said.

Os pointed at the ceiling. Her old English teacher had just died of Covid up there. 'Because your friends didn't live up to their fucking world beating promises.' Her chest heaved as she fought off the sobs and her voice revved up. Why was he looking at her like that? And, before he told her it was grief talking, can grief not ring true? If she'd been there when Cody came to remove the high-grade masks from Drinkstain's ward, she would have converted that high rise nose of his into bloody flats. 'That woman who died taught me more than literature, and now she is not here...'

'Maybe the woman didn't have Covid, it could be septicaemia from an arthritic knee but we don't let -'

Os shot a hand in the air. 'Don't patronise me. I know what I saw. But Mrs. Emmanuel should be grateful they didn't carry her from Coventry to York to Nottingham to Newcastle...' Os leaned her heavy head against the wall. A trolley packed with soiled linen trundled down the corridor. The way it flicked through the plastic curtains and disappeared reminded her of David's coffin. She paused and tilted her head as if to clear it of the darkness rising through it. Drinkstain patted her on the shoulder.

Another trolley creaked past, trailing an even more pungent smell of excreta and vomitus. 'They treat us like that, like shit,' she said, waving at the departing trolley. Drinkstain's friends could say what they liked about the NHS. Whether that someone has time for it or not, or cheered the pay cut for nurses or not, whether or not they said if you want an uppity nurse for a neighbour, vote for the other lot, when it matters to someone who matters, the NHS pulls out all the blinking stops. Which is why Trustraker survived, but her son, flesh and blood, born of a woman too, did not.

'He's the PM,' said Drinkstain, eyeing Os as if she'd lost all her marbles.

'Genies gimme shelter, does always getting the best treatment not only make you better, but make you feel you are better than others and make others feel you are better than them?' said Os. Where were Drinkstain and his efficiency-savings-seeking duckrabbiteer friends when the St. Thomas's guys were pouring taxpayers' oxygen down his friend's neck? 'Not one of them said, "Stop, you are over nursing him, you inefficient overmanned bloated NHS hustlers, why are you wasting the ITU bed? Stop the oxygen! Can't you recycle what he breathes out, squeeze every efficiency saving, every molecule of oxygen from that last litre before you turn that dial? Why can't he have a few free radicals, or try retooling his lungs to work without oxygen? Two whole nurses, why not one and a half? Where do they think this is? The oxygen replete Amazon forest?" Not one of you.' She raised a finger and puffed a long sigh. Through her moist eyes she saw Drinkstain fumble in the back pocket of his trousers and fish out a wad of masks. Os could have them. And she shouldn't let that they came courtesy of a Tory WhatsApp group put her off.

'As for Bojo,' he said, 'he is the best man for the job.'

She wagged a finger. 'Ah, ah, correction. Your friend is the best man for the job *he* is doing,' said Os. Which, alas, was why he was here and her boy was not. Os realised how loud she was when a passing consultant shot her a rude glance. Dropping her voice to a waspish hiss she said, 'How many will die precisely because your friend was in charge? One, two, three? None? Ten thousand?' She chased after the departing colleague by raising her voice. 'Or is that not a fair question to ask in polite free-speech-making company?' She wrinkled her nose against the smell of exhaust fumes from the long queue of ambulances double parked outside the doors.

'I'm a glass half full man, by God's grace this thing will be over before Christmas.' Drinkstain hopped again like a Test umpire and slipped into an overblown Lagos accent. 'God, oh, please come yourself this time, oh, this Covid is no child's play, oh.' He winced in self-castigation for the crass reference to mortality. '*Pele*…did you apply for compassionate leave?'

Os shook her head. Someone said compassion for NHS staff got its marching orders years ago and it hasn't looked back since. 'What of that reference?' she said, her toes curling up at the banality of her request, but it was her way of asking his take on whether she should still apply for the job.

Up shot Drinkstain's hands. He may be a glass half full man but giving a professor a reference was way above his pay grade. Why didn't she ask her friend Jeremy Corbyn for a reference? A turgid pause followed. Os sensed that she'd offended him but couldn't bring herself to apologise.

'Your health…mental health is the main thing…'

'What of my mental health if I do not apply?' said Os.

'Patients are not therapy.' He dropped his voice. 'Have you spoken to John? Ah.' He thought not. 'What of my Louise, the diplomat?' he said. 'Ok, park that one. What is it with you and Cody Hayes?' He pointed at the photograph of Cody above the entrance to the unit.

'Er, he's set up a disciplinary committee, kangaroo court…I don't know the man's problem…after everything…just because I wrote a few emails…' A curse at a nurse by a patient in a nearby trolley reminded her that, despite several calls, Simply Blue had not got back. Worrying.

Drinkstain hopped on the spot. 'You don't need me to tell you Cody's track record. That man, *na wa o*. Vera told me,' he said, shaking his head. Vera was his former personal assistant and as loyal to him as Rose Mary Woods was to Tricky Dicky Nixon. Os called her Vera the Improbable because she could find a grain of sugar in a snowstorm. 'As everybody knows, I'm a glass half full man, but as the words of the poem go, they want to gravel your face and your soul then make you grovel then shove you in a shallow grave with a shovel,' said Drinkstain with a shiver and another hop on the spot. 'The man is not bluffing.'

CHAPTER TEN

Three weeks and two days after David died, the disciplinary hearing set up by Cody took place on a clammy overcast morning in early September. Os did not see the waddling pigeons pecking at crumbs around her, or hear car doors clanging shut, or the squeaky rise and fall of the car park barriers, or the van crawling up behind her until it tooted, making the hairs at the nape of her neck, which she couldn't quite reach to weave into braids, leap. Blonde Barrie's over-the-top double thumbs up greeting from a passing van disturbed her. What did he know that she didn't?

The panel sat in the Hayes Boardroom, a hall the size of two HGVs, its ceiling painted duck egg with scenes from Greek mythology. Os sat at a table between the two jaws of an arc of mahogany tables. A minotaur with a fiery beard glared from the ceiling. At the head of the panel sat Cody in a brilliant white shirt, its sleeves folded above the elbow as hospital protocol demanded. He asked his friend, Ms Adele Harrison, former midwife, Putinophile, and co-author of his plain-speaking books, to co-chair the proceedings. Tanned Donald Trump orange, with hairy eyebrows and a penchant for Cuban cigars, Adele Harrison's bespoke mediation services to the NHS funded six months of ghost-writing waspish management manuals from a hillside villa on the Costa del Sol. In a green suit, discrete silver brooch on left panel, the self-styled queen of no nonsense free-flowing free-speaking prose sat a foot to the right of Cody, her eyes oscillating between Os, Georgina and Mrs. Kindolowo, the HR officer with the large biceps, as if she'd never seen so many black women in a room without the need for a whip to hand or a whip around.

'Can I call you Os? The rest is a bit of a mouthful?' said Adele, as she worked a page free from her bundle of papers.

'No, you cannot, with respect,' said Os. *Genies wept, Ossy, what next?*

Adele's head jerked up, a querulous frown creasing her forehead like a dried prune. 'What should I call you, then?'

'Professor Osese Sharp.' A male member of the six strong panel, one of Cody's pals on the Human Resources Research Group, swore under his breath, jabbed his pen down to tick a box on the last page of his thick bundle of papers.

'Time is our witness; we shouldn't keep him waiting. Georgina?' said Cody. Georgina, red lipstick as thick as a ploughman's lunch, plastered Os with a filthy glare. Os replied with her default English breakfast face which she managed to keep on, except for the odd gasp during Georgina's ten-minute presentation. From a carefully collated anthology, Georgina quoted witness statements from spies, the coerced and the genuinely aggrieved. Os knew Cody's modus operandus, to her knowledge, copied by many up and down the country. 'Ms Abakalaka, dear, where is that from *originally?* Nigeria, Uganda, Ghana? Papa worked there. I hear you are overdue a promotion? Taking part in peer review is crucial to your professional development. Then Cody would give them a big man's nudge and wink and slip them killer questions. Did Professor Sharp raise her voice, throw a wobbly, tantrum, cause you embarrassment or unease, play inappropriate music in theatre, cut you or a patient off mid-sentence, wear pungent perfume or gaudy clothes, exhibit any other form of intolerance or fanaticism, disrespect your values or the Royal Family or Christian values, Islam, snort at your bacon or beef, intimidate you or in any way, during team briefings for example, and undermine team cohesion? Examples of paranoia, mania or euphoria, hangovers? Sometimes he did the dirty work himself or delegated to others, and if they didn't dig enough dirt he sent them back until they found it.

Georgina went on with her report. Os made nurses cry and had favourites, such as Blonde Barrie whom she often chose to work with to the exclusion of other theatre practitioners, especially with private patients. Os ruined the schedule and the biological rhythms of the staff by insisting on starting work too early in the mornings. The professor denigrated the Trust Policy on PPE and undermined morale. Number twenty-three on her list. Everyone knew Covid was an extremely difficult once-in-a-life-time pandemic. Everyone pulled together, except Os. Was it any surprise that relationships in the department were strained.

Genies wept, this manufactured stuff gets everywhere. It's like microplastic waste, or the stuff in a baby's nappy. Their truth is their truth and they decide it. If they say they've been to Mars, who are we to say they haven't?

'Is this it?' said Os. 'Is this why we are all here instead of on the wards?' *Genies forgive them, for they know full well what they are doing. You shouldn't make it up but they do.* Os pointed at each of the four walls as she spoke. 'In theatre and in clinics, scalpels, bed pans and sexist insults are tossed or kicked carelessly around by my colleagues without as much as an eyebrow raised between present worshipful company, but the woman called Os so much as raises an eyebrow and it is against the Trust policy based on the expression of my facial muscles.' Blonde Barrie was sent to work with her because the other surgeons weren't *comfortable* with him, whatever that meant. They should ask them. He was one of the best theatre practitioners she'd ever worked with, which is why they got on so well. Whilst Os spoke, Adele scanned the ceiling as if looking for architectural ideas for her next hillside villa. *Genies wept, if she had a pound every time they passed her over for meaningful roles on committees - he wasn't going to complain to them, she hated their posing - or held important meetings behind her back or disagreed with her until they checked with a man, she'd have bought a few shares in Amazon before the pandemic shot the price and Jeff Bezos into the stratosphere.* Her eyes stung as she asked for a glass of water. Mrs. Kindolowo, taking not a blind bit of notice of the frowning Georgina, perhaps taking a cue from the discomfort etched on Os's face, scuttled up with a clean glass.

'Is the HR lady here to wait on us or take records?' said Cody, waving his pen.

'Give me a minute, will you Mr. Hayes,' said Mrs. Kindolowo. Os took some comfort from the snap in the officer's voice.

'Extraordinary. In your own time, then,' said Cody. 'Make sure you take complete records. Last thing we want is another frivolous accusation of misrepresentation, or is it under-representation? Or disproportionality?' Adele turned to Cody. She agreed entirely with the sentiments expressed. From his privileged vantage point on Mount Pallor he must find it difficult to keep count of the mounting accretions of reclassifications. She grinned.

'And politically ripe offence taken,' said Georgina, comments which brought a dirty stare from Mrs. Kindolowo.

'They are four or five hours behind us, not ready yet,' said Mrs. Kindolowo, glaring at Georgina whilst she rattled the keyboard.

'Then, whilst we wait, let's discuss the Professor's unprecedented behaviour.' With panache worthy of his family's place amongst surgical royalty, Cody described how Os overreached herself by ignoring the *Do Not Resuscitate* tattoo on a patient's back.

'Professor Sharp, you agree that the woman refused resuscitation because potentially she didn't want to end up a vegetable?' said Georgina, butting in, her eyelids twitching with fear that Os might escape grave censure.

Os shrunk into her seat, palpitations tapping through her blouse. What in Genie Thunder's name was Cody on about? But who was she to argue? If he says she did what she was meant to, he had the papers in front of him to prove it. She had zilch, no papers, and a blank mind. 'I'm afraid I...cannot recall,' she said, clearing her throat twice to rid her voice of its warp and squeak. She looked to the sky, her prized memory brittled by grief, crumbled under Cody's unexpected attack. Nothing in the documents before her, or inside her bag, Comfort, jogged to mind a fragment of memory to conjure and bluff with, as she had many times before. Os shook her head in deliberate ultraslow motion as if afraid to disturb what functioning brain cells she had left.

Her staccato utterances had the cadence of a drunken primate let loose on a keyboard. 'Who this patient was, is, tell me, in all honesty, I'm not sure… Are we talking of before or during Covid?' she said, to a snigger from Georgina. Os smoothed her skirt down to confirm it was still there and tore her eyes from Mrs. Kindolowo's sympathetic face because it threatened to melt her into tears.

Then it came back to her. It was a woman that Os called Mrs. Granola because the patient loved muesli. She'd had the ward in stitches because, when asked about her views on resuscitation, she said she didn't want to end up a *vegetarian* when she meant *vegetable*. Genies wept, they should be thanking her, not throwing bleeding brickbats.

'You owe me an apology.'

Georgina and Cody exchanged smirks.

Os asked them to confirm the name of the patient. Ah. Her voice waxed stronger as she recounted going to the ward to see her patient when this other woman in question collapsed. How resuscitating a patient in those circumstances could be deemed a casual disregard of hospital policy beat her. Does a fire officer stop to ponder the colour of wallpaper before they put out the fire? Thanks to our resus team, including young Dr Inuola who, by the way, will throw far and dent many managerial first impressions, she could say with reasonable confidence that the patient now had a fighting chance of enjoying her granola for many years. Os paused for effect before she put the boot in. Addison's, the same condition that nearly killed the young John F Kennedy, that is what the patient had. How come their pal Tim didn't spot it?

Cody rubbed his nose with his ballpoint pen.

'Typical,' said Georgina.

Oh, go and smoke that in your designer slippers, woman.

'Why not ask the patient or the daughter, or is that too much trouble?' snapped Os.

As for her recent emails, all she wanted was a proper and transparent assessment of PPE needs across the hospital, but she'd been treated like a bloody nuisance. The testing of the patients sent to nursing homes was a joke. Frightened ward staff used curtains to separate definite Covid patients from the untested. You didn't need that prescient World Cup octopus to tell you what would happen next. To say Os was scared to work on the Covid wards was like calling the Zong massacre an unscheduled stopover.

'Now the nurses tell me that you insist that we count each glove as an item of PPE. Who are we kidding? The virus is not listening. I ran into a junior this afternoon. He's on suicide watch. Someone sitting not too far away from me wouldn't give him time off when he felt unwell.' Os rested her accusing gaze on Georgina. 'He's convinced he passed Covid to the two gentlemen who died on his ward.'

Georgina shouted out, 'There are two sides to the sto—'

'Yes, same for a toilet seat, but it only fits one way up,' grunted Os. *Genies wept, look at the poisonous pair of them. Got fangs in those heads. Gravity bows down before them. They winch their pals up, dump the rest of us in Covid shit, then cover their broad backsides with varicose claims that wouldn't have a leg to stand on if they weren't marking their own homework. These were the same guys who couldn't wait to get their smug faces on the front pages of the local rags as NHS heroes of the pandemic. The guys who gave NHS badges to seven-grand-a-day private consultants to jump the queues at supermarkets and park ambulances outside the empty "Covid annexe" for a spot of PR. And she was the bad guy?*

'That is why you blab self-righteous crap to the CQC and BMA?' said Adele.

'I didn't want to take the credit for that, but if you say I said so, alas, word must have got out,' said Os.

Georgina snapped her head forward. Os was always complaining. Her thick lipstick made a sticky noise, like the amplified sound of pigs at the trough.

'Professor, you can smear us, but the Trust will rinse itself down and survive.'

The question Os had to ask herself was, would she?

Cody twirled his pen and asked if the Yanks were now ready. 'Ah, here they are.' A portentous clanging began in Os's head when the fuzzy faces of the American students, all female, two Euro-Americans and one African-American, appeared on the screen. One white one with a high colour looked as if she had been crying; the freckled one to her left looked like the sort of friend who'd wheedle a precious confidence out of you then send it viral. To Os she bore a strong resemblance to the Euro-American woman caught on camera screaming at African American Ruby Bridges for having the gall to darken the threshold of a school. *Genies, please, don't let us ever forget such stalwart defenders of freedom.*

But what now? Another ambush. Genies wept, this could go on forever until what? 'Nothing here about…students. Should I not have been told?' said Os, waving the agenda in the air but Cody leaned forward, eyes shivering with malicious intent.

Over the next twenty minutes by leading questions, gestures, beckoning and prompts, he teased the answers he wanted from the students. 'And how would you describe how she addressed you when she turfed you out of her cab?' he said at one point.

'She was rude to us,' said one.

'Can you be more precise? Any emphasis on, er, difference, colour, political correctness, that sort of thing?'

'Like, you mean racist terms? Yeah, certainly,' shouted the mean one, the words shooting from her with a whiny twang. The African American student nodded hard. Cody reciprocated with an elaborate nod of his own. He shook his head at Os over his spectacles whilst Adele made notes. Mrs. Kindolowo resumed the furious percussion of her keyboard.

'I gave them lifts but don't recall any of this,' said Os, rolling a post-it note into a tube. *What windy nonsense?* She remembered that night. It was soon after David died. But why was Cody doing this? Because of a few tetchy emails over PPE? She thought things were cool between them. Yes, she admits she was not in a good place when Ian called to ask her to drop off the students because their digs were in her neck of the woods. That he'd damned her recent article on post-op inflammation in younger smokers with faint praise hadn't helped either. And she remembered because she wanted to get home to comfort Louise. Nor did she care much for the way the young women crowded her space. With Comfort and laptop in the front and her unwanted fare in the back of her cab, a church steeple glittering in the moonlight had just dropped out of her rearview mirror when the students started a loud conversation about the death or murder of George Floyd.

Facial muscles beginning to clench, Os turned her radio down. You never know, Genies, we might learn something. Out fanned her ears, which by strange coincidence much resembled H-Mum's. 'They always say the guy was out buying a loaf of bread or something,' said one girl, bookending her words with sniggers. 'Like, we can't figure out what loaf of bread is slang for. Fricking predictable. How dumb is that, looting and shooting up your own shops and stuff?' she said, with a disgusted suck of air.

'Far more kill each other than killed by cops. And whites are killed too, like, maybe more? These guys should check the facts,' said the woman with the longer drawl. 'Cops are shitting themselves in the hood, like really spooked?'

Unable to think of a way of changing the impression she thought they had that she was Ian's insensate cabbie or side-kick, after revving the engine a few times to drown them out and smother her budding unease, Os had remained quiet, her grip tightening round the steering wheel, her heart bobbing like a pogo stick, face encased in leathery heat as she wrestled with herself for a killer response. Yet each time she thought she found the words, they felt too sharp or ambiguous or weasely and they seemed to hang around, crowding her voice box, as if aching to apologise for their inadequacies. Perhaps, she thought, she was being too sensitive. Or critical. It's their free speech, John would probably say. She should take it as a compliment that they spoke so honestly in her presence. They must think she was one of their own.

But from hard-wired experience rose also the troubling, but more plausible notion, that they spoke as they did because they didn't see her, she was invisible. Or they saw her but didn't give a toss. Or they didn't know that they had to give a toss. Or they believed that what they were stating, their world view, was as incontrovertibly obvious and as accurate as an atomic clock. Or they saw her and were trying to wind her up, for sport. Shock jock docs? Or, here the old paranoia or well-conserved instincts intruded, had Cody sent them as agent provocateurs?

This last notion came to Os much later and she dismissed it before it took root. But to think this lot are practising medicine for the next half a century. Bully for them, or "Champion!", as Ian would say. But she'd hate to be their patient, anyroad. Genies, they'd probably pay for her to go away anyway if she needed their help.

As they waited at a red-light, Os scratched her ear, fiddled with the dashboard, and coughed out loud. But one said, 'What folk don't get is that the cops are like us, like physicians, right? Like sent out to these hoods, risking their lives, right? Would you send doctors to the electric chair because they couldn't save some bum with a slug in his head? Get real, folks!' She emitted a triumphant tut. 'Cops are the last line of defence against anarchy, against losing our freedoms, that's my take on it. How can they do their job if they're not allowed to make mistakes?'

The engine rattled in the wrong gear. As she engaged the clutch, Os wanted to ask, yell out, as the late great Toni Morrison said, "Why no whites were shot in the back by these terrified cops?" Then, clearing her throat, and in the even tone of a detached academic, or so she thought, she asked if the shootings of the innocent kept happening because the cops thought or believed or were given to understand that they were above the law. One student sucked her teeth and said Os didn't "get freedom", maybe because she lived under a Queen in England. They'd got rid of all that in the States, said the girl.

Os couldn't let her get away with such a windy mouth fart in the back of her car. She slowed down to let a van in and glanced in the rear-view mirror. 'Funny sort of freedom,' she said, 'when half the workers in the "Land of the Brave" live from payday to payday and unfree visitors from Africa can't have a takeaway or ride a bus or stop to ask for directions without bumping into someone asking for a tip to help pay for bandages.'

She meant that tongue-in-cheek but the brunette shrieked. Os was talking about bums, losers, trash. She finished her tirade with a slight stamp, a disparaging cluck which Os, in her charged-up state, took to mean drive the car and shut the fuck up.

'Free speech can cost those least able to pay,' said Os, her lips a-quiver. 'Those shot dead by their neighbourhood cops had mums and dads and loved apple pie and played air guitar and just wanted to be, they were simply human beings too.' Her neck began to roast and ears pound and she found that she was five miles per hour over the thirty mile per hour limit. *Genies wept, this freedom of their speech in the car she bought with her money, without a subsidy from anybody was costing her more in thumping heart beats and soaring blood pressure and stressful vascular depreciation than she wanted to pay.*

She pulled up at the next Tube Station, tossed them a few ten pound notes and told them to get out and find their own way home.

'Excuse me? We're not too hot on using the subway?' said the brunette, then slammed the cab door shut so hard that Os's inner ear bones rattled.

When Os got home, she didn't tell John because he was in a huff, and although she knew she hadn't heard the last from them she was not expecting an ambush under duck egg painted scenes of Grecian minotaurs. She wished she'd kept her mouth shut. But then Cody would simply have found something else.

She fixed an unwavering gaze on Cody. 'Why would I use abusive -'

'Extraordinary. Next witness?' Cody clicked his pen at Mrs. Kindolowo. He pointed at an overhead screen.

When Lamide shot onto her screen, Os's stomach lurched. What in the name of the Horn of Africa was he doing here? It must be serious because he was wearing a tie, blue stripes on a yellow ochre background. Lamide hated ties. He called them "slave ropes".

'My name is Lamide, but please call me Larry,' he said.

Os gripped the glass of water to try to stop her hands shaking.

'Professor Sharp, surely you will not deny acquaintance with our witness, Mr Lamide Bamisetiti?' Georgina said, notes of baleful relish in her voice. On another day, Os would have wanted to punch the woman on the tumescent red lips until all her blood ran out. Today, she fiddled with a post-it note.

Adele began to speak. 'Larry, you've heard from the students and read what they had to say. Anything you would like to add? Take your time, imagine that you are having a friendly fireside chat with the truth,' she said, smiling for a few moments, then, with her chin on her domed hands, fixing her cruel gaze on a point between Os's eyes.

Lamide's voice boomed from the speakers, his West African lilt and North American drawl roughened by grief and a sniffle. From what he'd learned in his time with Os, he was not surprised to hear how she treated the students. It was this racialist attitude that finished their marriage. His deep voice tailed off and he blew his nose. He said that he was afraid to say it. Here he stopped and his voice dropped. This was what caused what happened to David too. Lamide paused once more to gather himself. He closed his eyes, tapping his lips for a few moments before he went on. They should please excuse him but he was not good in this type of arena. That is why he became a surgeon. They would not find what he was going to tell them in any textbook. This was his lived experience, a memory he could never escape. He tried to tell Os to seek help but she would not listen. She said she didn't want to be like him, an Oreo, dark outside and white inside. Since they split up, he'd met many people like Os back in the States. Os was suffering from what he called raciophrenia, a paranoiac delusional racial persecution complex. Hers was 'real deep': complicated by racialolism, an addiction to the cult of the racial victim. She looked up and down, north, south, east, west for slights, for ways to take offence at the smallest thing. Haba.

He shook his head and clapped his hands. The day she said tea bags were invented to stop the dark wet tea leaves touching the white cup, that was the day he knew she was going beyond. Still she would not listen. She said something similar about the colour of the manhole covers. She found reason to take offence at the medical textbooks, the names of instruments, nosology, classification of diseases, the description of rashes in dermatology, the interpretation of trials, say for blood pressure treatments or kidney disease.

She would ask him if he sussed the way the shopkeeper dropped the coins into her palm from ten feet, or how the passerby giving them directions spoke to her as if she was a naughty toddler. Lamide said he had so many samples of her ways, but only wrote down a few so as not to take too much of their precious time. But it is like a bug; if you are not careful you can catch it too, so he had to be vigilant. Os, the one-woman thin-skinned detective agency he used to call her. One more thing. Did they know that Os found pale chips revolting? They had to be burned brown, the colour of her skin? Lamide said, 'Maybe it was what happened to her dad on –'

'This is incredible,' said Adele, in the manner of an archaeologist at a stupendous find.

Os's face burned. She screwed her heels into the floor and scratched her palms in turn. The best lies are constructed from truth. Lamide was an expert.

'I know what you are going to say. That her husband is, er, white? It doesn't work like that, does it?' said Lamide and he finished his demolition job with obsequious thank yous to each member of the panel.

Os looked up at the screen then stared down at her steepled thumbs. How dare he strip her naked and let them scoff at her darkest days, stuff she'd tried her blinking best to bury? He'd even brought up her dad. *Jeerie me, human beings, eh? We'll be the end of humanity.* Everyone you were or are close to has a book in them – and it is about you. You just hope they never get offered the advance.

Back in their registrar days, when Cody wove his suffocating lies without any thread of doubt or dissent, Lamide resigned in protest. Fair game to him, as they say, though with David he didn't cover himself in glory. Wait till she told H-Mum that her precious Lagos boy had become one of those *anywhere dem belle face na front* people: slaves to the fast buck.

'This testimony does him little credit,' Os said. A smirk glowed on Georgina's square and ebony face.

After another half an hour of damning commentary on Os's behaviour, Cody, Adele, Georgina and the member of the Research

Group swapped papers. Os was to wait outside but she'd hardly taken a sip of the lukewarm tea when Cody returned to the room beaming like a newly commissioned lighthouse beacon.

'Professor Sharp, Professor Sharp? That is your name, isn't it?' said Adele, virtually bouncing on the leather like a teenage fan waiting for her idol.

Os's damp fists pulled Comfort to the chair beside her.

'We've seen ample evidence of disaffection with your teamwork, your breathtaking lack of insight into your racist attitudes, which, for a woman in your position, you had plenty of opportunity to give vent to…we have little option as–'

'Unprecedented behaviour. The panel recommends strict clinical restrictions,' said Cody.

'Patient safety is our utmost number one priority, morning afternoon and night,' said Georgina, ordering Mrs. Kindolowo with an emphatic nod to get those wise words down too.

Drenched through her white blouse in cold sweat, Os hadn't moved for ten minutes when Mrs. Kindolowo tapped her on the shoulder to ask if she needed any help.

CHAPTER ELEVEN

Days later, an email duly arrived. Purportedly from the CEO, it had Cody's DNA all over it. Os was condemned to quotidian gnawing, mind busting drudgery: scanning agendas, minutes of meetings, complaints and commendations and other odds and scraps onto a backup system. The furry green algae in the musty basement room rubbed stubborn stains onto her clothes. That did not concern her. She hardly noticed. But it was the long and idle hours, bulging painfully with guilty self-recrimination, impotent rage and frustration that cracked her up. And when the tears stormed fitfully from her swollen eyes, the rattling Victorian plumbing underfoot drowned out her breathless sobs.

Genies, ah, she cried, gimme peace, this pain is too much. I know it is my fault. One chance to run the experiment and I blew it up. Genies and H-Mum taught me about crime and consequence, but would I listen? No. Was it because many wing it and get away with it that I thought I'd do the same? Thought I'd leave him with John who should be alright, suiting this world better because he is white? How many people slurping coffee as they saunter past me on the high street can guess my secret? That since I killed my boy, it takes me ten minutes to add two and two and two or to fill a glass of water. I know it is ten minutes because that is how long the last hot flush lasted in the old days, BD, before David. How many know that my inflation of self has shrunk into contraction even as pain spreads under my skin? So, to those who say, "I'll leave the kids outside in the buggy for a moment whilst I lock the door, or in the room for a few minutes whilst I pop out," Don't! You don't want to feel like this! And to those who say "I'll just leave the smoking fag here beside the cot whilst I nip under the bed for the toy," I say Don't! Do you want to feel like this? To those who say, "I think she's being bullied but I'll call the school next week," I say Go now, you don't want to feel like this! Push that electric cable well out of the way, hide your pills, pack up the plastic bags, lock up the kids if you have to, because you don't want to feel like this. You don't want to feel like you've swallowed a blue whale of agony, a weighty dissecting emptiness in every fibre of your being, when every smile at you on the street weighs you down where it used to lift and neither your sore tongue, throat, nor your runny nose can help you taste what you eat. And you peel from your bed after a night in which you've again failed at that staged and voluntary surrender of some of your faculties because your mind has been racing through countless reruns of your days and still it finds tons of lashing mistakes. And almost every waking second during the day is so unbearable that you are tempted to take one of the merciful invitations to end it all. *Genies wept, I would, but for Louise.* Which is why I still take the blood pressure pills and went back on HRT because I didn't want to hide behind that feeling of riding a lion with its mane aflame. I do not deserve to hide behind my natural gynaecopathology if there is such a thing. No, Genies, she took it all back. She wanted all those who have not lost one to feel like she did for a few minutes once a day or week: as a warning. But will they heed it? She didn't. As she popped a throat lozenge into her mouth to soothe her sore throat a scurrying sound came from behind her. She looked over her shoulder and her eyes landed on the furry tussle between the pipes. *Genies gimme shelter, are those rats fighting over my egg sandwiches or my eyes making magic tricks?* She banged her chair on the floor. Shoo, get off you, Georgina may be coming. We don't want to frighten her off. She thinks she's being cruel but I mustn't let her know that nothing she can say or do can be worse than sitting here alone all day behind this steam age scanner.

Georgina did often drop in unannounced. Blood red lipstick glowing in the dim light, she came to tell Os how much better the department was running now that the Professor of Cactus Opinions had gone. Or she would recap, in granular detail, some ridiculous story about the speck on the varnish on her middle toenail, or the woolly towel she bought for her pet poodle, or about losing the house keys under her ergonomic pillow. Oh, how OCD she was! As if OCD was a joke.

Through all this Os sat with her chin in her hands, mute, her mind one of no fixed abode, wandering through sad incomprehension and dark indifference into nothingness.

One afternoon Georgina nearly tripped down the steep wooden stairs in her eagerness to tell Os that Cody had appointed Alfred "No Room For Society In Surgery" Enders as interim Lead of Cardiovascular Research. Enders dismantled in days the unit it had taken Os ten years of hard graft to build, getting rid of the brilliant Dr. Helen Mirano who'd come over from Mozambique on Os's invitation. When she heard the bitter news, Os put on her English breakfast face, shrugged, and made an offhand comment about the advantage of her regular hours and the solitude. When Geogina left, she gulped then wailed, pent up tears steaming from her eyes.

And she shed different tears for Dr. Mirano and others who relied upon and looked up to her. For letting them down. For giving them the impression that the world was her patient and it shall not want when it was not true; the world could go jump and fuck itself for all she once cared. Os lied to the world because she wanted the top jobs where, as Dad promised on a drizzly Tuesday morning two months after Semijeje died, she would find the room to be truly herself. But she was not blaming Dad. This was all on her.

Os was about three and a half when she asked her dad, as they packed their bags for the short move across New Cross, whether they were going home to Africa. Dad shrank into his twill jacket like a startled turtle into its shell. He looked so pale and pathetic that Os crawled over the gigantic trunk box with her name, Osese Adafunwa, on it, to bury her little head in his stomach. With a shallow laugh to stop himself from cracking into sobs, he picked her up in his short arms and swung her from side to side in a clumsy waltz. He'd left Lagos with such fanfare to study but dropped out of medical school when Semijeje fell ill. He was ashamed to return to Nigeria without a wife, money, or medical degree but felt guilty for trapping his dear sweet daughter here too. She'd never know what it was like to grow up, as he did in Lagos, not Black not White or on edge or on trial, free to choose when to blend in or stand out and given the benefit of doubt, even, it has to be said, by the mean police officer with the belly like a barrel and who lived on Kabiawu Street with his exophthalmic aunt.

'It's ok, Dad,' she said when he put her down. 'We'll be happy in the new house with Aunty Poju,' she added in a bright, teacher's pet voice, even as she sagged and died a lot inside because big grown-up tears gathered in Dad's deep eyes.

Dad kneeled before his daughter and took her hands in his warm palms, then, with the conviction of Martin Luther, said, 'You work hard and you will find plenty of room at the top.'

'Like in my story book?' said Os, to cheers in her heart when Dad nodded his wise head.

Years later, in a tumultuous expression of teenage pique, after a colossal bust-up with H-Mum, Os went to stay with a classmate's friend in the States. But she overheard her host's parents berating their daughter for asking Os round. By a process of elimination and an awkward shuffling in a game of silent musical chairs, by first accidentally then deliberately sitting in the wrong place at table, Os found out that they served her with cutlery reserved for the pet cat. When she told Lamide the story years later he said she was reading too much into it because the spoon was going in the dishwasher anyway. That night, after she shovelled the dinner down her reluctant gullet, to spare her friend the hurt yet hint at a grievance, Os gave her a plainly implausible excuse that her cat had died when everyone knew she couldn't stand cats. Os packed, spent two days sleeping rough at the airport then flew to Lagos where she could "get away from black people." She would also see where her parents came from. One day, in Lagos, as she raised a forkful of steaming *eba* and *egusi* to her mouth in a packed *bukka*, she recalled the high priest of Whiteanity Enoch Powell making what she preferred to call the "whip-hand" speech – to Os that was what the speech was about. And she recalled how she'd read from the beaky looks, sharp asides, and shivering silences and the way her dad walked and talked, that decent people who loved the Queen and Postman Pat and pet dogs and cats and hamsters and bingo and petunias, despised her kind on sight. And on that day in that roadside *bukka* to her mind juddered the consuming idea that the world was no benign comity of nations sharing a common humanity but, for black people, a soul pruning dystopia.

Nothing she'd seen in the years since had not reinforced her simple conclusion that, from your President Obama to your lowest of the lowest hobo on the street corner, they - black people - lived in a world white web, in a dystopia sicker, slicker, she thought, because it was real life, than any Orwellian nightmare ever put to paper. Huxley, Atwood, Kafka, the sardonic playful Roth or fantastical Tolkien, couldn't make it up.

To Os, a world in which, from Oxfam to the UN and the IMF, Chagos Islands to Falklands, Israel to Brazil, Sweden to South Africa, Ukraine to Russia, when push came to shove or didn't have to come to shove, blacks were the arm's-length other, the dirty stepchildren, the human bar of soap that scrubbed everyone else cleaner ('kaffirs' to Mahatma Gandhi), the people whose light-skinned brethren and whose "leaders" creep up behind or cosh upfront to lighten them of their wherewithal. A world in which black people lived a simulacrum of the life their wits deserved, in which they are more likely to deserve what they get than get what they deserve. A world in which, at the United Nations, the votes of blacks count for nought. They had no seat on the Permanent Security Council whose resolutions are ignored anyway unless the pockets of white men acquiesced. Worse of all, thought Os one night as she sat on the plane on the way back from a conference in Amsterdam, nobody fears us, our best hope is for tolerance – a virtuous quality so constantly signalled by priests in purple on Radio 4 and by politicians that she found it thick and tangled within the hearts of her white patients, tucked away under the leaflets of the mitral valve. Genies gimme shelter, she shouted at the radio after another lazy comment by one minister about popular music, it is blacks who kicked and punched the holes you rushed through. How dare they turn round, some of the most subsidised people in world history, to belch champagne bubbles in my face, lecture me from blood dripping pulpits about the good that free enterprise and trade will do us? Free trade? Genies, gimme air, gimme shelter, is that what they were shouting over the slaughtering chatter of machine guns? Maxims at the maximum? Why didn't they just wave over the waves from their boats and beg us for asylum, these religious and economic migrants?

Os didn't want the cast-off second-hand second-class life, the poor twin, the simulacrum, the penumbra of the life her wits deserved. *Aim high or you die a serf.* Os wanted what they had, what the Gladstones, Rhodes, Levers, Leopolds, Savilles, Putins, Bushes, Blairs, Cheneys, your average manager Mr. Slocombe of Acacia Avenue, had. She wanted what that football man, caught on camera dragging one of the to-die-for jobs in the game into a brown envelope yet drowning in million-pound offers, had. She wanted to feel at home on this planet, cocooned, serene and superior, colourless, colourblind, post-racial, indifferent, virtually untouchable too. Yes, she may have to sing louder and more sweetly than everyone else to escape her dystopian cage, put up with more to compete on merit, but it would be worth every drop of blood, sweat and lachrymosity, worth all the fine moral virtue signalling and the justifications and lies she typed on her CV. It would be worth every pot of sugar-coated sewage they dropped on her to stir, if she could, into manure, every bubbling hot English breakfast smile she served up on her cool meme-conditioned black face.

But she'd failed. According to H-Mum's three Hs, on a scale of one to ten of feeling at home in each domain, if she was being honest, she scored close to zero. Here she was, a professor of cardiac surgery scanning scraps of paper in a smelly hospital basement. Genies cried into their recycled bottles for her because she'd turned out, as they say on the football phone-ins, an absolute disgrace. Not fit to wear the shirt, or gown, or black skin. It takes guts to bear this skin well. Yes, she'd written a clever line or two, walked the walk, talked the talk, put in the extra work, for a gig, when they let her do it, she could do blinkered, with a hand tied behind. And for this they called her Prof. But her words counted for less than those of almost anybody else against her. Genies wept, her voice didn't count for much under her own roof in rural Surrey where her vote didn't count either because even the trees voted Tory and the dogs barked, "Woof-woof, Thatcher, Johnson. Ca-me-ron." And fly as high as she liked, she would always find waiting at the top those who paid lip service to progress but would rather go back to the days when women like Eunice Foote, pioneer in climate science, were not allowed to talk at conferences. The sort of people who called Rebecca Crumpler MD, the first black woman to qualify as a doctor in the States, MD for mule driver. Anti-woke they call themselves, code for facultative racism. Racism? It doesn't exist. To ever so meekly suggest otherwise is like accusing them of multiple suicide – an oxymoron, impossible. A fiction of the feverish special pleading of the dark and hapless nobodies justifiably swept aside by the forces of the free market.

One stifling afternoon after a sudden full body sob, Os was trying to restore her composure by working out 7 to the power of 3 in her head, when Georgina dropped in to say that Ian's job had been advertised at last.

'Thought you should know,' said Georgina, in a manner that would put off Alexander the Great. Os shrugged and affixed a suitably nonchalant look to face.

Yet events affect us through an infinite choice of wavelengths, some short, some long, and of varying penetrance. Neither Georgina, nor Os, could have known that their abrasive meetings, the gloating, sneering and scoffing on the one hand and Os's responses on the other, combined to work through her subconscious to gradually bring her closer to her old spiky self.

One day, months after David died and shortly after a typically irritating session with Georgina, a longhaired woman barged ahead of Os in a shopping queue. Instead of quietly conceding, as in the early weeks after she lost David, Os tapped the queue jumper on the shoulder and said, 'Excuse me, madam, am I invisible or dead?' and shoved back ahead of the shocked redhead. Os replayed the triumph in her head on the way home and told Louise. 'Just when I was beginning to think I might need to take medication.' John celebrated by letting Os help with his crossword and he made her cups of tea and baked a heaped tray of dominics. When Os woke up the next morning to find seven o'clock glowing in green figures on the bedside clock, which meant she'd had the first good night's sleep in ages, tears welled to her eyes because she didn't feel she deserved to feel anything like a normal human being when the remains of her son sat in an urn.

Drinkstain often came to provide moral support or quiet company. For some reason, or by accident, a few days after Os's mini victory in the queue, he pointed at the dusty scanner and said, 'That is so ancient, Noah's rejected it, health and safety...'

To which Os replied, in a flash, 'Noahs's sent a dove out for a copier, we're missing a base pair, or bear?' she said, then, admitted that, in spite of everything, she felt guilty to say it but she hoped Drinkstain would understand that she was beginning to miss her old job. She missed the quiet understated perspicacity of Dr. Mirano who was sacked by Alfred Enders. She missed the last stitch snatching of victory from the terrifying maws of surgical disaster. Missed the pleasure she got from taking a valve apart and putting it together again. Missed the challenge of wrenching words into shape in her head and onto page for publication and bringing trainees up to speed, watching the spring in their steps when they did something well, got a paper accepted for publication or for presentation, say. She craved the risqué banter with Blonde Barrie in theatre: "that Cody was so mean he used spider webs as firelighters" and "Georgina got that lopsided false smile from practising it in a silver foil mirror." She missed the delicious glee she got from feigning ignorance of rumours she started herself: the flabbergasted look on Professor Bute's face when Os said Instagram was going to take over his microbiology department to better display slides on the internet, priceless.

But, she asked Drinkstain, was she once again deluding herself? Was it not professional ambition that cost David his life?

'I'm a glass half full man,' said Drinkstain. 'But often the same qualities that got us into trouble, if well directed, can get us out,' he said.

One damp night, whilst having her hair plaited, and after a stupid tiff with H-Mum over the merits of stop and search – H-Mum for, Os against – to her mind popped the notion that the glass was fuller now because some saw that it was half full, or empty. Jeerie me Genies, Nelson Mandela could have chosen a relatively cushy time as a Cape Town lawyer, rands in the bank and an armoire packed with fancy suits, but he didn't. Instead, he gave up his life to light up the long walk to freedom for his people. And was it not because of what he and others gave up that she didn't need an iota of the fortitude of a James Meredith, or a Harriet Tubman, or an Ida Wells to be appointed professor of cardiac surgery? And though she still believed that she made the right diagnosis that the world was a dystopia, she'd chosen the wrong treatment and made it all about how she felt. *Genies wept, Ossy, people like you cannot afford to behave like that - anyway you like - not whilst "Black lives harder."* She raised her head and the half-plaited hair up to H-Mum with renewed conviction. Yes, in the grand moral morass of the universe, becoming Head of Department may not amount to more than a stringy or wavy particle's sub particle, but she was going for that job so that *no one*, BEM or WEM or anyone at the Trust, would have to rub themselves out to get on the right page.

'David would like that,' said H-Mum.

Drinkstain agreed but John asked if it was not too soon.

'Too soon to not go mad?'

CHAPTER TWELVE

Os did not have to wait long. One wet Wednesday morning in October Cody summoned her before a hurriedly convened Capability Hearing. He gave her less than two days' notice.

'Shouldn't detain us long. Georgina's summary makes the case as strong as I've ever seen in all my time as Medical Director for a referral to our friends in Manchester.' By that he meant the GMC, the regulatory council dreaded for various reasons by black doctors.

To Cody's right, under the duck egg ceiling, sat Adele in a loud black-and-orange striped jacket, beyond whom glared Ms. Ross, a consultant physician from a neighbouring Trust. Ms. Ross always looked pregnant, more so since, guessed Os, she must have consumed a mountain of dominics watching Second World War documentaries during lockdowns. Was she here for reciprocal back scratching? To help Cody and Co meet some secret target figure for suspensions and GMC referrals? To make them look as if they are hot on clinical governance? Or in return for some other murky favour at her Trust? Or did the madam fancy a day out because it would look great during her appraisal? There were two others, white males, one more bronze than beige, the other more beige than bronze, but both middle-aged and sitting shoulder-to-shoulder to the right of Ms. Ross. Os sent them a perfunctory nod and wink in greeting. If you've come to learn how to shaft colleagues you are in good company. The men couldn't keep their covetous eyes off Cody's gold watch, a family heirloom featured on the Antiques Road Show.

Mrs Kindolowo glanced once more at the panel and tapped her

keyboard. The three American students appeared on the screens. Seconds later, a shaven headed Lamide flicked on too, this time without a tie. Os squirmed on a chair which seemed to have been chosen to make her backbone bleed. She dabbed her flushed cheeks with a wet wipe, returned it to her bag to keep it moist, and had a quick feel of the USB in a side pocket. Earlier that morning she had handed a copy to Mrs. Kindolowo with a stern warning not to lose the device, or else. Os scanned the faces of her interrogators and served them each a quick lips-still-sealed smile. She received not a flicker in return. *Genies save us all, bet they wouldn't all be sitting here wasting taxpayers' dosh if the students came from Upper fucking Volta.* She shrugged her shoulders as she turned to Mrs. Kindolowo who replied with a filthy glare.

Thankfully, her John, who was keen to help, hadn't shoved his long-nosed pliers where they weren't needed and jammed the dashcam wires in the wrong way round. Would the thing deliver? It worked yesterday for the boffin from HR who couldn't come today. Maybe he was afraid. Don't hold it against him, Os, he may not know where his mortgage is coming from when interest rates begin the post-lockdown rise, as predicted by H-Mum.

'I will take no more of your precious minutes,' said Os. 'Ready?' She turned to Mrs. Kindolowo. Mrs. Kindolowo gave the computer mouse a little shake.

'I am most definitely ready, professor,' she said, eyes twinkling.

'Thanks to my daughter who taught me to download, or is it stream?' said Os, buoyed by Mrs. Kindolowo's air of complicity. Seconds later onto the screen popped an image of the cabin of Os's car. The sound of her sad voice again, recorded soon after David's death, brought a vague wistful ache to her jaw and she paused for a few moments. 'This is an unbroken timeline, the panel can have it verified by IT again, if it so wants,' said Os, then directed the panel to the overhead screens as the footage started to play. 'I apologise. The sound of me swearing because I was asked to go out of my way will not be to everyone's taste. I hope...' She stopped talking whilst the footage played, ending after twenty-nine minutes with Os asking the students not to use the cab as a pisspot and the sound of slammed doors and the whines of outrage from the students as they got out of the car.

'We know what we heard,' the students cried, unmuting themselves, their voices rising, whilst each successive nod of their African American compatriot got weaker, like the head of David's toy soldier when it ran out of charge. Cody Hayes's face turned two tones, pale on top and the colour of sump oil around his jowls. Georgina's looked as if she'd taken an unexpected right hook to the chin during a brawl at her wedding.

'Do our friends want to reconsider their testimony?' said the darker of the white men.

Tracey, one of the Euro-American girls, sobbed with head in hands. The other, Lindsay, let her blonde hair drop over her reddening face.

'It's not fair, it's a rerecording, or splicing? Fake news,' said Tracey. 'She has, hasn't she Dr. Cody, that's what she said wasn't it?'

'Dr. Cody? Dr. Cody? Yes? Can you hear? Can you hear us?' they repeated, percussing their keyboards.

Cody tugged first one flawlessly rolled-up white shirt sleeve then the other and fiddled with his silver pen. 'Quite extraordinary,' he said.

Genies pity them, shedding tears as if they've got onions strapped under their mammary glands because they know they are wrong. Or was it because they were busted; or because they believe they are always right; or they fear their birthright is not going to work this time; or to fucking damn well make sure that it does? To think, if she hadn't had the dashcam footage, this lot would be sitting in a plush library describing how they escaped this gigantic black woman in darkest South London by jumping out of her runaway cab. They wouldn't be short of offers from freedom lovers to ghostwrite the best seller: another Hollywood blackbuster in your cinemas now, nominated for nine Oscars, an unflinching, honest, excoriating examination of the impact of multiculturalism on the right to our cherished ideals and free speech.

Os didn't blame them. It's the culture, innit? Perhaps she'd be the same if she'd been born into, or indoctrinated by, the great American export, Whiteanity – the Bible-based Kamasutra in which whites must always be on top. An ideology that implied that if ordinary apple-pie-loving, God-fearing people can lynch, burn, hang and quarter, and gun down at a whim, celebrate the misery heaped on others in kaleidoscopic colour, sparkling Pulitzer purple verse and prose, it must follow that such hapless target creatures –bait – must be pathologically and genetically less than the ones who did the killing. Which is why when the black man goes to the shops, he risks a melanin-seeking slug in his back or cranium courtesy of the concerned corner cop. And when some want to kill to keep the privilege their colourless skin brings, their self-proclaimed babe magnet cheerleader - who was dragged screaming and tweeting from the White House - merely shrugs, says shooters are good people, they were provoked, and goes back to desperately fishing for likes for his hashtag preaching.

Over in Russia, Putin is seething in envy because he wants his share of the Whiteanity empire too, starting from east to west. It's his religious duty, Genies, his heritage and birthright too, you see. Silly Ukrainians, can't you see he is doing it for you too? It was this same birthright thing that did for her son. And she was complicit too.

Which brought her back to Cody and his too-clever-by-half coaching, *inappropriate for my status* and the rest of the bullshit he fed the students. Os looked up at the faces on the screen then at the fidgety Cody yards away. Look at his floppy face. Pitying its unprecedented owner. If his eyes turned round to tell him what they really thought of him, he'd refer them to the GMC for suspension, to be struck off for telling the truth. Yet, when he is old with a spine like a monkey puzzle tree and one green tooth left in his skull, and he sounds like a parrot with avian Flu, they'll read the myth story books he wrote with Adele and say, "No way, this man who single-handedly saved the NHS during Covid, how can he be guilty of as much as blowing his nose the wrong way?" They won't believe it when you tell them that when he, or any of his cabal, cock it up it's straight to the laundromate. The laundromate is where they go for a spot of friendly laundering behind closed doors to whitewash the sins of their mates away. They won't believe it when you tell them that at the merest hint of an awkward one, the chosen ones activate, aggregate, coalesce and congeal into a starry block, to bundle the intruder out of circulation. That job done they disperse at once, shredding and deleting evidence, so try as you might, Sherlock Holmes, you will detect no trace of the scuffle. Except on the isolated intruder. And their connections. Nothing gets in the way of the defence of reputations, double promotions, clinical excellence awards or that knighthood. Nothing. That's the truth. But who will believe anyone mad enough to tell it without a mask on?

Os tidied her post-it notes and tossed them into Comfort, then, when the tightness in her throat receded, raised her head to speak. Her voice was shaking.

'All I want is to go back to work.'

CHAPTER THIRTEEN

Yes, yes, yes, done it. She'd sent Cody and his pack of liars packing. Os hummed and sang along out loud to the car stereo, her heart adding its unique tremolos to the final movement of Beethoven op 132 – a late string quartet which seemed to mirror her feelings of triumph and rebirth after operose application and torment. Genies could have a rest now. She'd turned the corner. 'I told you, *omo yi*,' said H-Mum when Os called to tell her. '*Awamaridi*, God moves in mysterious ways.'

It was five past eleven, and Louise was in bed, snoring, coshed by her mother's crafty deployment of giant prawns and super honeyed naan bread. Os, tipsy with Chaquefort Roquegrave 2014, and in the striped shin-length night dress John bought her, crept into bed with him. Earlier that evening, on the sofa whilst he tried to read a newspaper under the faint glow of the table lamp, the merest hint of his warm olive gaze gliding over her bare shoulders made her tingle to the core. It had been quite a while and she wanted him. But did he want her? Had she been too harsh on him? Was her flesh still up to it after skimping on HRT?

'Sorry I snapped this morning,' she said.

John sighed, 'I missed you…love…'

Os stopped him with a kiss on the lips. 'Missed you too. Thanks for fixing the dashcam. Without it, Moby Cody Dick would have got me in his huge net…'

He winked at her and dropped the book he was reading on the floor. Os pulled him by the pyjama collar and smothered him in a long and languid full-throated kiss. 'Sure?' he said, coming up for air but she grabbed him and kissed him again and his steel erection shot up with its customary alacrity and she writhed his silky red top off his shoulders on to where she did not care and had him where she wanted him, between her legs, straddling him, preposterously filling and accommodating, sexual static, pumped friction, driving her to abandon, what must the earliest encounters have felt like before transitional epithelium evolved. Oh, there, he's got me, my head space whipped into a fiery cream. Why would anyone take drugs when you can feel like this for next to nothing? Feels as good as it ever did, thank the Genies. Nearly forgotten what it was like, this killing sweetly in and out and all over. His range may be limited but he was willing, earnest and hardworking. As they locked hands - was it abstinence or the celebratory glasses of wine? - John thrust in deep and did his trembling fish out of water thing, the way the late Prof Sleight once described it at the Cardiac Society.

'So much for sexual distancing,' she said, letting out a yell in a playful parody of her husband's whooping. She didn't reach the magic peak but this would have to do. Who needs the sort of highbrow intercourse that Ernie Hemmy or Fyodor the Dosty might write about – cinematic, ceaseless teasing and tottering on crests of excruciatingly exquisite near inevitability – when you can enjoy a connection you thought you might never make again?

'That was wonderful, thank you, Johnny, hundred percent. And for the dominics.' After an awkward knock of knees and elbows they swapped places and lay like spoons, she near the radio in his hairy arms. Os closed her eyes. Bathed in the salty metallic aroma of their mingled fluids, she swayed gently against him to the poetic rhythm of the shipping forecast.

"Fisher, German Bight, Viking, Thames, Dover, Cromarty...' went the radio. John joined in too. They chuckled. She felt his chuckling turn into thrusts. Genies above, what's got into his rhythm stick? It's stiff again. And oh my Genies he's moving in. Three heaves and, oops, a slicing warmth engulfed her and she shuddered and whooped and laughed and cried out loud and emitted notes even Ludwig her pal could not put down on a page.

Afterwards, she lay with her head on his chest. Maybe all was not lost. If only David were here. Oh, David. She closed her smarting eyes. Her nose dripped onto the pillow.

'Fancy a night out? Sort of locally, Wimbledon, Putney? Somewhere easy to get to?' John stroked her sweat soaked hair.

Os stifled a sneeze and reached out to turn the radio down. She rolled over to face him. His olive eyes lit up. Os closed hers. How did it come to this? They used to do so much together: took in the opera, a concert, four course meals out with friends. But past performance is no guarantee of future success, especially when the heart falls out of it, and since those halcyon days they'd dropped out of that exalted social league.

Os combed his thick chest hairs with her fingers and opened her eyes. 'I've got something to tell you,' she said. He started back. 'No, I'm not pregnant.' Genie gimme strength, the man has the imagination of a tea leaf. Os propped herself on an elbow and gave John a careful, pithy account of what happened with Simply Blue and Mr. Boardman on the day after David died. 'Before you say anything, I put my hand up. Should have checked whether Cody changed the order. Simply Blue did brilliantly, considering.' In her distraction that morning she could not be sure that her surgical notes were accurate. She'd tried to get Simply Blue back in to make sure that she'd carried out the correct procedure; but not even Vera the Improbable, Drinkstain's secretary could find the man. John rolled on to his back with his hands as a pillow. 'So that's a no to a night out then.'

'You're putting words in my mouth again,' she said.

'So you do want to go or not?' he said.

'I don't think you would want to go if you were me,' she said.

CHAPTER FOURTEEN

If Os thought she'd turned the corner at work she was wrong. Cody and Georgina stalled. Furious, Os said she'd see them in court. But where was she going to get the money? Something John had been quick to point out. 'You'll see,' said Os and made that long delayed appointment with her firm of accountants.

Muffled sounds of street life, a van door sliding closed, motorcycle engine revving, filtered through the open sixth floor window of MoWM accountants. 'Only doing our job,' Os said, squirming to praise for NHS frontline workers she knew she didn't deserve. The female trainee accountant in a woolly suit bowed to Os again and leaned stiffly to put the tea tray down on the glass table. The coffee was too sweet. Os pulled a face. The livid nick on John's chin again caught her eye. He blamed her for not getting him the right shaving cream during lockdown. Poor thing. Such a fuss over the loss of a few red cells. He'll live. David didn't. She repressed a surge of irritation by calling to mind a photo of Louise as Romeo in the school play. Don't bloody mess her up as well, Ossy. Or let anyone else.

Ms Jamieson sailed in. Aged about forty-five, give or take a season or two of Botox, with brown hair and high eyebrows and wearing a large houndstooth jacket, she had joined the firm weeks before Covid made British landfall.

'Morning both, again,' she said, laying a huge file on the table and sinking into her leather chair in one movement. Ms Jamieson's eyes dwelt on John for a fraction too long, rekindling an unexpected tension in Os's rib cage. She eased her chair an inch closer to John and summarised her predicament.

'I won all ends up but guess what?' she said. 'They want to look at the footage from my dashcam again. It will take months, they say, because the Yanks are threatening legal action. Meanwhile I'm to do what?' Os sighed. 'Then the other day he sends for me and with Georgina smirking beside him says he's had a good Christmas with his autistic son, so as a gesture of goodwill and after long and careful deliberation I could have my job back. The cheek.' She raised a hand. 'Wait for it. I could have my job back on one condition. Georgina shoves this paper at me and asks me to sign an agreement that I would not apply for Ian's job. Words to that effect.' She fanned her face with her hand. 'Genies gimme strength.'

'Which is why you are here, I presume…at last,' said Mrs. Jamieson. 'Don't worry, the matter about which we were trying to get hold of you is resolved. Loose end related to the last budget.'

'I tried to get her to come, but too busy, as usual,' said John, stroking the faint weal on his chin. 'But Ossy is right to be aggrieved. She hasn't been able to earn real money for months because of Covid and they've cut her salary.' Os bristled as John had said he doubted whether British barristers or accountants for that matter accepted payment in cowries. Even if they found a stash somewhere behind the Oba's palace in downtown Lagos, he bet that such was the exchange rate now, according to Goldman Sacks, that Os would have to pay for a couple of super tankers to freight the bulky fees from Lagos.

Os counted to five. 'My husband has a First Class Degree in Anthropology, that's if you haven't guessed already,' she said. 'But can you make my numbers work? It's for legal expenses. As I set out in my email.'

'It's why we pay your company the gold-plated fees, isn't it?' said John.

The accountant replied with a bright-eyed smile. 'But you are not blessed with great liquidity, that is the problem.' A soft West Country accent intruded and faint creases flitted around her warm grey eyes. She flipped through an orange file and shivered as if tickled by the ghosts of bankruptcies past. At a push she might find a few grand using some creative elbow grease but after that the figures were somewhat encrusted, in liability she said. Her fingertips peeped from her jacket, which gave her a furtive air as she drew two circles - one red, one black - on a piece of paper.

One represented the sum borrowed by Os, the other the total interest remaining on the loan. The latter was not shrinking but growing. Os felt like a one-legged woman teetering on the prow of a sinking ship. She dug her elbows into the arms of the chair to steady herself as she recalled that she took the loan to set up a limited liability company, Smartcells, with Ian Kennedy to exploit her insights into myocardial cell memory after cardiac surgery. All was great until, courtesy of Governor Mervyn and his committee at the Bank of England, interest rates went up. No worries. The company was comfortably washing its face and off she sent her cheque to pay off a chunk of said loan. Days later, a Roderick Barkson Esq turned up with said cheque and, on his laptop, a reminder that Os took out an "innovative" product to protect herself, but not as it turns out, if interest rates went up. Sorry, madam, but you personally owe just south of half a million pounds and rising with each ticking sweep of the hands of his exquisitely complicated chronometer. The man was backed up by the business support section of a too-white-to-fail bank, the type that does its silky underwear laundry in Latinate America. SMEs, your local riding schools, fast food outlets, hairdressers and drycleaners complained that they'd been stitched into the very small print itself. They could not escape. But the big bank was not having any of it and divided the investors, or debtors, into two groups: the unsophisticated, worthy of some redress, partial refunds, and the sophisticated, who deserved nothing more than tea and sympathy. Os, as an academic who should have known better, they put in the latter group.

'Genies gimme shelter, sophisticated, moi?' said Os.

Under Ms. Jamiesons's reproachful and theatrical grimaces and John's sucks of breath, Os fidgeted and curled her toes as she recounted how she raised the money to try to clear the debt. She accompanied Ian on his visiting professorial trips to Saudi, UAE, Congo, Angola, Burma, South Africa, Russia, the US, everywhere carrying out surgery on the most unsavoury characters dressed in Italian suits Ms. Jamieson would ever wish not to meet. When Os told how she changed diamonds for cash whilst standing on a bed above the flood waters in a brothel, Ms. Jameson shrieked and slapped her hands to ears.

'Shsh, I didn't hear that. Professor, let me give you a free piece of advice,' she said, putting a playful emphasis on the word free. 'Never open up to someone like me on a first meeting…' She blew on her fingertips. 'Prof, sue them if you want but if you lose they will threaten you with punitive costs well into six figures.' On top of what she already owed. Is that what Os wanted? To lose her house. Everything?

John stopped scratching his jaw, ignored Os's decapitating glare and gave his coffee a furious stir. 'Louise needs stability, after…sort of everything. It's logical and sensible to place us all on a firm financial footing as soon as practical…"

Os bridled, sensed Ms Jameson's eyes on her and raised a cringeworthy smile, wishing John would shut the fuck up. It wasn't his career heading for the u-bend. She was fed up to the back teeth with the inequality of arms between claimants and Hospital Trusts. Many whistleblowers or victims of managerial highhandedness dug into life savings to try to save their careers but the Codys of this NHS were backed by expensive lawyers, bankrolled in effect by the state and indirectly by the victim or plaintiff. 'Makes my skin crawl,' she said.

'But you can't risk the bloody roof over our heads. Please tell her,' said John and, as he turned his imploring eyes on Ms Jameson, Os felt another piece of her marriage fall away. *Atlas wept, my man's got less backbone than a ribbed condom.* This wasn't about Louise at all. It was about him and wanting-to-show-off-the-big-house to Jaundiced Matilda in his rivalry with Gary.

'Crowdfunding?' said Ms Jameson, rolling a pen in her fingers. 'Or you could take in tenants.' She knew of a foreign couple trapped by Covid restrictions. Or Os could remortgage. 'Check with your home insurance who might be able to help with some of the legal stuff.

Friends? Family?' Ms Jameson turned her gentle eyes on John. 'Your brother owns -'

'Never.' The words leapt from Os's lips before she could stop them. She wagged her head with great vigour. As Genies were her witness, she would rather lap her morning cereal out of a skunk's armpit than tap Gary for a loan. Genies wept, you soil your palm with their lucre and Matilda's nailing the IOU to the front door of the BBC, calling the bond markets, and appearing as guest on Songs of Praise to thank her stars that she insisted on a water-tight prenup before her son got into bed with that surgical gold digger. Out of politeness, Os made some notes whilst Ms Jameson spoke, but she knew that she had as much chance of raising the money as scratching her face with her tailbone. Maybe if she got lucky, wrote a catchy tune, a slogan for the government that then went viral. Perhaps try to "get the jab" or, as Drinkstain's friend would say, get the *facts seen*. Yet were facts not the last thing Drinkstain's bloviate friend wants to be seen?

Os shrugged her lips and made a zero with her finger and thumb. 'My options seem somewhat limited,' she said. Yet worse was to come.

***

A few days after what would have been David's eighteenth birthday, Os had just blown her nose after a quiet weep when Georgina appeared in the doorway.

'Are you ok…Professor?' she said, one foot on the step below. 'We should be more together, you and me, because out of the deepest valleys rise the highest mountains.' For example, Cody was really down after they took him off the complex surgical list but, she thanked God, things happen for a reason and now she and Cody were like a broadsheet. He calls her the broad and he is the print. They could not be separated and he was promoted to Medical Director and his wife has stopped fighting him for money and gave him more time with his son, Andy. She locked her fingers together. 'If someone with OCD like me can help Andy, then we can all work together for patient care.' Cooperation is better than conflict. Addition is better than division. Surely Os understood where she was coming from? Were they not both brought up in London?

The walls rattled from an air lock in the carious hospital plumbing. Os needed a homily from Princess Georgina of Clacton or wherever like a double break in the neck. Whatever happened between Cody and his family he brought it on himself. That he lost his prestigious post on the surgical team was no reason to raise his fists to his blessed misses or pour the procession of whisky bottles down his aqueduct neck. Os rolled her shoulders to a prickling unease. 'I could do with a new laptop, this one keeps crashing, but maybe you are too busy planning your wedding, or are you only good enough as Andy's maid?' Os said, seeking a sore spot through which to plunge her words, and, from the look on Georgina's face, finding it. *That will teach her.*

'You operated on two Mr. Boardmans that morning? Yes? No?' Georgina said, not waiting for an answer before she said, 'He was admitted to the ward.'

Ah, should have known she was softening me up. 'I think I know him,' Os said, her voice failing her. She coughed. 'Can I see him?' she said, to a fore and aft sensation in her stomach.

'He's dead,' said Georgina, with the elan of those who delight in delivering bad news.

'No way. What? How?' Os said, her heart slipping from one banana skin to the next as she tried to wrestle words into a plausible show of sincere regret. Simply Blue, her dad's murderer and her patient, was dead. What was she supposed to do? She bit her lip and, through the misty swirling in her head, she heard Georgina say that a return to work was completely out of the question. Number one, they had to complete the first investigation. Number two, now that Simply Blue was dead they needed to start another inquiry. Georgina's thick red lipstick made a chewy sound as she spoke. 'Number three, you know what Cody is like. If there is a bottom to this issue with Simply Blue, Cody will find it...'

'Champion. Smashing,' said Os, lapsing into Ian's way of speaking. She plastered on her English breakfast face and wriggled from her seat.

If only the awful man had come in for checks. But he said he was doing well. What the heck, what if he caught bloody Covid? No way was he coming in to be their guinea pig for the vaccine. A friend of a friend on their street who had her hip done, it was Covid wot did for her.

Georgina hadn't been gone two minutes when Os's head began to swim and pound. Her lips and fingertips tingled. She lolled against the pimpled wall. If this went pear-shaped, she'd be lucky to get a job testing Putin's bulletproof specs. Sweat sliced down her face. She grabbed the table for support, but her vision went black and she slumped out cold, wedged between table and wall for a few seconds, until she came round. Her head seemingly packed with soggy sandpaper, she dragged and pulled and rolled herself back into her seat and placed her head between her legs for a minute. If Cody got a postmortem and lined the ducks in the right order, saw the grafts in the wrong place, and if - big if - the grafts *are* in the wrong place… Just one will do - he'd love it, love it, milk it for all it was worth and prance to the GMC with the bits of Os between his teeth singing "Strike her off, Strike her off, She's not fit to practise." Then he's skateboarding to Scotland Yard and to Holloway rapping that she was not fit to walk the streets and that every room we've let her in she's blown the walls off in minutes. She recalled ruefully the blunt question Adele asked at the disciplinary hearing. 'Professor Sharp, is there nothing you are not bad at?'

Committing slow-bleeding hari kari she supposed.

Even the always-sunny-side-up and glass-half-full Drinkstain agreed that if Os was to survive with a career of any description, she needed the help of a heavyweight.

CHAPTER FIFTEEN

It was an unremarkable day roofed by a thick sheet of grey sky when Os arrived at work to see Ian, the only man in the world for whom Os, who hated heights with such a passion that a game of snakes and ladders made her dizzy, would consider doing a bungee jump. Defaced by graffiti and pigeon mess and on the left of the main gates, the poster of the local MP with David Cameron giving the hospital the thumbs up reminded her of the deathly vote of confidence familiar to doomed football managers. The kiss of death. On the other side sagged the dirty blue and yellow banner of the junior minister who promised billions to rebuild the hospital with the dividends expected from the runaway success of Brexit and the HS2. The minister had since been sacked, a shock because extrusion from the cabinet was quite an achievement, like a newborn stuffing its placenta back into the womb and following suit.

She found Ian at his sprawling desk surrounded by a ceiling-high library, shelves wilting under the weight of first editions, theses, file boxes, textbooks, registries, loose manuscripts and annual reports. A clammed-up laptop hung over the right edge of the desk. On it sat a dirty brown and green mug. Wearing black-rimmed round bifocals, Ian had an open countenance, a short sandy coloured beard and was wearing a frayed corduroy jacket he claimed a miner uncle had handed down to him. Back in the day, just over twenty years ago, he saw something of his younger gauche and prickly northerly self in Os at a research meeting. Despite warnings that he was wasting his time – had he gone bonkers, not heard of her suspect temperament and that she was a loose cannon, was she not a single mother for a good reason? – he took her on.

Puffing for breath after skipping up the stairs on her short legs, Os sat down opposite him, facing casement-leaded glass windows through which she spied a clump of darker clouds in the northern sky.

'Hot in here or is it me?' she said, puffing air over her face.

'Sure you're ok?' said Ian, his crow's feet digging deep into the side of his blue eyes.

Os shrugged and sank further into the leather seat. Her legs scraped against the stiff journals stuffed in the desk's deep kneehole. She waited for the gritty prickling in her eyes to recede then said, 'Thanks for seeing me.' She cleared the hoarseness from her voice. 'Means a lot...'

'Your ears must be burning, guy you saw in the clinic's been on the phone. Said he doubted whether you had sufficient command of the English language to convey the intricate details of a case as complicated as his. Which is why he insisted on his right as a professor to speak to the top man, known as Moi to you and me,' said Ian.

Os's belly began to squirm in sickly anticipation of the *don't take this the wrong way but* scenario.

'You won't believe it,' said Ian, oblivious to Os's discomfort. 'That black lady doctor told me nothing, he said. Nobody tells me anything, he said, then he said he had a mind broader than the Niger delta and it ran faster than the river Congo and had he not worked and taught all over the world, including Ethiopia, Uganda and Tanzania, and passed through Tripoli three times? He was only telling it as it is,' Ian's eyes twinkled. He polished his spectacles on the sleeve of his huge grey jacket. Surely a man should have the choice over who runs a knife over the intimate corners of his heart, or *moyo wangu* as they say in Swahili. Os got the patient's drift: with all the woke-ish political correctness, he needed a degree in multicultural palaeontology to get treatment in his bailiwick nowadays. She scratched her neck. Her bra felt sticky. Yet the residual working-class Geordie lilt to Ian's southern modulated accent somehow muted the impact of his words.

She replied with a stockphrase of her own, 'I'm sure he didn't mean the way...er...'

'I had to contain myself, Os. Because when I saw your sketches of his aorta and your neat writing and explanations sticking out of his inside jacket pocket I felt like I did when I had my first paper published; over the moon, But, as they say on the BBC, I chose my candid words with, er, the utmost care...and told him where to go,' said Ian. He stroked his lush sandy beard, a shimmering boyish eagerness for praise in his blue eyes.

Os's toes dug into the floor. *Genies gimme shelter, but what is a girl to say in reply to such a sideways endorsement? Thank you?* Or apologise that your boss had to go through that on your behalf? Ask if her etching for the patient came up to scratch? Did the man not have a point? Is the customer not always right? Os remembered the patient. Checked jacket and thick spectacles and transparent ears. Marched in like lord of the manor, flash of wintery discontent on his face when he saw it was her not Ian. Should she say that she didn't think too much of it? That until recently, she hadn't realised how much she was used to taking it. Jeerie me, what must these ready-made smiles and forced warm handshakes be doing to her blood vessels, DNA, and telomeres?

Os rustled up a bespoke smile and said, 'He might have had a bad day, partner kicked him out of bed? If he doesn't mind, I'll see him again to explain how I intend to replace his crumbling imperial aortic arch,' berating herself for betraying her irritation. Don't tell those who make or made you sick how you feel, woman. Then, whilst Ian was in this receptive mood, she launched her plea for help. If he didn't know already, in her honest opinion - and she had it on the good authority of others better placed - Cody was getting her ready for the chop. All she'd done was write a few shirty emails about PPE. Hardly a hanging offence. She hated to ask but could Ian have a quiet word? She knew he'd got her out of many scrapes but this one had the momentum of a flash flood. She didn't understand why Cody had it in for her.

'You know what the GMC are like,' she said, the flash of irritation in Ian's eyes telling her that her comments hadn't come out of her diplomatic top drawer. Ian himself was a GMC grandee. Os gazed at her knees as if they were to blame for digging the hole in which Ian found her. 'But what will happen to our microvascular energetics team?'

she said, referring to a unit she built single handedly but for which she let Ian take credit.

Ian polished a grey stapler on his sleeve with a distracted air. 'This unpleasantness with Cody has been rumbling for a long time, has it not?' he said, his forehead double dimpled by a frown. A most unwelcome intrusion he said, and his voice sagged, lips hardly moving behind his bushy beard. He put the stapler down and polished his spectacles on his jacket sleeve, put them back on and tapped the side of his nose. He was sorry that Os hadn't managed to keep her nose clean, as he'd advised.

Genies wept. Unpleasantness? Intrusion. What do they have to do with the pace of climate change? Cody's got her measured up for the gallows and here is Ian tongue-testing his latest evasions. For the sake of his triple-locked pension pot? An image of David's ashes intruded. Os lost her train of thought. 'Cody's been after me a long time you say, so has middle east apartheid. Doesn't make it right,' she said then flinched to the hot splash in her belly. Had Cody guessed that she didn't know he changed the theatre list on the day Mr. Boardman collapsed? *Genies, please no.*

Ian raised his bushy eyebrows. 'You don't do things by half do you, Os? Something's nagging. The day after…you know…after your son, er, passed, maybe you shouldn't have come in that morning. Could explain why your patient collapsed. I hear you were in touch with the patient? Simply Blue?'

Os wriggled her knees out an inch and dragged her chair back with deliberate care whilst she cleared her head.

'Any advice? My hearing before the committee is any day now,' she said.

Ian scratched his sandy beard and spoke so softly that Os leaned forward to hear him.

'The timing's not great.' He threw his pale hairy hands up in the air and brought them down on either side of a journal lying open before him. He'd already used up massive, and he meant massive, political capital in getting rid of Cody. 'But to go bull in a china shop now against him?' He shook his head. That would be like costing the lads the match with an own goal at the Gallowgate end in the last second of added time. 'Cody had rough patches too. Divorce cost him a fair wack, millions I hear. Lost custody of the two girls and autistic son. Family home. Takes its toll on a man you know.' Os was about to speak but Ian interrupted her. 'As the missus says to me the other day: Ian, time to look after number one.' He puffed his cheeks, shook his head and let out a long sigh. 'Gutted for you, for your loss, for everything but...' blushing, he bowed his head and stroked his chin. Then he gripped Os in his intense blue gaze. Cody had made her a smashing offer, all considered. Ian could tell her for the price of a Newcastle United jersey in Sunderland that the job was not worth the aggro. Os should go find herself a high-fidelity mirror, look in it and ask herself, after everything, in all honesty, if, in going for the job, she was really being true to herself.

CHAPTER SIXTEEN

'Don't stand there like a stick insect, close the door,' H-Mum said. It was just past seven o'clock in the evening, cold enough to need the cardigan Os was wearing and which she kept on as she followed H-Mum up the draughty staircase. The dimly lit living room was strewn with cards and photos, notes, copies of school reports, newspaper cuttings about David. Hymnal singing seeped from the radio. H-Mum brushed past Os and dropped to her knees. 'It's a new filing system,' she said, with a brusqueness that warned off dissent. Grumbling that Os should have given notice, H-Mum began a frenetic clean-up of the memorabilia, clutching cards to her chest, trapping them under her chin, but many slipped to the floor before she reached the carton behind the sofa she got them from. Through this, Os emitted phatic grunts, adopting a half crouch as if to help, but she couldn't bear to watch and, muttering vaguely about the diuretic effect of that last mug of coffee, she scurried to the toilet to have a little weep, give her nose a good blow, and splash water on her scorching face.

When she returned, H-Mum was looking at a favourite photo that she took of a four-year-old David on his first visit to a farm. He'd never seen a live llama and had been so excited when it fed out of his hand. Sensing Os's arrival, H-Mum threw the photo into the carton at her feet and smoothed her skirt down, her eyes swinging low behind the finger-soiled lens of her spectacles. Her lips trembled. She reached out for the arm of the sofa with her left arm and swung stiffly into the seat. Her eyes closed and head dropped into her palms. *Why, why? Did she not pray enough?* First for Semijeje, then Kola, now this. She shook her head. Os dropped into the sofa beside H-Mum and offered her a paper hanky. 'Are you reading your Bible? Will you come at Easter?' Genies wept, this was no time for H-Mum to lose her blinking religion. Os could barely keep going, let alone float H-Mum too.

'I'll stay overnight if you want,' she said. Louise could make her own dinner. She'd understand.

H-Mum smiled and tapped Os's knee gently, wiped her eyes and put her glasses back on. After a clumsy search with her feet, she slipped her shoes on and shuffled across to feel a radiator. Grumbling about the gas bills and the fickleness of the English weather she drew herself up, wiped her nose, and swayed to the kitchen. 'I have mackerel and the special fried rice from the pastor's take-away joint,' said H-Mum, with a warning in her voice for Os not to scoff. Nothing wrong with being a capitalist pastor; instead of, like some people, always waiting for manna from heaven. Os stood in the kitchen doorway, Comfort hugged to her chest, seeking an opening in which to insert the impasse with Cody. H-Mum popped the bowl of fried rice into the microwave. 'If you say he didn't call the police, I have to haccept…but a woman in your position should not hallow what was going on between them…'

'What's she been saying?' Genies wept, that Louise girl had a mind like a one-way wrench.

The microwave chimed. H-Mum ignored it. '*Omo yi*, do not talk to me as if I am an empty bottle. Only John knew what happened with David that morning and he is not telling the whole truth. Anyway,' she added. '*Wetin do the man bladder sef?*' John seemed to spend more time in the toilet than a tennis player losing at Wimbledon. She would not stand by and let Os deceive herself. 'As if I am a bad mother.'

Os's nerves screamed for her to leave before they snapped. But she couldn't because she needed advice. 'You want me to flog them like goats?' she said, a dig at H-Mum's brutal methods.

'Without discipline you think you will be a professor today?' H-Mum opened the microwave door, then seemed to have a second thought and closed it again. 'Without a good guide will you reach where Kola said…'

'So all professors are flogged? You lied, both of you. There is no room at the top…for–'

'The job of a mother is to dress her child in the best story she has. When the child grows she can wear any story she likes.'

Os emitted a grunt of token resistance. The ends justify the myths. Guided hypocrisy. Was that what she practised with David, encouraging and shoving him to do Medicine by telling him fattened stories about granddad?

'Kids nowadays won't accept what that–'

'How is work?' said H-Mum.

Her heart stopped. 'Getting there…' She gulped hard.

H-Mum kissed the silver crucifix hanging round her and raised it to the sky. 'Hail Mary I despair, oh.' What hon this God's earth did Osese mean by *getting there* by *nearly there*, ernh? In all her time travelling hon the London Underground she'd never hever heard of "nearly there" as a destination. 'Which line was it? Bakerloo? Northern? District restricted? Osese Sharp Line to nowhere?'

'Maybe it's for the best, not to apply,' said Os. She shifted her weight on her feet. H-Mum shouldn't jump down her throat but what if Cody was right to object to her application? Did a black woman not carry more aggro into the operating room from the outside world than, say, Alfred Enders, a familiar face, a white man who is comfortable and is less likely to be wound up by a rude police officer or porter or a security man on the way to work?

'Maybe if I take his deal…' She told H-Mum of Cody's threat to refer her to the GMC if she applied for Ian's job.

'*Babanla nonsense,* that man will cut your head off and say you gave it to him because your neck was tired. Osese, please say you didn't agree…'

Os replied with a timid shake of the head. H-Mum flung the microwave door open and asked why they wanted Os to sign their *yeye* agreement when she'd wiped the floor, shown them *real pepper* at the hearing. 'The man is trying to torture us with hope, then power-wash it haway.' He behaves as if he is the only star in God's firmament, and they all allow it. Including Os. Did Os not have the best surgical results last year and the year before and the year before that? H-Mum shoved her spectacles back on and waited for a response from Os that did not come. 'So, Osese, my dear, why are you making my mouth twist and shout like Chubby Checker, ernh?' If Os didn't behave the way Cody imagined *he* would if *he* were a black woman, that was his problem, not Os's, but Os shouldn't come all this way to jump about like oil in a frying pan. H-Mum donned multicoloured gloves and landed the bowl of spicy fried rice on a tray. Garnished with fish, prawns and peppers it was the London version of Lagos fried rice as H-Mum adamantly claimed to remember it. 'I will say this, then shut my mouth. Osese, I see why you are confused. Your husband thinks heveryone should be like him. Cody thinks he is better than everybody and Lamide still does not know what kind of man he wants to be. But you need to go back to the trinity of what we all need, to be at home in the head in the house and houtside.' She pointed at Os's head and heart. Os bristled and hugged her bag closer. Silence teetered between them, their knuckles touching and bouncing off each other as Os helped H-Mum serve up. When H-Mum turned away to wash her hands at the sink she tossed a question over left shoulder. 'I hear that man, Simply Blue, died…true?'

Os's heart seemed to scramble for cover. She cleared her throat and, as if H-Mum had not spoken, picked up Comfort and sidled out of the door to tidy the living room. On the piano stool sat a black bag, the same simple design as Comfort. She hadn't seen the bag for years but before she could have a closer look H-Mum appeared with the tray of food. They sat side by side at the coffee table. Os picked at the rice and the vegetables for a few minutes then apologised and said she wasn't as hungry as she thought. H-Mum stopped munching. Why did Os look as if a battery was leaking acid inside her head? Was Louise alright? Or was John grinding her down as well?

'Speak up,' said H-Mum when Os mumbled.

Os massaged a tense calf. H-Mum was right. Simply Blue was dead. She stammered through a recap of the mix-up in theatre with the Mr. Boardmans the day after David died. What if she made the mistake that killed Simply Blue? Os made a tortured and torquing action with a fist into her head but couldn't admit to H-Mum the fear that in the fugue of grief on the day after David's death, she may have taken her dad's dying words *not to let them get away with it* to mean that she should avenge his death. What dad really meant was that Os shouldn't let whatever happened to him stop her aiming for the top.

'Cody was in the theatre on the day,' said Os, grateful for the time to think afforded by an ambulance screeching past. 'Cody is going to get a post mortem. What if he knows that I didn't know he changed the list. What if I made a mistake?' she said, cringing with guilt, with self-hatred for wasting H-Mum's life-long support for her.

In the ensuing viscid silence you could hear your neighbour's tinnitus. Os's head stewed as she prepared for a dressing down, the extravagant variations on a theme of put-upon single parents – *haba, this girl, see what you've done, your only son gone, hall my hard work turned to quicksand and steam you cannot stand on*: and so on. But H-Mum raised her crucifix to her lips, relief jostling with shock and guilt behind her spectacles as if Os had that moment resurfaced after life-saving surgery for a terrible accident that H-Mum caused.

'Osese, you must not punish yourself.' When Os's dad died she blamed herself for everything: for forcing Kola to wear the Nigerian/Union Jack shirt she bought for him, for allowing him out in the wrong shoes which meant he couldn't run fast enough to escape Simply Blue and his gang, for buying a flat in New Cross when she could have had one in Peckham or Lewisham. Why was Os beating herself up about that man, ernh? Had Os not dragged herself out of bed that morning? The morning after her son died, she went to work to save the life of the man who killed her dad. Her eyes deserved to rest on medals, not tears.

Os shook her head. 'Mummy, your mouth is dancing ahead of what I was trying to say about–'

'Wait, ah ah, let me talk, ah ah. People do what they like nowadays and laugh in your face.' Had Os ever heard a foreign aid worker hapologise to the mother of the innocent African child they sacrificed? When they take the money they could spend on antibiotics and give it to buy water because they want to save others? Did they give the bereaved mother a medal, the child a state burial? '*Nibo*, for where?' Did cultured and civilised men not bomb little women and children into jigsaw pieces then get a Nobel Prize for Peace? Not long ago they were hanging us from trees for fun. If not for that fine girl, Darnella Frazier, and her mobile phone they would say that poor man, George Floyd, strangled himself to spoil the fine name of the wonderful super police department. H-Mum kissed her silver crucifix. May the Lord forgive her for knocking on the door of heresy or blasphemy but, even if Os minced Simply Blue's heart and fed it to greedy pigs, good luck to the lovers of bacon. Her eyes blazed with a frightening conviction and her tone was both invigorating and caressing. '*Omo mi*, we are only here once. Do not let life slide you by when right is on your side...'

'Is that where right has been all this time?' Os made a paddling motion. 'Get thee right behind me and shove.'

'I am serious.' H-Mum pointed at the black bag that looked like Comfort sitting on the piano stool. 'Your CVs and floppy discs? Is that what you called them? From around Lamide's time. I was going to tell you, but my memory is getting bored with its owner,' said H-Mum. 'Remember them and that *penkelemesi* with Cody?'

With a deft flick of the wrist, she opened the bag and out slipped a dozen discs. Os sat on the stool beside H-Mum, turning and reading the discs, her neat writing and the dates on the well-thumbed stickers evoking wistful recollections of the difficult days as a junior. If she smashed more runs before tea than the rest put together, they said it was a great batting wicket, conditions favoured her. Her great CV was only a piece of paper, a piece of vainglorious fiction, naturally, as it was self-penned, a "guide and not a rail". Cardiac surgery is mentally draining and backbreaking work, not for any Tom, Dick or Jane Doe. She got the message. Then, as now with Cody, she found out what they really thought about her when she made a mistake, or they thought she made a mistake, or they thought she thought she'd made a mistake. She had an idea. Os waved one of the CDs in the air. If she could only tempt Cody into a game he was sure she could not afford to lose...

CHAPTER SEVENTEEN

Thus began what came to be known as the Clash of Sarf London Scalpels.

Os contacted Selina Mantle, a former medic who had retrained as an investigative journalist. Selina started the Doctors for Justice group to support NHS whistleblowers. Deliberately way over the top in her tweets and blogs, relayed and retweeted by Selina's close to half a million active followers, Os accused the Trust of giving Cody and his ilk a free pass. They work by nods and winks and unwritten rules, she wrote. And if you dare ask "Excuse me, please, is he not born of woman too? How come he is getting this and that directorship and double money and more double taxpayers' money for failing at Surgery and made director of this and that forever without a vote by the rest of us or a manifesto or a means to get rid of him if he's fucking us up?", they say, "Go and check with him first. See if he agrees not to be head of this and that." Then they roll eyes and say to this woman, "You are making them pretty, pretty uncomfortable in the mental health department for raising these issues and presenting the service in a bad light. How dare you say the staffing on ITU is inadequate when they had an adequate "mix of skills" on the ward? We are inclusive. That is why we count the domestics and cleaners as members of the team. Had the inspectors not seen how quickly these colleagues change rubber attachments on vacuum cleaners? Does that not count as an intubation skill which can be reengineered at short notice for the benefits of patients? And it ticks the boxes on diversity, as nearly all are from our BEM and/or LGBTQ+ community or recent immigrants. And it is cheaper than using agency staff. So, doctor, be careful before you make these baseless and reckless accusations. Draw a line and think of the consequences for your GMC revalidation.

For weeks, her quarry didn't bite. Internet trolls bayed for Os to be committed to a psychiatric hospital and threatened to rape her and subject her to various forms of sexual degradation. But from the man she wanted to bite, nothing. Os was beginning to despair, until one morning, she was sitting in her basement office when she received a text from Selina. 'He's on,' she said.

After Os's relentless tweets and retweets, in the end, Cody couldn't resist. Helped by his friends in the media, he recounted his crucial role in fighting Covid to a standstill. Extraordinary. Unprecedented. This was typical of Professor Osese Orise whatever-her-name-was Sharp. She hated us and "our way of life" and wanted to impose her egregious zero-sum identity politics by spouting grist to the mill of the diverse enemies of "our NHS". He had a son with autism himself, for whom he would do anything, and he had empathy for the grieving Os's impassioned blunderbuss outbursts, but on the matter of the wider administration of the NHS she has gone way over the top. If Os really cared about the NHS why didn't she cooperate with him in drafting his Cody Hayes Bill, meant to strengthen protection for whistleblowers? This extraordinarily unfortunate chapter in the glorious history of our incomparable NHS must be binned and buried or incinerated like the recent Ashes series England lost.

From her Mediterranean retreat, Adele Harrison helped Cody relaunch their latest book, "Proud Face of our NHS". It had an airbrushed photograph of Cody in white coat on the cover and a foreword by a pair of American Republican Party senators. Crammed with numerous examples, some apocryphal, of Cody's consummate buccaneering managerial derring-do, devil take the naysayers, anti-woke management style during the first wave of the Covid pandemic. Effusive praise from sportspeople - a male jockey, five cricketers plus two historians, one actor, and politicians and journalists sick of stories about the murder of George Floyd - filled several pages of the slim volume. Os was one of those practitioners of the dark arts of identity politics who believed in destroying cherished monuments. God help us. How could anyone advocate tearing down statues of benevolent philanthropists? Worse than burning books. These were the innovators in mass transportation and production in the New World. What next? Bombing private yachts? Ack acking Lear jets because you disagree with their carbon footprint? Desecrating the graves of your parents because they supported a porcine loving football club? Dance, ululating, around the bonfires of the hot dogs? And, whilst he was at it, the culture of victimisation insidiously infiltrating certain sections of the NHS and wider society needed confronting. This Slave Trade they bang on about is the excuse for, as well as the result of, their inferiority. But he wouldn't go as far as to call it a myth. Because there were all sorts of slaves: white, black, yellow and brown. All slaves matter.

What Cody did have on good authority - and apparently corroborated by government think tanks - was that the Atlantic trade was a forerunner of the modern Olympics and the Americas' Cup. As Cody understood it, and he quoted many bogus sources provided by Adele and those of similar persuasion, if you look closely at the drawings of the so-called slaves lying packed together like sardines in the holds of the ships, look carefully without pinko-tinted lenses, the oars have been airbrushed but those people are rowers, the cream athletes, soldiers, iconoclasts, dissidents of their societies, and just as fit and committed as any you would find in a modern team. The ships were really racing schooners and had unisex teams, women and men on the same team, and children too; if you were good enough, you were old enough. And like Formula One today, wealthy backers in the 16th century, such as the Royal Africa Company and shareholders in the East India Company, competed for the prestige of owning the fastest boat across the Atlantic. Why else would Queen Elizabeth I give her blessing? And Sir Francis Drake and Sir Walter Raleigh get involved. Why would the Pope of all people, and the Jesuits and the Churches carve the oceans between the seafaring powers if not for friction-free trade and sport? One of the ships was named after Jesus, for Christ's sake. Why did sharks learn to seek out these ships during this so-called Middle Passage of the contest? Because the competitive Africans were eager to win, and you see the evidence during the modern Olympics. Jamaica and the hundred metres are synonymous, Ethiopians and Kenyans don't give or ask for a quarter. Back then, it was the Africans who tossed the bodies of the dead, dying, and the deadweight into the ocean and when they landed in America or Brazil or Guyana or any number of destinations, disputes broke out between tribes over who won the race, over cheating, times and dates, ballast and fuel loads, displacements and the size and weight of the anchor, the number of sails deployed, over tiny innovations like front wings and back wings. These disagreements exposed old African tribal rivalries and wounds, spilling into pitched battles and wars. One war lasted for forty years. Christian charities, not the Arab slavers, absorbed the veterans and survivors of these encounters into the local economy, split them up from their families and tribes to avoid wars. Children were not sold. They were taken into the care system or sent to work away from their parents for their safety. Of course you cannot rule out the odd bad apple, but some of the stories - burning alive, buried alive, beaten to death, dismemberments and lynching, rapes - were grossly exaggerated, boys being boys boasting about their conquests. Where is the fossil evidence? The Africans did well producing sugar, cotton, tobacco, just as immigrants are absorbed into flexible markets today, picking strawberry, lettuce or cockles at Morecambe Bay, say. Nothing is new under the sun. History is Darwinian – it repeats in a certain way because it is the best fit, like water trickling down a rut invisible to the naked eye.

The internet giants loved Cody for the revenue streams he attracted to their platforms. What little money they had left after the punitive 10% taxes, they spent on searching for and recruiting teenage Codys. In the House, MPs ducked debates and lucrative outside interest sessions to watch Cody's flowing monologues on TV, gawping at screens in the foyers of Westminster or in groups on College Green. In secret meeting rooms, die-hard Corbynistas watched with begrudging admiration for his communication skills. Lib-Dems spliced his phrases to slip off forked tongues in crucial by-elections. The BBC, worried about the threat to the licence fee from the duckrabbiteer junta, gave Cody and think tank friends hours of air time, slipping him in around a history or an antiques road or auction show or documentary, on which, by the way, Os is still waiting for one of the guests to say, in response to questions of provenance, "You know what?! Great granddad stole it."

Genies wept, grow a cerebral cortex, Ossy, but who would come on the show with such booty?

Once, with his full panoply of self-endearing performative grunts, fleshy cheeks flapping like weathervanes, Cody went off on a long-winded exposition about dumbing down and cancel culture and the underrepresentation of people like him on TV. When the anchor interrupted to ask how many of Her Majesty's Subjects with the privilege or misfortune to attend a £170,000 a year school in Switzerland he wanted to see on prime-time TV, Cody threw his hands up and blamed the media for culling the right to free speech. He abhorred, with every elastin fibre left in his middle-aged pale skin, trial by social media, reverse discrimination, and inverted snobbery. Why should he be blamed for what his dad said about Jamaicans? If - big if - a few black people on the island of Jamaica crossed paths with the Hayes in the past, did it mean that his dad had to like them? He, Cody, didn't like his greens when he was in short trousers, but was he not a great patron of green and rural England in all its diversity? And what about white slavery month? Did not all slaves and slavery count?

Genies wept. Os thought that Hegel, Kant, Hobbes, Powell, and the other architects, bastions, cheerleaders, of the dystopia - as well as recent local boy, Boris Johnson, and the denizens of his Equality Unit - were bad enough, but this stuff was what she would call ambitious. Below-the-belt, transgenerational gaslighting posing as high culture. Cody's people had made their first killing in sugar by working and caning Africans to death in the Caribbean, later laundering the proceeds through the Mississippi Company of John Laws, then banks, trusts, and piles of real estate in Bristol, Knightsbridge, and Liverpool. When several times over great granny slept her way to the money he is spending today, Cody was not there, Os wrote. Of course he wasn't. And when, in 1784, granddad raped at will and put the products of his rapeseed to slave for him for life, Cody was not there, can't remember, doesn't want to know. But he knows how many buttons Henry VIII had on his tunic when the king sang Greensleeves. Ok, fair play to Cody, he can't know everything. Nor has he knowingly come across his naturally brown cousins in Jamaica, Barbados, and Liverpool. Anyway, she's not asking him to give her or any of his cousins any money, nor the billions in compensation the taxpayers - including her granddad - must have forked out from their pensions to his folk. What really got her heart juggling fireballs was that unlike in, say, the start of a quintessentially English cricket season, when each team begins the season on zero points, Cody's lot not only got to carry the gains stolen over the centuries, but also to pass them down the generations; his lot are born with the keys to all the pavilions. The rest of us are born way beyond the boundary with neither ball nor bat in hand. What on earth did plebs need maths teachers for when we'd never earn more than four figures? What a waste of time setting up a Nanny's Health Service and pensions for brutish lives mercifully destined for brevity.

By July 2021, the ordure from the tweets and counter tweets were lapping at the doors of the Trust Executive Board, the CQC, and Whitehall. One incensed MP told "this so-called cardiac surgeon" to go sheathe "his hammer and sickle": the best man should always get the job.

'Did you know that the surgeon in question is a woman? You could be accused of misogyny,' said the puzzled journalist.

'I abhor all forms of misogyny, whether directed against male or female,' was his riposte, uttered in a self-satisfied Oscar Wildean tone. Os chuckled at her radio. May the Genies forgive her, she was no Churchill either, but never a more satisfying clanger rolled off a loftier tongue. Furious with Cody for exposing the family to cruel and merciless social media scrutiny, the scions of the Hayes surgical dynasty called a meeting in a mews in Kensington — the magnate magnet, same borough as Grenfell. Why had he got into the gutter with that god awful woman? He was to get Os off his, and their, case or they'd do it for him, which wouldn't do.

Cody summoned the Trust's Management Board. This woman was a loose cannon, a troublemaker. What did Cody propose, asked the CEO, as rehearsed in private with Cody earlier. Cody tapped his nose, slowly turned his papers, closed his eyes in apparent careful contemplation and, after a suitable interval, clicked his fingers and said he'd come up with just the thing. 'A hybrid meeting.' Had they heard of it? The other members of the Board shook their middle-class heads. Cody beamed. He rolled up the sleeves of his brilliant white shirt and said, 'A hybrid meeting provides extraordinary flexibility, combining elements of a public inquiry, an employment tribunal, and the GMC's fitness to practice procedures inside one time-conserving, convenient wrapper.' He flicked a finger in front of his face and said, 'Let's say she's done, dusted, disposed of.' Murmurs of relief and approval went round the room.

CHAPTER EIGHTEEN

For appearances sake, Cody set the hybrid hearing not in the sumptuous Hayes Boardroom, but in a draughty first floor office above the tradesman's entrance to the Maintenance Department. Representing herself – the BMA had run out of patience with Os's "irrational personalisation" of her complaint against the Trust – Os sat alone with a sleeveless vest belonging to David under her tie-dyed blouse, on the distal limb of a horseshoe formed by a jigsaw of tables. Her strategy was risky: to inflict more damage on Cody than he did on her. Nerves, and a cold draught from the window shivering up her spine, to counter the impression some may have had of her as the angry black woman, Os bravely reset her smile. Each attempt, because she was out of practice, fell within seconds to the onslaught of lactic acid.

Facing Os across the room and representing the Trust at considerable cost to the taxpayer, sat Ms K Flanders, the barrister with stacks, "bundles" of evidence, witness statements and notes. Round shouldered, with pinched pale grey eyes, Ms Flanders had lost only one case out of fifty-three in ten years and that was on an arcane, seventeenth-century technicality. Georgina sat to Cody's right at the top table. Cody, of course, was co-chairing the hearing with Dr. Windsor, the nominal official chairperson, who sat to his left, her blue-rinsed hair like a conning tower. Beyond her sat Mr. Thomas Hunter, aged about 60, whose broken left cheekbone gave him a permanent sneer. Another white male layperson completed the panel. A clerk and a secretary sat at a separate small formica table by the entrance. All handpicked by Cody.

On a signal from the clerk, Dr. Windsor pointed her conning tower hair at Os, at times sounding like a foghorn. 'I want to stress for the record that we are here to address your fitness to practise, not because of some imaginary vendetta.' She turned to bat her eyelashes once more at Cody. Georgina ground her teeth, the veins standing out on her trembling dark brown pate.

Cody slicked his hair back, which made Dr. Windsor blush, double-clicked his silver ballpoint, which made Os wince, and began to speak. The Trust had been fair to the professor. A more meticulous approach to any process you would struggle to find at NASA or in the making of baby milk. 'Lindsay, I mean Dr. Windsor, is correct in every respect,' he said, at which the face of Dr. Windsor, who really believed the spiel that Cody was born in Windsor Castle, dissolved into an unctuous smile. Os sighed and checked to see if her witness, Dr Mirano, had managed to log on. Call her paranoia panoramic, but she wouldn't put anything past them. Had one Trust not tried to sabotage an awkward doctor's whistleblower's crowdfunding page and another not bugged a consultant's office? One employed a handwriting expert to uncover a whistleblower.

Cody stopped to hand some papers to Dr. Windsor. Waving at the blocks of files on the table and the mountain of documents on the table, he began to speak. 'Shame our American friends couldn't attend. Er, pressure of work, but…we've got dates and times of misdemeanours, how she made the staff cry or dread coming to work, how she picked favourites, her vaunting self-righteousness and the rest of it.' His plummy tones appeared to grate with Mr. Hunter, but Dr. Windsor gleamed like a licked receptacle.

'Why is Mr. Cody Hayes sitting as judge on the panel as well as witness?' Os said out loud for the benefit of the online audience.

'Point of fact,' said the barrister leaping in before Cody could reply. She was going to paint the picture and Cody was merely here to set up the easel. Cody frowned at his silver pen. Os doubted if he'd ever been called an easel before. She winked at him to wind him up, but her smile crashed from her face when Lamide appeared on the screen. She squirmed and cursed inwardly as he reprised his theory of her raciophrenic racialolism. 'The past is our sleeping partner, but kinda contributes more to our business than we can figure out,' he said when he finished, sounding pleased with himself. One lay member of the panel eyed Os with undisguised abhorrence, as if she'd attempted to bomb a creche.

After a short coffee break, the barrister took over, her long dark cloak lending her a cunning, corvine look. Her voice had a slap and scraping quality, like the sound of a trowel on wet grouting. Tapping her hand on the desk for emphasis, she asked if Os had done everything in the right order on the morning she operated on Mr. Boardman. Os should please restrict her answer to the question asked. Time would not look kindly on them if they wasted it.

Os sucked in a deep breath. The click of the barrister's ring against the tabletop had set her nerves on edge. She counted to five and reminded herself what H-Mum said: "*Only thing to hopen to the world is your bowel.*"

Pouring a splashy glass of water, deliberately spilling some, she wiped the table and put on a good-natured frown. 'Restricting myself to the question risks squeezing the truth out of view.' She sipped from the glass of water and, just as the barrister was about to speak, said, 'But to return to the question about the order of events. I often teach my students that before and after every problem is its solution. It is quite simple,' she continued, in response to the indignant expressions on the faces of the panel members. 'We anticipate complications from experience, but in treating them before they arise, a lay observer may misinterpret our actions as the wrong way round. Why are they suturing up when they have not started, that sort of thing. We have many such examples in surgical practice. From simple purse strings to drains and vents, to prophylactic cardiac support machines and pumps.' Genies forgive me, not quite in the Socratic class, but then even King Canute said he couldn't do everything.

'I apologise Professor, with due respect, let me reframe,' said the barrister, cocking her head one way then the other. 'There had to be a list, the order of ops on the day. Was there not?' Or did Os operate in a fog of unconventional ambiguity? Clasping one wrist between chest and abdomen, the barrister waited for Os's answer. Cody couldn't have looked more delighted if the ghosts of his distinguished swashbuckling ancestors had spilled cut diamonds at his feet. The layperson on the far left, the only member of the panel Os hoped she might flip to her side, puffed his cheeks.

Paddling furiously away from charging pessimism, Os played dumb, and for time. She said she didn't understand the phrase "unconventional ambiguity".

'I meant to say, do you operate in a fog of ambiguity at the intersectionality of intuition and voodoo surgery? Never mind, let me lift that mist to be more specific,' said the barrister. Well-briefed by Cody, Ms. Flanders knew how to make you look to the world like a terrible and incompetent doctor. She tapped her diamond stud earring, to the envious stare of Dr. Windsor, and asked Os how much sodium, magnesium, potassium, and selenium Mr. Boardman was allowed at breakfast in the run-up to surgery. And, since the professor was so keen on the before and after, what was the weight of the patient's right lung before and after surgery? With each question the lawyer's sarcasm waxed with self-admiration and boggle-eyed anticipation whilst Os shook a head that seemed to have filled with foam. Bombarded by unreasonable, irrelevant questions, you couldn't answer even if you had the case records open before you, she writhed and evaded, her career prospects fading like the prospects of tolerable customer service in a Soviet gulag.

Seconds after Os's latest pathetic whisper of "I don't know", the screens dimmed and the brassy noise of a whining toddler blasted from the microphones. Mrs. Boardman, the wife of the white Mr. Boardman, apologised, grappling with the child as she fumbled around with the keyboard until she found one, speaking for several seconds before she learned that she had the mute button on. 'So that is why Jim collapsed,' she said, aiming her suspicious remarks at Os, her voice erupting from the speakers in an adenoidal rush.

Os got on well with Mr. Boardman but clashed with his missus.

These minor chemical and temperamental incompatibilities and imbalances happen and were ordinarily not, as they say, a hanging offence. But had Cody weaponised this for the occasion? A prickly flush fanned under Os's scalp. Shouldn't have scrimped on HRT. Dying to roll the glass of water over her broiling neck, she said, 'You may be correct, I couldn't say for certain at the time but I will do my best to explain.' First of all, she'd like to refute the charge of arrogant incompetence. She made a mistake. Who here doesn't make them? Even the great Roger Federer erred on match points on his own serve at Wimbledon, twice in quick succession, for Genie's sake. Os paused for a sip from her glass of water. She'd already admitted grafting the wrong branch during the first Mr. Boardman's operation, but no way were they going to hear from her grainy mouth that she didn't have the foggiest that Cody had swapped the list, not unless mama barrister loaded mouth and fired the question point blank. She drew herself up and smiled at the layperson to the left of the panel. 'What is more important? Who said what about what they remembered or what happened to the patient? He is hale and hearty, is he not?' she said, choosing her words like gems lost in a minefield, like a politician sent to lie for the cabinet on TV. 'But I…if… if I can just finish,' Os said, raising a forefinger to give her online supporters the impression of a rude interruption from a Goliath on the other side. She wondered what Selina thought of her performance. And Drinkstain and H-Mum? What would David think? The layperson twiddled with a ballpoint. From Mrs. Boardman came a sceptical harrumph. Try as she might, Os felt her prospects dropping like the value of the currency of a banana republic after the president's latest lavish double wedding. Yet she straightened the collar of her blouse and put on her most polite voice. 'Mrs. Boardman, do you remember that your husband developed a sudden liking for curry?' Os was going to add that they joked about Mr. Boardman's preferences on the ward but she changed her mind. *The only thing you open to their world is your bowel, woman.*

To the question about her husband's sudden liking for curry, Mrs. Boardman replied with a wary snort.

Jeerie me, granny could try to be more forthcoming. Os flipped through her notes, then explained that, on reflection, stressing the word for the benefit of the panel, on *reflection*, not until after the operation in all honesty did she connect Mr. Boardman's new love for curry to a loss of his sense of smell and taste. Smell and taste are like the thumb and fingers. To titillate his taste buds he needed sharper dishes, but loss of smell is a symptom of Covid-19. He probably brought the infection into the hospital. And if she had said it once, she had said it a hundred times at departmental meetings that the older heart-lung machines the Trust thrust on her, unlike those offered to other surgeons, carried tiny particles to the patient causing coagulation problems and wide-spread inflammation in susceptible patients. Until they disbanded her research unit, she had once had Dr. Mirano's research fellow working on the problem. Did they want her to spell haemophagocytic lymphohistiocytosis and myocarditis: feared complications of Covid? 'I've not seen a heart remotely so bulky or knobbly or patchy in all my years of practice.' She felt compelled to wipe her burning face. 'Neither have my esteemed colleagues. This is what caused his collapse, not my mistake...'

'This scrambling about for straw for a strawman does you no credit at all, Professor,' said the barrister, pronouncing Os's sobriquet in an arch tone.

'But he is ok now,' said Mrs. Boardman, sounding so supportive that Os's head popped back from her eyes. As far as Mrs. Boardman was concerned, the lady professor did her best. The men turned him down because he was a difficult case. The lady professor has put her hands up and said she corrected her mistake but it looks as if the men were ganging up, just as they did against her daughter who works for a top London newspaper. If he needs another operation, would the Professor do it for him?' Os clasped her hands together, thanked Mrs. Boardman, but she wouldn't lie: in all sincerity she wished there would never be a need for a *next* time for Mr. Boardman. *Genie Thunder, listen to you, Ossy. Where did you learn to talk like that?* But putting on a pantomime of smarminess never hurt anyone's bank balance.

Dr. Windsor attempted to interrupt and the barrister let out a husky sigh. She turned and raised two long fingers in the air. 'Two patients collapsed, one on the day, one died much later. I hope it will not be necessary to trolley the body of the patient known as Simply Blue up here to convince you that the poor patient you operated on is indeed dead.'

Os turned right to the clerk by the door to gesture for more water, but the bespectacled officer yanked her eyes away as if her sight depended on it. A jangling pitter-pattering gathered pace within Os, the early knockings of a panic attack even as she crashed in and out of mental cul de sacs. If she'd put in the wrong grafts and written up the surgical notes incorrectly and it looked as if she hadn't come clean, they'd call her a bolshie danger to the public: a fraud worth not half the price of a cow's fart in an abattoir. But, Genies help her, if she admits to a mistake she didn't know she committed, or to a crime she did not commit, same bloody terminal result. They'll say "Ah, why didn't you say so from the beginning?" and that will be the end of her. She could not bring herself to blame any mistakes on David's death because that would be like using the grave she put him in to try to keep out of one she had dug for herself. And Cody would simply say she showed bad judgement in coming to work that morning, when she knew that, if she hadn't, this very prat gurning inside his white collar would have rolled his blessed eyes, tutted, looked at his pals, tossed exasperated looks at the corniced ceilings and asked why the long face and blubbery lips and ears. Had Professor Sharp never heard of the Blitz spirit?

Os's vision began to thicken and narrow to a wavy darkness tinged with yellow. Sweat broke on her brow, but her mouth seemed to have had an emergency damp proof course. She gestured to the panel to give her a moment and dipped her hand inside her bag, Comfort. Her hand emerged with a pill in a blister pack. She couldn't read the label. *Genies wept, could be anything, even Louise's Pill pills.* Her head pounded. She lowered it further, aware of the eyes of the world on her neck, or so it felt. Lowering her head seemed to help. Her eyes cleared. The pill pack read paracetamol. It would do, as a prop. She waved the silver foil in the air and gestured for more water. The nausea subsided but her heart continued to punch out erratic beats. Thank the Genies, a close-run thing but she hadn't fainted. Oh, for just one hint of the way that post-mortem report leaned.

'Come on professor, you heard what our barrister said about the time,' said Cody, triumphal grin twinkling his eyes. Os leapt, as if into a dark void to pull on a thread the strength of which she could only guess. 'How they can bring a case against me based on an inconclusive postmortem is beyond *my* competence to decipher,' she said and paused to take the temperature of the room. Arctic malice and contempt crackled from the table. Dr. Windsor looked left and right as if to ask the rest of the panel if they'd ever heard such high-grade nonsense. But was that a subtle flicker of uncertainty on the tip of Cody's fine nose?

'The postmortem will be inconclusive, difficult to interpret, especially if the gross anatomy of the heart is ambiguous, or, shall we say, if the heart is in some way damaged?' she said, rolling and stretching the same thread as far as it would go. The layman began to take notes. A welcome memory oozed to mind that a text from Drinkstain's secretary, Vera the Improbable, said the police had accompanied Simply Blue's ambulance to the hospital. Two officers stood guard outside his ward. When Simply Blue died, Cody forbade all but essential access to the mortuary. Could it be that Simply Blue was involved in a criminal incident, or an accident? Was he tearing along at 70mph without a seatbelt? Did he have a stroke? Or did he have a stroke whilst he was driving fast or a stroke and a heart attack whilst he was driving fast? The man was too old for fisticuffs, but you never know. He could have been attacked. Os decided to go for a vague description of a stroke. She aimed her words at the layperson.

'Forgive the technical jargon, but in traumatic situations the hypothalamus and pituitary, the axis we call HPA, fires up and results in surges of catecholamines which can cause cardiac arrhythmias and, if he crashes or receives a blow, for example, direct physical impact or the impact of the hormones released may damage vital organs including the heart.' She preferred this pat, conscience-salving narrative to the more disturbing scenario that Simply Blue had had a heart attack at the wheel because of what she did wrong the morning after David died. 'Sixty pack years of smoking is like a smouldering powder keg in the vascular tree, so to speak,' she added, trying at least as hard to convince herself as she was the watching public, of her hypothesis.

The barrister pulled on the skin tag on her chin. 'That is not what I asked. It is quite simple, is it not?' Did Os perform the correct procedure or not? Yes or no?' she said, hectoring Os.

Os dabbed her sizzling cheeks with a moist wipe. *This barrister mama must eat the pancreas of her victims for breakfast.* 'What I am trying to say is that it is possible that I did not in every single respect do everything exquisitely perfectly, but that is not a crime or admission of –'

'That is not what I asked and you know it…'

'Know?' said Os. 'What we know, can and cannot recall, or never knew, defines what we claim to know, but can we recall the exact detail and order of everything we do?'

'Hate to interrupt,' said Mr. Hunter, a layman, leaning over his copious notes. 'In the interest of time, I think you will find that the postmortem concurs roughly with what the professor is saying. Medicine is not like drawing lines on a screen, or like awarding marks for ice skating or ballroom dancing. The pathologist has decided that the postmortem is inconclusive.' He got up, walked the long way round, past the clerk, to hand Os a copy of the report. Cody and Georgina swapped glances, but no smiles.

The layman's words, bar the cries of her newborn children, were the most beautiful, exhilarating, life-affirming sound Os had ever heard. Her stiff shoulders sank to their rightful anatomical position and her breathing relaxed as she scanned the report of the postmortem. Os put the paper on the table and raised her hand to speak. Battling to keep her composure, she asked them to excuse her if the words came out wrong. 'Memories thrive on repeated visits,' she said. And heaven knows that she'd revisited the events she was about to recount more times than she ever wished. She turned to Mr. Hunter, the layperson. 'If you go to the GMC archives you will see why I objected to Mr. Hayes sitting in judgement over me, or anyone else at this Trust or elsewhere…' It was now her turn to state her case.

The clerk typed away as Os told the meeting how, in her early days as a research registrar under Professor Turner and eight months pregnant with David, she had waddled into the department for some data she needed for a paper she was writing. 'I looked everywhere that day,' she said, but imagine her shock and disappointment when, a week later, when she found Cody Hayes presenting her work at a seminar. She complained. Professor Turner did nothing. "Could she not be mistaken?" he had said. "Has she not by any chance heard of pregnancy brain? Did she not lock herself out of her room the other day?" Some said she was troubled by fear of exposure because the baby didn't belong to Lamide but to any one of the hunky hospital porters. A photo of golliwogs noosed by a toy stethoscope landed on her desk. Team building badinage they called it.

'Extraordinary. Hogwash,' said Cody Hayes. 'Hogwash,' he repeated, louder this time, turning to Dr. Windsor whose manner suggested she couldn't imagine the industrially arrogant and obnoxious Os giving birth to anything other than a feral wolf.

'I imagine you can substantiate these allegations?' she said.

Os placed her hands back down on the table. 'Remember, Cody? We didn't have USBs in those days, but little squarish discs?'

A long and tortuous midline vein bulged on Cody's forehead. Georgina kneaded her wrist. 'You've got just two more minutes, Professor,' said Dr. Windsor, sounding as if she had just missed the last train out of Siberia.

Os explained how at the time she wasn't able to work out how Cody had got her data. On a wild hunch and in desperation, alongside the Bonferronis and other well-known statistical terms, she had sprinkled the odd reference to Obalendic analysis. She had derived this made-up term from Obalende, a suburb in Lagos. Os had then tipped off the university through a sympathetic registrar who would remain nameless.

'I heard what happened later,' she said. 'When the examiners asked Cody Hayes about Obalendic analysis, he didn't have a clue. His MS thesis is still in the bin, metaphorically speaking…' Os turned to Cody who looked as if he was going to be sick.

'It must have hurt, surely, but imagine how I felt to have my data go walkies into another's field.' She made a big zero with her hands to show what the GMC did. 'If they had done the right thing, we wouldn't be sitting here washing our dirtier undies in public. More importantly, Dr. Raga would still be alive.' Os dipped her head in regret because back then she didn't pay much attention to the Dr. Ragas of this world because she thought such a predicament befell only melodramatic foreign graduates, not phlegmatic, English born, bred, and trained doctors like herself. But as H-Mum said, the hand that pokes fun at the foot stuck in quicksand may soon find itself mired in it too.

'Who is Dr. Raga?' said Mr. Hunter, the layperson, suspending his ballpoint over a fresh piece of paper.

'Ridiculous,' Cody said. 'The data is departmental property and, sadly, Professor Turner is not here to defend himself from these baseless cowardly attacks by blowhards—'

'Prof Turner and "good name" in the same breath?' said Os, boiling under a blouse that seemed to have shrunk two sizes under her armpits. *Genies wept. You cut your entitled conscience to fit the crime and you can get away with anything.* 'I have one witness.'

Dr. Mirano's light brown face, short curly hair, appeared on screen. She had come from Mozambique to work in Os's department until Alfred Enders had disbanded the research team. 'Happy to be here, not happy but you know what I mean, glad to have a chance to explain what happened to Dr. Raga after so many years,' she began. 'I don't want what happened to my cousin Dr. Raga to happen to anyone else.' In a calm and confident voice, she described the case of Dr. Raga, the eldest of six children of a paraplegic farmer in Mozambique. Dr. Raga came to the UK on a scholarship and Professor Turner had asked a Nigerian doctor, and Cody Hayes, then a junior, to help with translations and literature searches. Cody's research was not going well: a couple of lousy abstracts and a case report. Desperate to impress his distinguished parents, both of whom it was said shelled landmark papers for fun whilst still in nappies and spoke ten languages between them, he presented Dr. Raga's data as his own at an international meeting. When Dr. Raga reported the plagiarism to the departmental head, Prof. Turner, the good professor had doubted whether this person from wherever, down there somewhere, who couldn't rub two English words together without turning them into combustible material, had done the work on her own. Devastated, Dr. Raga took an overdose and died. Prof Turner felt unable to avoid setting up an inquiry, but it was chaired by his wife, Professor Bulkden. Conclusion: Dr. Raga suffered from homesickness, long winter nights, or seasonal affective disorder. Recommendation: southern hemisphere fellows should undergo a rigorous period of acclimatisation. How could anyone unhinge over a few misattributed test tubes? What rotten luck for Professor Turner. All this aggravation when he was only doing his bit for the advancement of these fellows.

Dr. Windsor nodded her conning tower at Cody then accused Os of barking up several trees in the hope that someone would toss her some bony rumour to chew on; this was nothing short of an elaborate but rather clumsy and desperate contemptible attempt to besmirch good people. Georgina's head wobbled like that of a puppet on springs.

'Please, I don't need from them lectures about anything,' said Dr. Mirano.

'From him lectures about things,' said Cody, imitating the Mozambiquan doctor's accent and word order, and chortling to himself. Dr. Mirano looked bemused. Os raised a hand to speak but onto screen flicked Lamide, the whites of his eyes glowing and gigantic, like those of that man handcuffed to a cow on a Lagos runway. He was wearing a light blue shirt, striped tie loosened.

'I want to remind you that we have a duty of confidentiality. I rolled up here to testify to the truth, not for or against anybody,' said Lamide, his mellifluous voice sounding just as Os imagined David's would have – if he'd lived. But she didn't have time for reverie because when Lamide said, 'It was not Cody's fault. I gave him the data.' she went blind. Disbelieving flies on the walls of her skull clapped their wings all at once.

Lamide said he took Os's data for their sake. Cody had promised to put in a good word. But he didn't. Lamide had left for the States because he was ashamed and not, as he put it at the time, to protest Os's treatment. He came back to England to make it up to Os and David but then came Covid and he lost his son and he was just going to have to figure out what he was about. His voice cracked, then he screeched and gave up.

Os stared at the screen, her eyes spitting frying oil round the back. Lamide or Larry or whatever they call you should be with the CIA or Mossad or Putin's FSB if he wasn't too two-faced even for them. He and his pal Cody could have ruined her for life. Kicked into the darker shades of depression by these bastards. But for a train strike on the day of her appointment with an eminent psychiatrist who diagnosed psychosis in all black women, she would also have ended up on an eccentric and destructive experimental drug regime that blighted families for generations.

Cody had gone green around the lips, as if he'd been asked to lick vomitus off a pavement. Georgina interrupted Dr. Windsor and, waving a piece of paper, said, 'Why is Lamide just telling us this mumbo jumbo story now after saying—'

'My name is Mr. Bamisetiti if you don't mind. I have both my FRCS and I successfully defended *my* MS thesis.'

Dr. Windsor called the meeting to order by rapping the tabletop with her knuckles. She patted her documents into a tidy pile. She pouted, swung her jaw left and right and said in her hectoring voice, 'I'm afraid, I have to admit that the professor has no case to answer.'

'Thank you,' said Os, as glorious arias echoed round her head. Now the world could see flipping Cody for the silly but dangerous shit he was. She wished David were here. How cool is that, hey? Your mum's only gone and taught the man who made - and makes - her sick, the guy born with golden everythings within reach, a lesson he should never forget.

CHAPTER NINETEEN

She'd heard enough.

'Thank you, no please don't be sorry, it's not your fault, Dr. Gauge, honestly, not that...'

It was difficult to stifle the angry tremor rising to her voice. The park smelt of mouldy grass cuttings and of the wet cigarette stubs dropped around the bins. Between them, two huge clouds gripped most of the grey sky. Os closed the call and dropped the phone into Comfort, which bulged with sticky tape and balls of string and other items to help pack up for the move back to Sure Lanes. It was a Saturday morning, a few days after the hybrid hearing and John was waiting beside a noticeboard, in his hand a packet of AA batteries. He smiled and blew a kiss but Os turned away, feigning distraction by the police car wailing past the southern gates. Her brain fizzed and smarted.

They walked up the gentle rise side by side, with Os trying to keep a semblance of control over the fires raging in her head. A clump of skyscrapers, the tip of the wet Gherkin, sparkling orange in a rinse of broken sunlight, loomed into view.

'Did you hear what I just said?' said John.

'Partly,' she said, but her attention had turned to the little black boy wrapped in woollies racing a woman out of a grassy declivity. He looked just like David at that age, broad forehead, clear eyes. His excited yelp stabbed Os to the quick.

'How do you know it was "partly" if you weren't listening?' said John.

'I guessed, even the best quiz shows, even exams, allow you to guess,' she said. Her nerves shrieked.

'Who was on the phone? Not Larry again?' he said.

'It wasn't. He's Lamide, not Larry.' Os had called him twice to see if he was alright. After all, he'd lost his only child. And his job.

'Don't bite my head off,' said John. He tugged his collar straight and said he was glad they were going back to the big house on Sure Lanes. He couldn't bear the dreadful notion of Gary's Cynthia making snide remarks about squatters taking up indefinite residence at her husband's flat. He was thinking of taking his mum on a guided tour first so she could take in, imbibe, in her own unique way, the impressive ambience. 'They made a really good job of it, the French doors, the brook dug out, silver birches trimmed.' He kissed his fingers, raised them to the mottled sky. 'You'll love it, so will Louise.' Of that he had no doubt.

They came to a man reading a crumpled sports page on a bench. The conical red waste bin overflowed with plastic bottles and face masks. She slowed down, her guts screwing up, as if it were they, not the bin, which brimmed with maggots.

'You never know what's around the next corner,' she said, hanging back a stride to pick up an empty plastic cup and prod it through the slot of a plastic dustbin. 'They'll be paying for the upkeep of some surgeon's Ferrari with their blocked arteries one day,' she added, pointing at the hillock on the left where children huddled around the hot dog stall of *"Eddie's in the Right Ball Park."*

'Can't we go for a walk without you launching a petition against your feet?' said John. 'It's called freedom of choice. Which, if you haven't noticed is in short supply…'

The nauseating smell of frying oil wafted up her nose. *Genies wept, so that's why he called the busies on my son?*

'Freedom of choice! So is drinking until you are brainless and your liver turns to stone,' she snapped, all the more determined not to return to Sure Lanes. 'You may not know what's round the corner, but you know what happened at the last one and you don't go back the same way again.' *Genies wept, Ossy, stop faffing about.* 'Fancy a coffee?' She needed to get that smell of frying oil out of her skin. Her eyes settled on the cluster of metal tables beyond the north-eastern gates and she decided it was more civilised to talk there than within earshot of a queue for hot dogs.

'But we've got coffee at home. Look at the time,' John howled. He peeled his sleeve back to stare through the scratched face of his wristwatch, a gift from his late dad. 'Tells the time just as well as the monstrosity Gary bought Mum for her birthday. But guess what Mum said. It tells the time *and* the world what a great time she was having.'

'She doesn't ask him how he offsets the life of a dying child against tax,' said Os who knew the story well. Matilda had whacked the precious cricket bat John bought her into a broom cupboard. Os quickened her steps, cringing at the knowing glance her bored expression drew from a woman in blue passing by. 'No two siblings are born to the same parents,' Os said out loud, for the benefit of the passerby. But what did John have to moan about? He's still here, is he not? David wasn't. 'By the way Buckingham palace doesn't call them offshore investments, they are known as *onward* investments,' said Os mimicking the royal high pitch squeak. She sensed his displeasure but didn't care. At a small puddle spangled with rainbowed droplets of oil, two women jostled with buggies for a dry strip of crumbling tarmac. John opened a sprung gate to let a black woman with heavy shopping stagger through. The woman stabbed Os with a disapproving look. Os replied in kind. *Genie gimme strength, can't even have a peaceful stroll.* The little black boy who ran up the hill earlier skipped past hand in hand with his mother. Os sighed. That was her once, with the future perineal chancellor of the Exchequer. She waved back, and her womb kneaded a tense emptiness, a referred memory.

Five minutes' walk from the park and two doors down from a boarded-up laundromat, they came to the café. Its smart yellow door opened onto a smattering of wrought iron chairs partly shielded from the rain by brown awning. Rows of tempting snacks, pastries, donuts, apple pies, sausage rolls, tarts, lay behind the sloping glass of the display. Os and John stood feet apart, each deciding where to sit. A scream came from the park. Then came a wicked laugh from an older mouth. Os's heart flung a beat back up her neck. Was that David's last call for help too? She bit her lip and sat in the sun at a round table outside the cafe. John made a playful aside about the sugar and coffee in a scene from Blackadder goes Forth. David liked the show too. Maybe the only thing he and John had in common apart from feeling that they owed the world their last word on its state. Another errant heartbeat hiccupped into her throat. She waited until normal beats resumed, counted to five, put her cup down, and said, 'John?'

'Yes?' he said, with such eager innocence that Os hesitated. Berating herself, she tried again.

'I want to change my will, give a share that would have gone to David to charity, educational trust perhaps, I haven't thought it through…'

John clapped his hands. 'Great minds, great minds, same wavelength,' he said, almost breaking into song. Wasn't it sort of great that by happy coincidence he'd been asked to revise the history curriculum. 'To make it more inclusive, diverse, sort of,' he fluttered his hand and added, 'multidimensional.'

Os paused for a moment. 'Are you taking the mickey?'

'Struck a raw nerve, have I?' he said.

Os shrugged. 'No way, the neurons saw you coming.'

John frowned and rubbed his chin. 'It's a dumbing down exercise if you ask me. Bite sized nuggets for chavs unable to digest words with more than one syllable without throwing up. Too many dates and events fucking doing their head in. That's the new age reason for shirking, isn't it? Mental health.' John tugged on his shirt collar. 'A monumental educational catastrophe in the making,' he proclaimed.

Os kneaded her lips with her teeth. *Genies help, in ten years of austerity seven million kids went through school. Shortchanged generation. They won't get those years back. And this is the answer?* More myths and white lies? 'Where will you start? The Daily Genesis? Let there be light and Big Ben rang out? My mistake, better to keep telling them that they are world beating, naturally, from the day they were born. They should rely on the smiles shone by the toothpaste spat out by their betters. When they come up against the rest of the world and things don't turn out so good some messiah guy - who couldn't possibly know better - will come along to tell them it's the fault of the boats bearing people with odd names, melanin, and unusual diseases,' she huffed, swallowing the rest of what she was going to say because a lady carrying a brown poodle underarm collided with a chair. 'I want to sell the house.' She sat back in the afterglow of her achievement. A strange anticlimactic melancholy threatened her with tears. She clenched her teeth to stifle a deep sigh.

'You haven't even got the bloody job yet and you're like a cat on a hot tin roof,' whined John. As he searched her face, the glow in his olive eyes subsided into a frown. He scratched his neck. 'Louise doesn't need any of this…angularity…' He wagged the point of his jaw at her, condescending twangs in his voice. If he said it once, he's said it a hundred times, things will be fine once she settles back in the house. Of that he had no doubt. He shook his head, downed the coffee and, with a rattle of his head, shot off his chair and made space for Os to come with him. His jaw jutted forward because Os remained in her seat, Comfort against her shins. She gave her head a gentle shake at him. *Genies wept, he is so used to me tagging along, bending over so far for him.* 'I'm not ready to go home yet,' she said, her firm tone seeming to swing him back into his chair.

'Ok, let's sort of agree to diverge on the merits of my pedagogical approach,' said John. 'Ah,' he added suddenly, his voice lightening up. 'This will cheer you up.' He fished a flyer for a local concert from a pile on the next table. 'Remember the fun we had at The Proms?' he said, the corners of his eyes wrinkling into a bright smile. 'Don't tell me now you didn't enjoy it, you were well away, and as for the *après* Proms? Spicy. Come on, po-face, admit it,' he said, poking the tip of his tongue through his lips.

Os recoiled at a memory she now found debasing, of her love making when they got back home after the orgiastic celebrations at the Last Night. She could not deny that in the early days she enjoyed throwing herself into all that and his ways of life, for both their sakes, and, she told herself, for David's. Genies would bear witness to her wholehearted commitment as she belted out the "never never shall be slaves" songs with the best of the Albert Hall promenaders when the younger teenage Os would rather have gargled with hot lava. For years she told herself they were engaging in a harmless expression of steam. Letting your hair down. Her resolve to whip herself into line for him survived until the whiteianist preaching gathered pace on the coattails of the Great Recession and the stirring hostile milieu of the Brexit referendum campaign. Then, despite her attempts to suppress them, the old New Cross insecurities reemerged from their silos. And by the mid noughties her calculated insouciance crumpled and, as The Albert Hall echoed to its dome with songs of how for centuries they got away with crimes against humanity, she wept, ashamed of herself. She never told John that her four-times great grandmother on her dad's side was a slave in Brazil, that H-Mum's five-times great grandfather was one on Sao Tome. That in the last few years, if a branch whipped into her by accident in the garden, she often thought of them, flogged for sneezing, for the wrong look in the eye, for a black back or knee not bent right, whipped until the whip hands tired and there was no skin left hiding on the victims' backs. Enoch chose that whip-hand metaphor well. If she, an amateur, could think of a hundred awful ways to use a scalpel or whip, what chance did anyone have at the hands of those who were paid to humiliate, maim and kill? They burned them alive, for sport. To think that the only reading material allowed them for 300 years were the myths in the Bible of their oppressors. They weren't even allowed to read it themselves. Anyone caught teaching them how to read at all risked a horrible death. How on earth did those white people get away with that? And still be able to joke and dance about it. How on earth did black people get through that? And still be able to find anything at all to laugh about? In the last few years, between the referendum and the pandemic, after the show, when the singing was over and the conductor's white shirt and black bow tie were wringing wet, Os looked round at the puffed-up faces and that of John beside her in his calm post orgiastic fulfilment and she asked herself a terrifying question. If push came to it, and the IMF or Bank of England, or the bond markets or the Institute of Directors said they needed to "grow the economy" for tax cuts and new "freedoms after Brexit" would this lot here present - for all the piety of "Lest We Forget" on Remembrance Days - vote to impose by stealth the Great African Calamity again? Discreetly vote to park the workers offshore - or "onward" - on an overseas territory; Chagos Islands, somewhere like that, far away? And the poor BBC, addicted to the licence fee, wouldn't - for fear of the duckrabbiteers who owned the rest of the media - be allowed to call it slavery. For the sake of "impartiality" they'd call it labour drift by competitive selection, quantitative easing of potential population hubs, transformative re-balancing of the global economy, facilitated flexible commonwealth workforce strategy, re-equilibration of the north /south capital labour environment. All this while human supply was turned on and off like a tap, windrushed in and windrushed out to zero contract hours, sans holiday, sans sick leave, sans maternity rights, sans passport, sans pension, sans minimum wage, just like in the old days with Colston, Gladstone and Drax before those woke self-righteous spoilsports like Granville and Equiano and Wilberforce stuck their oars in.

'You're doing it for love, I kept telling myself. I tried, Genies know I tried, but all I did was break my spine, bit by bloody bit.' She shuddered. 'If I told you earlier, about how I felt…maybe David would still be here. And I'm sorry…'

The barista sensed the cooling atmosphere and slapped a napkin over his shoulder as if to swat a fly as he tiptoed away from their table.

'I'm not going back.'

They sat in silence. Os tapped her lips with a bunched fist and pretended to study the menus. John turned his coffee cup clockwise whilst gazing into the distance. A pair of male cyclists in leotards raced past, in disparaging conversation about a woman at work. Os hoped the subject of the conversation had a bullet proof constitution.

'It's the ordinary folk in Africa I pray for. Because, if this Brexit thing shrinks us, and we can't dig up the staff readymade from Europe and our demographic bomb explodes, who is going to wipe our geriatric bottoms, eh?' In Os's nightmare scenario, in return for the promise of hard cash, the Africans, their so-called leaders having run out of things to dig up for sale, would be forced to take their kids out of nursery schools and creches and drag their students from PhDs and cut off their balls to make British cast-off underwear fit. And if they complained we'd whip around and say how uncouth of you, heathen, you're lucky to have a job we can bear to hand you instead of feeding you to the sharks of the Atlantic. Genies wept, if she could make it up in the shower, in her cab and basement office, whilst cleaning her teeth, surely those multibillion-dollar right-wing think tanks could too. The terrifying difference was that they had the power to make it happen, or transpire, as John would say. She mimed a banner in the air the way David once did.

'Independence, autonomy, what's not to like, eh? I must confess, they nearly got me too, but sneaking off behind my back when we agreed, you don't see how that was like a king-sized slap in my face?' She squeezed her eyes shut and shook her head. 'Forgive me, but it's who you couldn't wait to vote with. *Them*.' She tried a thought experiment on him. What if their roles were reversed? They were in Africa and he was the physically obvious migrant, carrying oppressive historical baggage or not – it makes no difference to the story – and she rushed in weeping for joy because she couldn't wait to tell him that she voted with the racist Ahuruwuru Party and the Assembly of Ebony Humanity that hated white people. All because they promised unlimited eat-your-fufu-and-have-it independence and endless feasting on yams and pepper soup? Too far a stretch, was it? Because he couldn't bring himself to reimagine the last 500 years with his people below deck? She could no longer live behind his veil of innocence.

'You never stop telling me how you feel and how I should feel about how you feel, but have you for one nanosecond thought of how it feels to be me? Not as an accessory or appendage, but as me? For Genies' sake, you're the one with the fancy degree in this sort of thing. Honestly, all those field trips, wasted......' She raised her hands in the air. 'I don tire oh,' she finished, in imitation of H-Mum. 'I'm sick to the back teeth of constantly recalibrating myself, for you.' David was right. An elegiac lowing in her heart joined the long-limbed ode to her son.

'Can't you tell a solid argument about sovereignty from one based on frothy emotion? You twist everything. Did the same over Louise's braids.' He folded his arms and sat back.

'Jeerie me, more evidence of those wasted field trips. Anyone with half a neuron knows that hair goes way deeper than its roots,' said Os.

John's lips began a frightening clonic twitch. 'After everything I've done. Mum warned me. My career parked in permanent neutral for your blinking sake, to be kicked under a bus…'

The words she tried to spare him steamed from her mouth. 'Don't you dare. It was David…my boy under the bus. For my sins I was in there with you, but it was you at the bloody wheel. I had a word with the guys upstairs. You know, our neighbours on the second floor, the always fighting pair. Mike he calls himself. First, on the night of the funeral he said he didn't know who called the busies.' She pulled Comfort back up towards her midriff. 'Later, we got talking, maybe he felt awkward and didn't want to say at first, but David used to bang on the ceiling to ask them to keep the noise down. The day David was arrested this Mike guy says he heard the noise in our flat and looked out of the window and there were the police. He guessed some other pissed off neighbour must have made the call…'

'Well, there you are then, although I doubt the veracity of…let's leave it…' croaked John, polishing the face of his watch with a thumb. Then he seemed to gain a second wind. 'It's not beyond the bounds of possibility that someone had it in for David,' he said. He ran a hand through his silvery hair and puffed his cheeks.

Os wagged her finger. *Genies gimme shelter, he really does think I'm as dumb as my hair looks?* 'I got the detention centre to send me records.' She stammered as she tried to keep her voice down. Did he expect her to fold her pretty wings in prayer and wait for some anodyne report? She got a switchboard recording of John whining about his black teenage stepson running amok, and that there was a girl in the house. 'That's what Dr. Gauge called me about…this morning in the park.' She shook her fists on either side of her clenched eyes, saw David's body lying in the mortuary and snapped her eyes open again but the image would not go away. 'What did you think would happen when you called them, eh?' But he just couldn't help himself. When they were little boys Gary said John couldn't hear a twig crack under the foot of another without running off to tell mummy. "Public spirited" John called it, but inviting Cressida Dick's finest under your roof because you want the loo? And knowing the right buttons to press with the cops to make them hurry up. Stepson, can't quite get my tongue around his surname?

John's tanned face faded to coconut milk white. He folded his hairy arms then unfolded them and folded them again as if they no longer suited him, then leaned forward to rest them on the table, beads of sweat glinting on his hairy chest. He scratched his cheek but did not speak.

'Go on, a feline got your fancy lingua franca?' said Os.

He mangled the paper napkin in his hands. 'It sort of got out of hand. Dreadfully, dreadfully sorry. If only I, sort of, you can't imagine…I thought we could put it behind us…' It started to drizzle harder, the odd raindrop rolling off the awning to smash into the pavement.

'I'm never setting foot back there in that house…again. Ever.' To go back there would be like dancing on David's coffin. 'But for your sake, Louise won't hear what you did from me.' Os tucked Comfort up closer again and stretched her hand out to test the rain. 'We're done.' She got up.

'You're going back to fucking Lamide, aren't you? Doing a Madame Butterfly on me!' Os saw his sweeping backhand a fraction too late. She took the impact on her right wrist, ducked and fended him off with Comfort as she rocked into a metal table, toppling it over with a loud crash of metal and crockery onto the pavement.

'Sorry, didn't mean it,' he said, his voice trembling. Os shoved him away, waved two twenty-pound notes at the barista then shoved them under a cruet and limped as fast as she could from the scene, lowering her eyes and crossing the street in the dreary drizzle to avoid curious gazes. She took the first left turn away from the busy park and found herself in a dim broad street. The wet facades of the townhouses, with their pointed finials, wrought iron balconies and black windows looked like the helmets of opposing subterranean armies set in a concrete truce, and reminded her of a hymn she used to sing with H-Mum. "Soldiers of Christ, arise and put your armour on." But Os felt stripped naked, and she grunted to a jolt of angry self-reproach as she stumbled on, her faint short shadow rising and falling off the front walls and the cars parked in the driveways. After a right fork down a footpath in a valley formed by six-feet-high slatted fences, she turned sharp right again to find herself near the foot of a rise on the High Street. It began to rain again and she let a few tears join the drops on her grim cheeks as she bumped, ground and dragged her heavy legs through the buggies and window shoppers and huddled bus queues until she found herself at the door of the flat. The door rasped open.

'What happened?' The explosion of shock on her daughter's face felt like a steel capped kick in the gut.

CHAPTER TWENTY

'You know I'm not that sort. I swear it will never happen again, ever. I love you, Ossy, trust me,' said John as Os brushed past him with Comfort on her shoulder later that day.

'That's like a heart attack promising not to do it again,' said Os.

'Or cancer saying it won't spread or come back if you leave it alone,' rejoined Louise who was a "thousand percent" behind her mum.

They moved in with H-Mum who, whilst not exactly singing Hallelujahs at the prospect of sharing a bed with Louise, exploited her role as accidental landlady to comment on the breakdown of Os's marriage. Jesus knows she prayed, but this was always going to happen. And before Os jumped down her throat, this was not to do with John's Oyinbo status, the colour of his skin. It was his ways. Yet, because they were in Hengland, they all cut him more slack than they did Lamide. In Lagos no woman would dare address an in-law the way Matilda did here. No way. *Nibo?* Any woman who does not know how to control her mouth will not last one minute before she is thrown naked into the nearest gutter with her dirty teeth scattered to the sun first.

A recurring ache of failure joined the heavy emptiness in Os's stomach. Every Genie knew that the man had fault aplenty but Lamide would never call the police on his son. Yet he was history and so now was John. She loved John still, she thought, and felt sorry if he believed she used him to get on; but she also knew that whatever the whys and wherefores she could no longer live with him. Was his assault the last straw or an excuse to go? Or was it the sneaking off to the Brexit vote? Everyone has a nonreturn valve. Once breached, time to go, before serious irreparable damage to body or soul. Back in the big house, until it was sold, John was in a state of putiny, feeling sorry for himself because his latest attempt at a hostile takeover of a neighbouring school's history department had failed.

Meanwhile, the Trust had set up a panel to consider Os's return to full time work. It was headed by Amanda Springer, a feisty general surgeon with dark brown eyes and short hair, ever-changing colour, usually brunette. In an irritating expression of so-called solidarity, she insisted that Os call her Amandla, a once popular rallying cry of the African National Congress during the fight against South African apartheid. But when Cody and management had initially started the witch hunt and Os asked for support, Amandla cried off pleading previous engagements. Os didn't hold it against her. The poor woman had twin Lamborghinis to feed.

It was a bright but cool Tuesday morning, punchy with birdsong. Os, three minutes late, jogged from her basement office past the long queue of ambulances, their engines idling, stretching a quarter of a mile from the A&E department. The boxy and blue cladded HR department hastily erected to house the backroom staff brought in by the tenth CEO appointed to the Trust in as many years called to mind the puppet shows Os watched awestruck on TV as a little girl.

Amanda smelled of the expensive musky perfumes she favoured. She tossed her fringe back with a hand and beckoned Os into the white walled interview room. In it squatted a dark brown table shaped, ominously and presciently for many departed consultants, like a pear. Three grey power strips for laptops ran down the centre of the table. Os sat in a concavity with her back to the door trying to keep her face cool with surreptitious puffs of breath. Her moist arm stuck to the table and she wished she had listened and put on the long-sleeved blouse Louise got from the big house and not this heavy cotton and polyester shirt. She really must ask where Blonde Barrie sourced HRT for his missus. Blonde Barrie, the operating department practitioner and amateur dramatics enthusiast from Lagos, knew how to get anything except enriched uranium. During the first lockdown, "whited up" like

Ira Aldridge as an experiment to see if he would get stopped by the police, he drove a van of bootlegged and contraband PPE to desperate care homes and hospitals. A "sarf" London team ran the scam. Word on the street was they acquired PPE through contacts close to friends of the government, then re-bagged kosher PPE with cheap knockoffs for resale.

Amanda sat opposite Os, fingering a blackfaced designer watch and glancing up to Mrs. Kindolowo who repeatedly dashed in and out to drop boxes of files on the table. Just as they were about to start, Mrs. Kindolowo squeaked and scurried out for another batch of papers. These she kept to herself. The sight of the mountains of paperwork for what she presumed was a simple slam dunk return to work meeting raised a scratchy unease to Os's epigastrium, but she put on her English breakfast face and leaned Comfort against a shin.

With one more glance at her blackface designer wrist watch then the door, Amanda sent Os a few sheets of paper. 'I think you should have a read.'

Os didn't need a degree in forensics to spot Cody's and the barrister's droppings on the page. Vaulting phrases referring to natural justice, presumption of innocence, statutes of limitations gave them away. Genies gimme strength, should have known when they split the damned transcripts into three and blacked out whole pages. What was the phrase again? Clinical and commercial confidentiality. We are owned by fucking private equity now, are we? What did these white-collared pedigree terrorists care about natural justice? Os sailed the document across the table to Amanda and, as its pages splayed out halfway across the table, in marched half a dozen clean shaven black barristers in charcoal suits. Os grinned to herself at Amanda's wide-eyed expression of surprise. *Genies wept; the woman must think you've got the brains of a wet windsock.* The men sat down and opened their designer briefcases. Mrs. Kindolowo ground her teeth, peeled her laptop open and shoved a wad of papers across for Amanda to pass round to the visitors herself. Amanda shot a look of disdain at the HR officer before snapping a toothy smile on and turning to Os.

'My favourite cardiac surgeon ever, but for the benefit of our legal colleagues can you confirm your full name?'

'Professor Konibaje Oritsejolomi Osese Sharp,' said Os. 'It says so on my passport.' *But how much longer would this go on for? Jeerie me, what in the Horn of Africa was this in aid of?*

Mr. Newton, the barrister sitting to Amanda's immediate right, rubbed his wedding ring and asked if Os had any objections to a review of the evidence she gave at the hybrid hearing. He was a much lighter shade of beige than Louise, about the colour of a peeled peanut. In Nigeria he would be called a white man if he wanted. In the West he was Black, whether he was or not, liked it or not. Heavily built, he reminded Os of the then-leader of what used to be called the "powerful 1922 Conservative backbench committee" during the South African Apartheid friendly days of Margaret Thatcher. He spoke in clipped almost sibilant tones, acquired at great expense and subsidised by the poorest in the country. Os wondered when he lost his racial innocence. When he was three, as in her case, or later as a teenager when he was battered by the store detectives for walking too slowly down the aisle, stalked by another shopper; frisked for bombs in Tel Aviv; scoffed at by the history teacher when he wrote an essay about his granddad's role in the war of Europe? And how did he or any of the other barristers cope now? By sneering at black people, by whistling Vivaldi and smiling out loud to the back teeth with his hands on show in the air when they went out at night; buying a not too flash car, getting a white man or woman to vouch for them; by waving a double platinum credit card at the entrance to posh restaurants; by middle passaging their tongues between the buttock cheeks of the likes of Cody Hayes? Yet, she sympathised. As H-Mum would say, 'Man must wack.' You have to make a living somehow. 'Correct me if I am mistaken, but I smell a bucket of whitewash paint here,' said Os.

Mr. Newton, butted in. 'Professor Sharp, your tweets and emails breached several of the confidential codes in the Trust's statutes of governance. We suggest some form of retraction or apology to your colleague, Mr. Cody Hayes, the medical director, then, after a suitable period of rehabilitation I am confident that we will see no further legal impediment to a recommendation for revalidation and a formal resumption of your normal professional activities, of course this depends on…you…'

Genies give us shelter, the black woman's dilemma again. Come across as, what was it again – bumptious, vexatious, antagonistic then they'd make it all about them, and they will say to all and sundry, "You see what we've had to deal with?"

But weep for your dead son and what you've been through and you are being melodramatic and embarrassing. And if you don't weep and put on the phlegmatic show it must be because you people don't feel pain in the same way as colourless people like Cody would. Or, with ingenious circularity, conclude that there couldn't have been much wrong in the first place because if there was, they'd expect people like you to make a drum out of your thin skins to concoct a song and dance out of it. But you can't say any of this because it is not politically correct or prudent – they own the show, the stage, the sets, the props, the limelight, copyright, and will pay the impresario's out-of-pocket expenses out of your pocket. They decide what is political, correct, or politically correct, and if you say so, they howl, "My history, my history, you're rewriting my history." Because they know that what they think of you counts more than what you think of them, end of. Lump it woman; your skin colour lost.

'Can we at least agree that I want a proper investigation into PPE, and that you do not? An investigation into the plagiarism of my colleague and you do not? That is what this is about is it not?' said Os, the throb behind her eyes raising her concern about her blood pressure. She had stayed up so late the night before, she forgot whether she took her pills.

Mr. Newton's hand shot up. He asked Os to name one member of staff she *knew* died *because* they didn't have PPE? 'Name one. Give a hospital number or date of birth? Those who died may have succumbed anyway or died even if they dressed in suits made of antibodies. And they could have contracted the virus anywhere.'

He checked his notes and looked up again with his glasses perched on the edge of his nose. Was Os's friend the doctor still alive or not? Was Os sure what time she saw him without a mask during the resuscitation of a patient? Did the patient have any underlying conditions? Did the doctor receive contaminated parcels from Nigeria days before he fell ill? Who prepares his meals? Did he eat takeaways? Mr Newton licked his lips and swept his hand in an arc. 'My learned friends do not accept the proposition that the Trust was in any way to blame for any staff illnesses or deaths from Covid, or anything else for that matter. Whilst we are on the subject…'

'This seems to be a regular pattern with you, Professor, we've been here before,' said another barrister, in a pompous tone, like a Dickensian headmaster about to flog a hapless student.

Been here before, said William the Conqueror – the sort of rhyme David would compose.

'We've been here before because nothing changes,' she said, belatedly remembering to reassemble a neutral face when she finished speaking.

As Amanda began her reply, Mrs. Kindolowo tutted at a vibrating phone and trotted from the room to return shortly with two middle-aged white men in light grey linen suits. Os squinted at their temporary identity cards and when she saw where the men came from, her heart leapt from the frying pan to a well feathered bed. The men were from NICOR, the National Institute for Cardiovascular Outcomes Research which monitors the hospital treatment of patients with cardiac disease. Data she tweeted via the Selina's Doctors for Justice group must have reached their screens. Os held her breath.

'Welcome, sirs, we have been hoping for a similar rapid response from other subspecialties, but it was not to be,' said Mrs. Kindolowo, eyeing Amanda sideways, her biceps bulging the short sleeve of her green and white blouse as she dragged two extra chairs along the tiled floor.

Amanda's chin turned gravelly and dark. 'Will someone tell me what is going on?' she said in the general direction of Mrs. Kindolowo who turned to ask if the gentlemen wanted anything. Tea? Coffee? What sort of biscuit? Digestive, chocolate, plain, oatmeal? She fussed over them for a hectic five minutes, then sat down, beaming like a bride on her wedding day.

'As far as *I* know we are not expecting any other unexpected visitors,' she said.

'I ask again. Who authorised this?' said Amanda, staring at Mrs. Kindolowo.

'They are doctors. After all it is a hospital,' said Os. She rose to pour herself a cup of black coffee from the side tray. After a quick exchange of supportive glances with Mrs. Kindolowo, she smiled at the older of the newcomers. Round-faced with kind eyes and a soft voice, he reminded Os of kind Mr. Aggett, the local chemist who had encouraged her to read medicine. The other man wore a permafrost scowl. She knew him from Cambridge. Charmless George. No change there then. But he probably said the same about her, with justification.

'Professor, but why did you not refer this to the CQC?' said the avuncular older surgeon. Os had once sent them the figures she got from Vera the Improbable. The mortality rate at the Trust between 2015 and 2019 was 3.6% – 1.6% above the national average – but if you took out Os's excellent figures, the mortality rate for the Trust leapt to around 4.0%.

Os muffled her chuckle. CQC? Was Big Uncle having a laugh? 'I tried once but the CQC automatically took Cody's word over mine. Told them I was a troublemaker and it was all a flipping storm in a teacup. Yes, he could have handled it better, but it had nothing to do with patients or clinical work.' Os rubbed her hands and paused but no one else seemed ready to speak. 'Why would I risk my health when every little genie in a bottle knew that the regulators hang the whistleblower out to dry whilst the ink is still wet on their anodyne report? Carry on, Trust, they write, your floor is immaculately polished because you knew we were coming; we can see that you've temporarily emptied that investigations unit out of the broom cupboard because you knew we were coming. That takes commitment. Nobody died, they write, but whistleblowers can go and do just that and decay where the stench of rotting flesh won't reach their delicately regulated nostrils.'

Os had always wondered whether the whole legislative and inspectorate industrial complex were in it together. Where was their benchmark? America, Cuba, Scandinavia, Germany? Or were we comparing average with average to fit in with the Treasury models for the economy? Or stalling for time until the 350 million quid a week Brexit dividend Boquacious promised arrived? Don't hold your breath. Genie Thunder, but perhaps we'll get it when the sterling in our pocket is worth ten cents and inflation a cricket score and we are scouring Europe for a foreigner to run the Bank of England because the local boys have got us relegated from the premier league by playing rigid systems made up since around 1619 when labour laws were so much more flexible and you could have people - and their children and their children - working for you for life without paying them a penny. But when a scandal like Mid-Staffordshire or Telford breaks, the same Honourable Members - who paid gooey lip service to the duty of candour and who ducked out of sight when someone knocked the cover off the cover-up for gaffs that came from gaps in funding are all over it, scapegoating both doctors and managers. 'I know what this is about, to stop me getting back to work in retaliation for what happened at the hybrid meeting. But at least I've had a semblance of a career to look back on.'

Had they heard of Usha Prasad and Chris Day and Linda Fairhall and Peter Duffy and Alison McDermott and a hundred others who were selling the family silver to save the families and roofs over their heads from the depredations of predatory managers? Fighting against teams funded by the taxpayers. Just for speaking up. *And they ask me why I don't go to the CQC? Genies split their bottles with laughter. You couldn't make it up.*

'Yes, we've been there before but we wouldn't be here now if they'd taken action then,' she said, smacking the table.

Mr Newton picked up his briefcase. 'Not taking any more of this.' He growled at the door because he tugged it the wrong way as he tried to leave. Lugging black briefcases, the other barristers marched out after him.

Two days later, Os was in her basement office drafting a letter of complaint about Amanda's conduct when Blonde Barrie called, lapsing into Lagos demotic and yammering so fast she had to tell him to slow down.

'Come see wahala for Chief Ex's office. People dey come, people dey go, police dey come, police dey go.' He never saw so many pots of tea made in his life. For CQC. He swore he saw uniformed police as well. 'One of them was only a small pickin, like, twelve years old?'

For Genies sake, it was probably one of their kids doing work experience. 'He sat at my disciplinary hearing, the only one who sided with me,' said Os, her laughter echoing achingly through the voids within.

'I'm serious, Prof. They said the face of Mr. Hayes was like a burned pancake,' said Blonde Barrie. Spooked by NICOR's visit, and despite the threat from rising cases of the Kent variant, the CQC must have sent in one of their rapid response teams. Two days after the call from Blonde Barrie, Os met the three officers from the CQC in an office. As they say on the radio phone-ins, she left it all out there, words tumbling out of her uninterrupted for 56 minutes – about the toxic culture at the trust of distrust, low morale, poor quality meetings, the anti-black racism practised by blacks, including herself she had to admit. At that her interlocutors went strawberry red.

The CQC placed the Trust in "Special Measures." Out went the CEO with a mighty cheque he'd be mad not to pocket. That he took the cheque vouched for his state of mind. Cody Hayes survived.

'He looked at me with his cocky eyes and said he was on the fucking transition team because they needed some grownups in the room to sort out the mess. The very mess he made himself,' she told the convalescing Drinkstain over a drink at his house in Tooting Bec.

'At least you get revalidation and your job back,' said Drinkstain.

'Shouldn't have lost my blinking job in the first place,' she said, and how the truth must weep in its latest grave because the CQC report said nothing about Cody stealing her work; nothing about the games they played with PPE at the expense of front-line staff; nothing about the money given to Tim's company to buy PPE; nothing, because his fleet-footed team of barristers, led by Mr. Newton, splashed their redacting pens over the awkward bits. 'Ear-drumming silence, honestly, Drinkstain, you say anything against Cody and it is like polishing your teeth with his earwax. Have you seen the latest job description? Chalk and cheese compared to the original I saw early last year…' She let out a long deep sigh. The interview was set for Friday the 13th of August. She dug into Comfort for a copy of the job description and handed it to Drinkstain. 'Hot off the press of Vera the Improbable,' she said.

'Previous experience in running a department at short notice would be desirable?' said Drinkstain, looking up for an explanation.

Os let out a groan. 'That's because Enders acted up when I was locked up in the basement.'

'A desirable specialism in molecular cytology of myocyte kinetics?' said Drinkstain.

'That's to suit him too. You haven't got to where they say "unalloyed and sustained sympathy for the cherished traditions of British science", though.'

Drinkstain flipped the page. 'And this bit…ah, ah, here it says "uninterrupted clinical practice, *recently*". Ha!' He threw his head back, clapped his hands. This couldn't be more skewed if this Enders man wrote it with his doting grandmother. He drew a wicket in the air, in lieu of leaping on the spot and launched into pidgin English. 'Ossy, my sister, dis don pass me, na real original *juju* you need, oh.'

'The Genies are locked in on it,' replied Os.

CHAPTER TWENTY ONE

'You'll smash it, Mum,' said Louise over breakfast.

'But will they notice?' said Os as she snatched a few minutes of the Choral Symphony on her laptop. Something in the calm, deft authority of the timpanist during the octave leaps of the second movement got her going.

It was the 13th of August. The day the Taliban decided they wanted their country but also the day Foreign Secretary Dominic Raab, the man who didn't think much of British workers, remember, was not rushing home from his holiday in Crete. And whilst this indomitable Foreign Secretary, who would not genuflect to anyone but his wife and the Queen, was standing up for attention to detail in sunny Crete, Os readied herself for a more prosaic battle against a group of well dug-in white males in South London.

Half an hour after she left home, as she teetered on her toes waiting for a wheelchair user to go past, a trolley carrying soiled linen careened round the T-junction and crashed into the same hip bone she had banged against the table in her scuffle with John at the cafe. A dark stain spread down her good luck orange suit; the stench so strong you could virtually see it rise from its nidus. Brilliant, just champion brilliant. After all you've waded through, to be tripped up by bags of non-weight bearing material. Limping slightly into an alleyway, she shook her phone out of Comfort and warbled to the registrar that she was going to be late. Then she hopped to the theatre suite for a shower under the frustratingly feeble trickle of tepid water. The stiff theatre togs she borrowed from the changing room felt like wearing a wooden cabinet. She rummaged through Comfort as she scampered to the interview. Please, Genies pretty please, she hadn't dropped the USB into the yellow bin with her dirty laundry. She hadn't.

In the oak-panelled room behind an intimidating expanse of polished oak, under the portrait of a bewigged ancestor, sat Cody Hayes. To his immediate left beamed the latest Acting CEO. To his left reigned the great Professor Sir Peter Mortimer, the panel chairman, who said to Os's face that she had as much chance of getting the top job as a camel had of passing between the brake pad and disc of his latest sporty runaround. Os recognized two recent professorial appointees to Southampton and to Plymouth, as well as Mr. Briars, cousin of another of the candidates, and the sybarite, Mr. Inglewood. Retired surgeon, recently married for the fourth time, he sat three places to the right of Sir Peter. One other, balding with thick hairs sprouting from his ears, sat with folded arms across his chest to hide the coffee he had spilled on his white shirt in his excitement at meeting Sir Peter at last.

'You're late,' snapped Sir Peter, staring at his gold wristwatch. Os bowed. Glasses of water and cups of coffee poured and drunk, papers pawed over, murmured greetings and Covid anecdotes long shuffled and reshuffled, the members of the panel, eyes fixed as if starched, reminded Os of a row of disgruntled football directors at a home thrashing. Os gripped Comfort hard. *Genies wept, woman, why are your knees clapping their caps? You should be used to this for fuck's sake. Remember, to succeed, your doubts do not have to fail, and failure does not have to succeed your doubts.* She bowed again. Her self-deprecating joke about Friday the thirteenth fell flat the moment it left her doughy mouth. She raised her English breakfast face – toasted lips spread over grilled teeth with salty eyes frying behind – but it fell off its hot sweaty scaffold in seconds and, try as she might, would not return for hours.

The Acting CEO, accomplished cellist, spiky haired, sparkling diamond ring on right ring finger, tapped his pencil on the arm of his black spectacles. Brimming with conceit, presumably for not putting a foot wrong so far with Sir Peter, he beckoned Os into a seat. Os had exactly ten minutes, no more, to tell them how she intended to run the department, "going forward". This would be followed by an interaction with the panel, whose academic and debating juices had been whetted by having to wait so long for her arrival.

Os rose to her feet. When she finally trembled the USB into the correct side-port, a tall white woman in a plum-coloured suit, who had been watching Os with an air of ill will, flounced across the room to draw the grey curtains. Os counted to ten whilst the lights dimmed. If they could not see her in the dark would they be any wiser if she mimed to someone more articulate? Nina Simone, Eartha Kitts? The title slide for her presentation, "From Cell to Bench, Bedside and Beyond – Pocket Depth and Premature Cardiac Mortality Rates," came on. Each time her coarse cotton togs rubbed against her legs; a disconcerting sound similar to that of a motorbike engine revved from the microphone. But just as a boxer way behind on points needs a knockout punch, and an injured tennis player tries to keep the points short, Os cut out half her slides and put all she had into her attack at the top of each section. Only the word *mortality* snagged in her throat.

'Thank you for listening,' she said at the end with a stiff but elaborate bow. The lights came on and the curtains opened to show a watery blue sky and an atoll of chestnut grey clouds.

After a quick shuffle of gazes between them, questions started with Mr. Briars, first cousin of Os's main rival, Alfred "there is no society in theatre" Enders. He billowed out of a tight black jacket and waistcoat. 'Surgeons get in, put the fire out, get out and leave the wheres and wherefores to those who didn't have the talent, innit,' he said, adding the latter word in a mocking street accent.

Clean-shaven, with a flat tipped nose, Mr. Briars cultivated a reputation for calling a spade a spade and seemed to have made up his mind, based on what he'd read and heard, to treat Os as a dangerous anarchist, a sleeper for some foreign enemy, seeking to insinuate herself into the heart of the medical establishment. He said this was an interview for the Head of Surgery, not for the local chapter of the shop-sweepers' union. 'Newton discovered laws which apply to us all. Do you want class-based science? You take exception to the laws of gravity applying to your lot?'

The CEO got in first. 'I'm sure he didn't mean your lot as in–'

'I meant what I said, thank you very much,' said Mr. Briars. 'Your lot as in your fate. Is that clear now?' he said, staring down the CEO who, to Os's wary cheer, replied with a glare of greater intensity.

'Namby nannyism will be the ruin of all of us,' said Sir Peter Monthouse and tapped the table with a fingertip for attention.

Her tonsils steamed at the comment but Os put on a neutral face. This guy is so far up his own arse he should be called Montcolon. Must think wind farming is something you do in your underpants. Or was she being unfair? Bet he didn't tweet namby pamby nanny when they chucked billions at the banks and Osborne stoked the property market then sent 35 billion of created-out-of-nothing QE money back to the Treasury when interest rates were rigged to the floor and real kids couldn't see the teacher at the front of the room for the curtain of rain falling through their school roofs.

Os looked Sir Monthouse square in the eye. 'We should auction the roads and speed limits so the highest bidder is allowed to go fastest?' If Sir Peter didn't mind, since he raised the point, she saw the economy as a giant ring road on which a relative few whizz round having fun on its steep camber with easy access to the wide spaces beyond whilst the rest are trapped inside the ring, scraping and scrapping to live off scraps, dying as much as fifteen years earlier than the privileged who couldn't give a toss, except to toss off their cast offs – until there is a big crash. She said, 'When there is a crash it's, oops, folks, we are all in this together, Blitz spirit and all that and the Queen is wheeled out and everyone comes out to help in the hope of better treatment next time whether it is levelling up or hosing down or feeding up or settling down in a house on the other side of the tracks with the hose pipes and spotlight turned on those not quite fair enough to cross the road without being spotted, except perhaps on dark and cold nights. But once the clean-up is over, off drive the first-class patriots, claiming the crash would never have happened if they'd only been allowed to go faster without this ridiculous regulation dreamt up by lefty beadledoms in Basle.'

'Does Sir Peter need any further clarification?' said the CEO.

'I don't think she's quite finished her...manifesto,' said Sir Peter, who sounded as if he was enjoying Os's self-immolation.

'It is in reply to Sir Peter,' said Os. 'If one man or woman owns tobacco, lardy fast-food outlets, ciggy factories, sugary confectioneries and has a near monopoly on medical instrument manufacturers, has us covered from cradle to grave with his vertical integration model, so to speak, do you, Sir Peter, say "Good on him or her - to intervene, to prevent diabetes and coronary heart disease will hurt investment and the economy?' She puffed her cheeks and dabbed at her damp forehead. What are they thinking? Look at the one on the left. If he had a gun he'd shoot me. 'But I agree with those who say there is nothing more illuminating than differing points of view.' Which, in all honesty, is why she became an academic, because scientific enquiry provided the best metaphors for the truth. Her job, if she was appointed, was to work to make her job obsolete by moving knowledge on and banishing the scourge of preventable coronary disease.

The men stared at one another as if Os had exceeded their wildest forecasts of her insanity. A hot flush rose to Os's neck. She'd run out of HRT tablets, and H-Mum's remedies, some seeds she bought in little Lagos, Peckham to you and me, were as good as trying to fan your face with your armpits. 'Specifically, I am looking to see if certain blood markers of inflammation we found in the poorer patients presenting for surgery damaged their hearts and blood vessels, or are due to poverty, or cause poverty and so on. An important area of research that might help guide policy.' Os smiled and waited from one sign of encouragement from the seated panel. None. Gee, if she didn't get this gig, Cody would snap each cell in her body on a rack one at a time.

After an awkward pause, whilst he fiddled with his earring, the CEO asked which was more important in the workplace – diversity of physical appearance or of points of view? 'In short, do you think we should appoint you because you are a woman?' said Cody, curling his lip.

Os counted to five to stop her sawn-off emotions going off. She gave the example of blinded auditions for places in symphony orchestras. Other examples stampeded to mind and she could not get them out fast enough. Gimme strength, it wasn't so long ago that they thought women couldn't paint serious art because they weren't supposed to be able to think in three dimensions. 'I am not saying you should appoint me for any single characteristic. To paraphrase my husband, we are each a corporeal coalition of contradictions wrapped or trapped in varying layers of melanin. It is your job to choose who to have on your teams. But how much earlier could we have worked out DNA if we hadn't tied women down for centuries?'

'Extraordinarily disingenuous as always. So, you do want us to appoint you because you are a woman?' said Cody, cocking his head to one side then the other, revelling in the sagacious grunts and barks of support. The CEO's delicate eyebrows drifted up and Cody turned to his colleagues with renewed gusto. 'The professor *does* profess that she is the best candidate because she is a woman,' he said, which sent a cat's claws on tin sensation up Os's spine.

'Have you never considered the possibility that you were appointed medical director and are still here sitting in judgement in spite of everything because you are male *and* white?' she said.

From the shock of red to Cody's cheeks, either these questions had never occurred to him, he misheard her, or he deserved an Oscar.

Sir Peter looked distressed, as if vandals had smashed up his famous wine cellar and built an unflattering statue of him with the bottle corks. 'This, er, race thing, erm,...' He rolled his wrist whilst he searched for the next words then added, 'I'm Homo Sapiens for God's sake, never held a heart in palm and said, "Peter, it is a black heart or this is a white woman's heart," never. It lies there beating, or not, as the case may be, daring me to touch it up or fail...'

'Hear, hear!' said the young professor from Southampton.

'Hear, hear!' said Cody. 'This is extraordinary, unprecedented. What are we to make of these utterances? From an academic?' He hesitated because Sir Peter made a sound. 'People are individuals, not classes or races, these divisive ideas should long have been confined to the sarcophagus, don't you think, Sir Peter?' He leaned round the back of the Acting CEO to catch Sir Peter's approval.

The Acting CEO's eyebrows drifted up. 'Professor Sharp?'

Os surveyed the panel. *Go on, shuffle your fucking feet, wipe your blocked noses. Ask me to comb your bleached, beachcombed comb overs.* 'If we are as colour blind as we say we are, it shouldn't offend if we are shown the shades we miss.' *Ah bless, look at the shock on their lovely faces.* 'If trying to prevent horrible histories repeating is divisive then we all have some way to go, whether it is preventing heart disease…infectious mono–'

'So, the way to prevent a repeat of these so-called horrors is by arson and rioting?' said Mr. Briars. Cody nodded his ballpoint and head.

Jeerie me, they truly have made up their minds about me. Why didn't they ask her more questions about cardiac surgery? 'Poverty causes riots in the mind, then, after a long gestation, these spill on to the street, as if by magic. Then we throw our hands and eyes up in the sky and ask the Archbishop of Canterbury to keep schtum, it is none of his business.'

The CEO thanked Os for her frankness and asked if she had any questions? Buzzing, yet drained, Os asked when she was likely to hear the outcome. *Genies wept, Drinkstain was right, she needed a miracle. She'd smashed it alright, the bottle with the genie in it. She'd have to come to work in blinkers and disguise, until she found another job, almost certainly abroad. After this, who in the Great British Isles would allow her near?*

In a week or two, said the CEO after a quick canvass of opinion in the room.

'Covid permitting, of course, as we have three other excellent candidates,' said the secretary to the panel.

Outside the interview room, to her surprise, Os found Ian Kennedy sitting on a bench, a neat inch trimmed off his sandy beard, suited and booted with his battered briefcase at his feet. What in the name of the Horn of Africa was he doing here? She didn't know whether to stop for a stilted chat or to run and risk being seen as rude.

'How's retirement?' she said. Ian resigned shortly after the CQC visit. In an awkward visit to his office as he packed, Os had wished him good luck, gifted him a pen shaped like a scalpel and hewn out of crushed velvet from the north-east. She thanked him for his support over the years. He said he did nothing.

'The only reference anyone needs is the one they write to themselves. Good luck, you'll need it,' he said.

CHAPTER TWENTY TWO

To get H-Mum to Heathrow in time, Os had to get away by seven thirty latest, or she and the whole of the global south wouldn't hear the last of it. H-Mum was going back to Lagos via Heathrow even if she had to walk to Terminal 3, or was it 5? Whatever. Os decided to give Ian five minutes, ten tops, for old times' sake. Now remember, woman, if he asks about John just say "good" and move on. Anything else, put on a face as if he asked you to dry-clean his arsehole, turn him 180 degrees and push him through the door. H-Mum awaits. And she had Louise to pick up from school first.

A few months earlier and four long weeks after the interview, Os was in the surgeons' lounge waiting for her next patient when Beethoven rang out from her phone. It was Mrs. Kindolowo. Os's gut strings twanged with apprehension but, 'Congratulations,' said the voice. Os stared at the phone. Was this real or a Drinkstain windup? Had they got the right person and gender? It wasn't that long ago that they gave the award for best picture to the wrong film at the Oscars.

'Are you sure?' she said, a little dizzy, her ears ringing.

'I checked many times myself, but it is true, praise be to the Lord,' said Mrs. Kindolowo, pious wonder laced with deferential irony in her thundering voice. After, Os went to stand outside in the corridor, and, with her eyes closed, dropped her head against the cold window pane in lament because her son was not here to see this day.

Ten hectic weeks flashed by in a flurry of interviews, presentations, meetings, trips abroad and the gratifying discovery of a privileged source of HRT on the continent.

'I know your government doesn't like us but that doesn't mean I want you or any other woman in the UK to fry,' said Os's pal, Professor Ingrid Svedberg, when they met over a coffee in Stockholm.

The pleasant aroma of new venetian wooden blinds wafted over Os as she looked out of the window. Through the inky blue darkness in the distance twinkled the glass and concrete columns to riches in the City of London. Money could not buy how she felt when she got the job. Black lives harder, makes making it all the sweeter. A shiver of melancholia went through her and on the teary film in her eyes the streetlights began to sprout watery fur. Os dabbed a wet corner of her eye with a knuckle, turned to return to the red leather chair she had coveted for so long. She'd only recently learned to call it her chair and not Ian's.

She put Comfort on the mammoth desk, shoved her watch up her thin wrist again. It was six thirty. Ian was late. Always late. What was it with some people? Was it not bad enough having to hang around on the ward earlier because Boquacious was doing the rounds to preen himself with vaccine roll-out glory; getting in the way of clinical staff too polite to tell him where to go. You have to laugh. It's like Tony Blair going to Northern Ireland every weekend in memory of the Good Friday agreement or Thatcher flying to the Falklands every Sunday to count freed white sheep. But what in the name of the Horn of Africa did Ian want? To check if she'd erased all traces of him? To mess with her head? Tell her she wasn't worthy, or being true to herself; that this was a dream and that the committee was high on cocaine and that she should have read the small print? That she was only warming the seat for Alfred 'there is no society in theatre' Enders? Yet, believe it or not, she'd checked many times. It was her name on the door and she'd brought Louise along to check.

Seconds after a vacuum cleaner hummed back to life next door, came a surprisingly loud rap on the door. Os skated across the shiny wood floor, ready to guillotine any small talk, but her stomach shrunk into a hard ball because it was Cody, not Ian, who stood outside her door. Surely, he couldn't be lost. His dad's Foundation designed the bloody place. What did he want? An ache spread sideways from the area around her gallbladder. Cody smelled of coffee, with bags under his eyes and a cunning smile on his lips.

'Oh, hello,' she said, not sure whether to shake his hand or tell him to sling his hook.

'Apologies for the subterfuge. Ian sends his best wishes. Busy?' he said, his blisteringly white shirt collar open at his neck.

'Busy? Hell no, just pretending,' she said, pointedly lingering over her wristwatch as she stepped back, so she didn't have to crane her neck to see his face. What would David do in this situation? Or Louise? She waved Cody in and turned on her heel, the ache in her gallbladder waxing into her jaw. 'I have to go in a few minutes…airport…'

Cody looked round in the manner of a grudgingly impressed estate agent, with his nose in the air and a querulous slant to his head. 'Extraordinary, it's Aladdin's cave without the treasure in here,' he said, pointing at the large gaps between the volumes lying on the bookshelves. 'Who looted this place? How those curtains have stayed up so long is a miracle.' He pointed past her to the venetian blinds. When the workmen came to take Ian's curtains down, they crashed onto the threadbare rug releasing overwhelming blasts of blinding dust, as if booby trapped. 'But you kept him,' he said, with an approving nod at the alabaster bust on the desk.

This Galton, no relation to Sir Francis Galton, didn't believe women should study medicine. Os kept this symbol of patriarchal condescension for inspiration: the thought of sliding back to the dark and backward days he stood and died for, and for which millions yearn again, she found gut wringing and terrifying. 'I have to go,' said Os, stabbing her watch, but, 'Great,' said Cody. She'd got rid of the god-awful rug. Picture of Easington colliery was it? Cody gave the left corner of the room the privilege of a once over then sat across the expanse of desk from Os. She remained standing for several seconds, seething, before she sat down with her fists clenched on the desk.

Cody wafted a cheque in the air. 'Yours. For the department. No strings. Equipment, travel grants, conference hosting, to get you going…

we can work together…if you wish?'

'In all honesty, if I ever turn my back on you again it will be to reload,' she said, with great force. 'Not after what happened to Tim.' For some reason Tim the Terrible wasn't on Cody's laundromate list: list of mates whose sins he would wash away.

'Ah, that,' he said, waving the cheque as he spoke. 'I warned him about the dodgy provenance of the PPE but poor Tim, chips on shoulder from the day he was born, couldn't resist the treacherous lure of lucre. Alright for you, Cody, he said, you were born in a castle, words to that effect. So he and the CEO ran this PPE supplier thing on the side.' He shook his head and decried the kerfuffle over a measly hundred grand the Trust paid Tim for PPE. He'd covered up for Tim for years. Wasn't it ironic? 'A man on the make brought down by face masks,' he chuckled. His long blink renewed the glint in his eyes. 'Ah,' he added. Os should look under her own roof before she pointed her fingers at anyone else. She and her blinking boss, Ian northern boy Kennedy, properly stitched him up.

Os's jaw began to ache. So that was what this visit was about? To whinge about his lost spot on the complex cardiac surgery team? Scanning the massive desk for a spot to land her gaze, her inadvertent shove on the nameplate brought a muffled rattle from the counterpoise lamp. Yes, back in the day Cody's figures were not the greatest but neither were they the worst; it was his attitude that Os didn't much care for, the way he gave people like him special treatment but couldn't be bothered to come back in if a salt-of-the-earth pleb had a complication. And, of course, she wouldn't be human if she didn't enjoy nailing him. Which is why, after she came in one night to bail out his patient, she had convinced Ian to get Cody off the complex surgical team. Genies may claim that was perhaps not her finest hour but where was the justice in letting him get away with stealing her data? Even Greek gods got up to stuff they weren't proud to tell the grandkids, and Genies cast spells they wouldn't confess to their bottles. Which reminded her that the Yank medics weren't going great guns in the conscience department either until they were forced to come clean because the black one, peeved to be left out of the conspiratorial loop, threatened to go to their Dean.

'I didn't know you were having trouble with your son, at the time,' said Os, to a crawling sensation in her spine. 'But if I'd asked you to take some time off until you got sorted at home, I know what you would have said. "Tell the black cunt to fuck off to Kilimanjaro…" or words to that effect. Don't deny it.'

Cody scratched his fine-tipped nose and the red glow on his cheeks subsided as a lopsided smile returned to his lips. If Os really believed that her charm offensive at the interview got her this gig then she had as much insight as a headless chicken.

'I…Sir Peter? How?' said Os, with an awkward start, not sure whether she wanted to hear what he had to say, but Cody went on anyway, swiping the air with the folded cheque in his hand. 'Must have been your lucky Friday the 13th.' Extraordinary. The blasted CEO should not have let Ian in. Ian Kennedy was like a northern powerhouse that morning. He sat in his Durham uncles' cast-offs and sang like a nightingale in support of Os. 'Pure unprecedented perjury.' He went on about how Os had changed after her son's unfortunate accident. 'I suppose he felt guilty for letting it slip that it was you who got him to take me off complex surgery.' The CEO had a soft spot for Ian. 'He's from some spot north of the Watford gap too.' Cody rolled a sleeve down and back up his left arm. Sir Peter wasn't having any of it but the CEO put his foot down and said he wanted Os. 'Poor Enders thought he had it in the bag. It was Ian wot won it for you. Extraordinary,' said Cody, leaning back in the chair, and shaking his head, a smile barely parting his lips.

Os lolled against the desk and felt her way backwards to sink into her chair. Genies gimme strength, what is wrong with these guys? Beat them fair and square, but can't take it, won't admit it. Got to wheel out the alibis and excuses, codicils and clauses of token or affirmative or sympathy or historical redress appointment. Nothing to do with working her backside off, losing herself and her son and her men and two marriages. Nothing. She just sat around waiting for them to winch her up. It's always up to them and down to them. Yet she was flattered by the news that Ian took the time to come and support her. He didn't have to. Was that really because he thought better of her or worse of himself? Cody and crew could say what they liked. They lost. And it was what she was going to bring to the table and the lives of others that counted. She flicked a paperclip, sending it tinkling further than she wanted, into a glass tray.

'We all need an Ian, just as Thatcher needed her Willie, which is why I am sitting here and your Enders guy's crying into his ice cream.' The ache in her jaw receded. 'I really have to go…'

'Was it also you who got the CEO to strip me of the Medical Director job? Happy now?'

'First I'm hearing of it,' said Os. 'Congratulations.'

'Very droll. I spotted that chip on shoulder look on his face the moment he clapped his eyes on me. People like me...we get it in the neck too, you know.' He crossed his wrists to make his point. 'For something that was supposed to have happened years ago…he gave me the chop. Lamide and I were always swapping stuff, data, for talks and presentations.' But, he should have known. Nowadays commonsense succumbs to mob rule by social media. And what was the kerfuffle all about? A few figures and graphs swapped between consenting adults. His voice dropped. In the glow of the counterpoise lamp, he looked jaundiced. The ache in Os's belly returned. *Genies wept, Os, you'd think it was you who stole data from* him. Os gave her jacket sleeve a gentle brush, gathered herself to her full height and glided as smoothly as she could to look out of the window, even as her blood pressure nudged upwards. So that's why the rat fucker is here? He wants his old place back on complex surgery so the CEO doesn't turf him out? Now it's his thick neck in the chopper's sight, he reels up with a cheque and sad, fallen guy eyes to gentle Ossy meek and mild. And he expected her to do what? Fake amnesia? Euphoria? Thank him for shoving her so nearly out of her mind, for booby trapping her career? For years she yearned for a day like this. In her mildest dreams she'd shaken Cody until he rattled and grovelled and wailed for mummy and daddy with her foot on his precious neck until his cervical bones crackled and popped. This kick for stealing data. That heel grinding your teeth down for lying through them. That elbow in the socket for the doctor with "too many vowels in her name" who you drove round the bend and laughed at as she packed her bags. This punch in the guts for threatening to have me struck off, and phoning around London for extra rivets to bang into my coffin: and this for the goons you sent to spy on me; and for pretending to help when my eyes were on her dead boy's body only because you wanted to squirt your poison onto me. Were the shoe on the other foot he'd be straight up to the CEO and GMC before you could say "I beg you." Os watched him stew whilst she weighed his fate. Sending him packing was too easy. That was the old Os but the new Os-in-the-making decided that if unsung heroes, black women, could embrace and forgive the killers of their daughters and sons and, out of centuries of enslavement and debasement, sing golden tunes to love and peace, then she would forgive Cody.

'On one condition,' she said, tapping the desk.

His half salute didn't do much for Os's good intentions. 'Anything.'

'But, as I was always taught by my H-Mum, you do not wield the toilet brush with your mouth wide open,' she said. Cody could have his old job on the complex surgery unit back provided he worked with her to implement the changes to the department recommended by the CQC. The Trust must establish a robust and transparent process for recruitment and advancement as well as a scheme for managers to take out indemnity cover. 'If we doctors have to do it, so should they. About time they took responsibility for their decisions.' No more of the mortgaged to the hilt sole whistleblower against an army of state sponsored terrorists. He had six months to report to her. Os waved a V-sign at her eyes to warn him that she had her peepers and sixth sense on him. One wrong step and he was out.

Cody agreed on the spot. His eyes swept round their sockets as if to search his memory for victims of his Damascene conversion.

CHAPTER TWENTY THREE

On the walls, blank spaces framed by fuzzy rectangles marked where H-Mum's photos had passed their years. Stifling an itchy sneeze from the zesty aroma, Os tapped the wrapped presents this way and that until they looked right against the conical stand, then crawled from under the massive Christmas tree which had a six-foot span and touched the low ceiling.

'What are you going to do about the Citroen?' asked Louise.

Os spun round so quickly the carpet burned her knees. 'Can't you cough or turn your headphones up or something when you come in. Nearly gave me an aneurysm,' she said. The tree lights flashed an erratic sequence of more reds and greens than blues and yellows onto Louise's doleful face. It was midmorning, crisp and bright. Louise was wearing a crumpled, petulant face and an equally wrinkled pair of pyjamas under a silky cardinal red gown. Her hair fell in thick tendrils down one side, the other half of her head was covered in frayed cornrows at least a week past their best before date. 'Are you going to get dressed or stand over me all day like a leaning telegraph pole? H-Mum is going to call in an hour and she won't be too happy if…' Os, still on her knees, shrank back from the storm gathering on Louise's face. She wondered if John was having an equally blistering time at Jaundiced Matilda's. Served him right. Os pointed at her hair. 'Now H-Mum's gone you might have to cut it short like mine. Saves time, darling. Easier to control, wash and comb and go, environmentally friendly hair.' She put on a TV announcer's voice. 'No crude oil products were harmed in making this up. It grows on you.' She wrenched up a smile but Louise's face had grown the length of South America. *Genies wept, she was John Sharp's daughter alright.*

'Why did you let her go?' said Louise, tugging at the belt of her gown as she dropped a knee onto a sofa.

'Broken up with Kevin or Kelvin, have you?' said Os.

'Don't change the subject.'

'Na my country, for me, for me, for me, me, I like am like that, yeah,' she sang in imitation of H-Mum's Lagos accent. 'She said she didn't want to die here. And you should respect that…'

'You sneaked off to the airport behind my back to save on cremation fees? Worse than dad.'

Os's elbows dug into her ribs. *Genies gimme strength.* If she'd spoken to H-Mum like this when she was young, H-Mum would have thrashed her to within an inch and arraigned her before the Supreme Court. 'Jeerie me, Louise, how many times? I said sorry. Cody held me up. That's why I couldn't pick you up.' If David was around he might have taken Louise to the airport; but if David was here, H-Mum may not have left for Lagos. But ifs and buts are for the history books. Os tossed a blood pressure pill down her parched throat and chased them down with warm honey and lemon water. Did H-Mum get any beauty sleep, what with electric generators snoring outside her window all night? How was she going to teach maths in Lagos if her head weighed more than a planet from lack of sleep? *Genies wept, Ossy, you sound like John. You'll be asking if she's shaved her tail next.*

On the sofa, Louise sniffled, and wiped her nose and said, 'You promised to stop her…' But Os's stony face cut her short.

'You think you are the only one who is missing her?' said Os.

The tiny Christmas tree lights in the living room flashed through another brief yellow and green sequence. Os punched the air, two-fisted.

'Come on, let's get started, it's Christmas,' she said.

'Tell H-Mum I had to go out,' said Louise.

'But everything's shut,' said Os, her throat beginning to ache with the effort of keeping her bile down.

'The streets are not,' Louise muttered to herself and sneered at the

Christmas tree.

Os counted to ten. Jeerie me Genies, give me patience, my BPs through the sphyg. Telling H-Mum Louise was in the gym was not going to wash. Os tugged and plumped up a cushion on the sofa, had one more look at the small stack of presents under the tree and, for want of anything better to do, went to the kitchen to make herself a cup of black coffee. It takes two to friction. Surely, even Louise couldn't keep this po face for much longer. The tree lights went through another frenetic sequence.

'I'm supposed to say to H-Mum what exactly? That the daughter of the woman she spent her life looking after can't be bothered to say Happy Christmas?'

'Your problem, not mine.' Louise turned her nose up as she scanned the room.

Boiling blood thrashed to Os's face. 'You think I'm to blame for a woman returning to her country because it is not convenient for your hair?' she said. 'If this is not, er, what's your favourite buzz word again, appropriation, I don't know what is.' The tremor in her voice betrayed the fact she'd been just as selfish herself.

'Duh, to, like, equate my hair to me not wanting H-Mum to go… You know what? I give up,' Louise said, tossing her chin up and turning for the kitchen. Os heard a cup slam on a board and she hurried after Louise, who was leaning over the sink, face strained and suffused.

'I had to let her go, darling,' Os said, feeling the day careening out of control. She hugged Louise, who, thank the Genies, yielded a fraction, then buried her head on her mother's shoulder, with rasping jerky sighs.

'Look at us! If grandma Jaundiced Matilda could see, heaven know what Christmas jeers she'd toss at us,' Os sensed a slackening of Louise's neck. Their eyes met, Louise's boggy and red.

'I keep messing you up. Sorry, Mum…'

'Members of the same team are allowed to fall out. It's not a sin,' Os said, reminded of Ian's horror when Lee Bowyer and Kieran Dyer of his beloved Newcastle United came to blows. 'We're missing a big player but we have to step up to try to fill the gap.' Like others who'd lost loved ones, they'd have to reassemble David from memory and imagine him making the memories he did not live to make. Clamping her lips, Os flicked a paper towel off its roll and handed it to Louise who blew her nose and wheeled away to look out of the window, the sky a dull and low dun canopy.

'I got you a present,' said Louise, drying her eyes as she half turned to her mum. 'Coming?' She dabbed her nose and scurried past Os, to return with two boxes wrapped neatly in silvery paper and a ruby bow. The label read *To Mum from Louise the Santa.* It was a biography of Beethoven by Jan Swafford.

'Brilliant,' said Os, curious at the strange coincidence. She flicked off the howling kettle and skipped off to get Louise's presents. One was a box set of female Jazz greats, Fitzgerald, Billie Holliday, many others, including Ma Rainey.

'Gosh, Mum,' said Louise. 'You are a heart reader as well as a surgeon, this is what I've always...' She clapped her hands to her cheeks and Os realised in that moment that they'd both taken their cues from a Christmas list David left in his room: perhaps the last thing he wrote before the police took him away.

'You found it too?' said Os, her voice coarsened by a vague fullness in her throat. Before Louise could speak again, Os shoved a second, larger, box at her daughter. Wrapped in shiny crimson paper, it contained an album of the dozens of photos taken of Louise and David over the years. Louise took one look and slammed it shut like a fire door. She raced from the kitchen and Os found her crouched over the living room sofa, tears bombing the matt black cover of the album.

'I'm ok,' said Louise, after another tremulous sigh, wiping each cheek awkwardly with clenched palms. Os kneeled beside her and teased the album open again. 'That's you two in the pool in Barcelona. And at the piano.'

Louise wedged a page open with her thumb. 'That's him in the atom structure t-shirt,' she said and paused, cleared her throat, and added in an imitation of David's deep voice, 'Electrons have more personality than you think.'

'And you argued over whether it was the electron itself or the stuff around it that made each special.' Os turned the page.

'What was he doing here, Mum? He looks as if he's lost it big time.'

Os dropped her head for a moment at the memory of David tap dancing to the presto agitato of the Moonlight Sonata. He'd ended up hopping about like a crazy rubber ball. 'If a deaf man can write this…'

'…then a boy with two left feet can dance to it,' said Louise and she flung her arms around Os. They clung to each other under the changeable sparkle of the Christmas tree. Presently, Louise fished a card out of the pocket of her dressing gown.

Os opened the card. It read "Best mum in the world ever, Love from your David and Louise. Proud of you." Os looked at the floor, squirming her toes to an almighty rush of prickly heat inside her head.

'Billions of mums in the world, I'm just one who–'

'Mum, stop now. I can't believe you are talking like this. Remind you of someone? If you are down on yourself, how can you do good by David?' Os had forgiven Cody hadn't she? And Simply Blue. And Dad? It wasn't Os's fault that the police took David away, or that he caught Covid. 'Have you never made a mistake at work?'

'That's different,' said Os, without conviction.

'No, it's not.' Louise squeezed Os's hand. 'Listen. If your patient dies, you still, like, carry on, don't you? Sometimes on the same day. You don't, like, stop operating forever?' So why was she giving up on her life because she thought she made a mistake? It's not what David would want. She got it. Girls are brought up to think that as mums they will be the family goalkeeper, the indispensable one in the specialist position, the last line of defence, the silent sweeper of the mess others make, ducking and diving to quietly save the day but taking the blame and windy nonsense when things went pear-shaped. But it was not right and it was not fair. It wasn't even true. Os said it herself. A family is a team. Teams win and lose together. She'd say it again, like, until her blood ran purple. That David died was so not her fault. She gripped her mum's hand again. 'You'll stop punishing yourself, now. Promise? Promise?'

'I promise,' said Os. She looked up into Louise's imploring eyes, fragmented by the flashing Christmas lights, and as she wondered how and when her little girl became so wise, David came to mind, wrapped in the memory of a dry afternoon in the Spring of 2019.

The clocks had gone forward the week before. John was out with Louise. David and Os were pottering about on their special mound of tulips in the garden.

'What's her name again?' she said and flicked a six-inch earthworm off her glove. The day before, she'd raced miles down the A3 to Guildford with a proper pair of shoes and a dress shirt for David because the club wouldn't allow him in wearing trainers.

A bright crimson tulip in a large wooden tub swayed stiffly as David tugged at a dandelion. He held it in the air as an angler would a prize catch. 'Melissa, I think, or was it Miranda?' he said. He chuckled to himself as he chucked the weed into the wheelbarrow. A gnawing sensation reached from Os's stomach to her neck. But before she could think of what to say, David pointed at the robin which had just then hopped onto a shard of clay pottery a foot away.

'Hey, my friend's here,' he tweeted.

'It must like you, the poor thing,' said Os.

David sent his mum a querulous look. He crushed the clumps of soil in his hand onto a craggy rock. 'Shame, these tulips here by the rock haven't come up.' He moaned at a deep hole in the mound, crawled backwards and brushed himself down. 'I'll set Louise's trail cameras on the greedy things and track them down with my thief seeking gear.' The robin redbreast hopped into the dip David left behind.

Os pulled at a trouser leg. 'Excellent deterrent indeed, that's if they don't drag the camera off to take selfies. That'll teach you to be more careful next time,' she warned as she swapped knees in the grit. 'Care less and you lose those who care for you and what you care for,' she added. She waited for a reply and when she got none, said, 'You're going to be one of the good boys, I mean, with girls.'

'Me, a geeky good boy? I'll press skip on that one.' David half swivelled towards her, sighed, turned away and dug his trowel into the soil. Sparks flew because it struck a piece of flint. 'No, you are right, you can't be too careful.'

'I'm being serious,' said Os, pinching her nose against a gust of dust.

'So am I,' said David. He leaned his shadow away from a crimson tulip. 'To make sure that people are not, like, smashed or dug up before they can kinda come up to shine. And that is why I solemnly declare that I want to be a doctor,' he intoned, pointing his trowel at his puffed-out chest. Then his voice rose. His eyes blazed fiercely, and he jabbed the trowel in the air. 'Jesus, Mum. Didn't Louise tell you? She must be slacking. You know what? I hate girls. Hate them, hate them, hate them, more than the pesky deer that gobbled up my surfinia,' he barked. 'I want to grab them by the ponytails and dash them against the -.'

Os grabbed his hand. 'Have I said something to -'

'For peace's sake, Mum, why don't you just spit it out?' He looked down, quivered for a moment but he left Os's hand where it was on his wrist and added, in softer tones, 'If you must know, I did make sure Melissa got home safely.'

Os blushed. She'd been afraid to ask because she didn't want to find that her son had turned out like his flakey dad or for that matter, John. 'Er, to be honest, I don't know why -'

'You know. And you know that I know why. I'm not going to be like...him...like them...' He shrugged and dabbed his sweaty forehead with the back of his hand. 'I was a good boy. Press play on that.' Then he muttered at her as he leaned over to tackle a broadleaved weed. Why did *his* mum have to slide around the point? She did it all the time. Like when she talked about grandpa, or about H-Mum, or her work. Now it was about him and girls.

Crack went a vial in the wall of her stomach. Ah, Genies gimme strength. These kids will be the end of you, Ossy.

'Hang on a second, darling. You are telling your own mother to her face that you never served her up a cold bold-faced lie?' Os paused for dramatic effect and as the doubts played on David's face said, 'Who was it who added a year to his birthdate on the union card so he could get into the Grosvenor to meet the England Rugby team? Or was I dreaming last night when the dodgy card fell out of your shoe?' She gave him another moment to stew then allowed a smile to play on her lips as she added with wicked relish, 'Press play on that, MC Saint David.'

David had squeaked, his hands shooting to his lips. A sharp prod from Louise ended Os's daydream. 'Mum, you've got your sad happy eyes again,' said Louise, but her eyes glowed with the same bitter sweet sentiments when she heard Os's story.

'You should have seen your brother's sheepish face. CGI couldn't make it up,' said Os, her wheezy sigh segueing into soft laughter as she dabbed a tear in the corner of her eye with a knuckle. She leaned over to give her daughter a big hug but to her dismay, Louise recoiled and her olive-green eyes dimmed.

Os's breath caught in her throat. She cocked her head in silent inquiry. *Genies gimme shelter what now?*

'What if it was me?' said Louise, her tone, wry, sardonic, like that of an immigration control officer.

'What if it was you what?' grunted Os, heat and pressure backing up from her jugulars to her face.

'Would you bring me gear to get me into a club?' said Louise.

Os hesitated for a moment because, to her shame, she'd never really considered the question seriously. But that's because Louise hated clubs, she told herself. 'Hypothetical, darling, hypothetical...'

Louise flinched. 'But what if?' she said, clicking her fingers and gripping Os in her vice-like glare.

'It's not the same,' Os insisted, squirming. *Genies wept, surely my girl's bright enough to know that.*

'Duh? So it's kinda one rule for David and another for me?' Brilliant.'

Os fumed. 'Yes, as a blinking matter of fact, darling, yes...'

Louise punched her knee. She knew it. Knew it.

'Oh, stop getting your Christmas knickers in a twist. Of course it's absofuckinglutely not the same. I'd bring the shoes to get you in and bloody well park my cab outside to take you home when the club closed.

If you think different you don't know me,' she said, taken aback by the rawness in her voice.

Louise face glowed afresh. 'Got you there,' she chirped.

'It was a windup?' cried Os.

Louise nodded, an impish grin playing on her lips. 'Gee mum, thought I'd better stop before I blew your gasket.' For a few moments she vaguely groped the base of her neck where her headphones usually hung and said, 'That was for winding David up.' Her voice was coarse. The grin faded and her hand fell awkwardly past her knee.

Os's lips twitched into an uneasy smile. Struck dumb by a sharp intake of the past, she stared at the floor, bracing herself, grimacing, and swallowing hard. But the aching lump in her throat clung on, like an embryo to its mum. In the keen silence, her heart swelled and shrieked as if its strings were striving to be heard above the thundering, sudden crescendos of its systoles. Carefully, she raised her stinging eyes to find somewhere quiet to land them. On the Christmas tree perhaps, out of reach of Louise. But these same eyes, as if of their own mind, reared up and to the right, shuddering to a halt, snagged by a sniff and a watery glint. And between mother and child slid a look too deep or sweet for words, an all-consuming look too strong to hold for long.

The world is our patient and it shall not want, for it is our healer too, thought Os, as she rested her watery eyes on the floor.

ACKNOWLEDGEMENTS

You've almost certainly forgotten me now, Debi Alper, but I'd inflicted an early draft on you and in reply you sent me that link, with advice that I needn't throw in everything including the kitchen sink. I've tried to follow that advice, though bits of the sink kept sneaking in.

I am grateful to Delphine Gatehouse for leading me where I dreaded to tread in Os's grieving head. I sincerely hope that I've done justice to her predicament.

Thank you Jessica Chapman for your witty asides whilst you cut my meanderings down to size.

A big shout out to Angela Mackworth-Young, Chris Loft and Jody Cooksey, brilliant writing pals, for your gentle nudges, the wise and timely nods and winks.

And to James Willis, Stefan Proudfoot and all the staff a t S piffing Publishing a big thanks. Without your magical publishing midwifery, this bashful tale would remain but ink twinkling on the latest nib of my unfortunate fountain pen.

Finally, to Mau and the boys - and the two little pettys. You are everything to me. Don't roll your eyes to the kitchen ceiling when I shout "new book!" I think I may be pregnant again.